Praise for A Storm Blew in from Paradise

'Anyuru's searingly poetic style ॥
bleakness and sentimentality al
lies we live by.'
The Independent

'A tense, sparse re-telling of a life. This novel is a shining
example of literature's ability to give its readers a new
perspective on the world, and an excellent way to learn
about the emotional consequences of war and exile. I can
honestly say that *A Storm Blew in from Paradise* is the best
Swedish novel I have read in a long time. I would advise
anyone interested in the writing process, in familial and
national ties, in pain, healing, loss, and rediscovery to
read it.'
Swedish Book Review

'An intense, beautiful novel that examines rootlessness
and identity.'
EDINBURGH INTERNATIONAL BOOK FESTIVAL

'A strikingly beautiful text pierced with today's doubts and
theories about what creates true meaning in the life story
of a single human being, as well as in history. This is a
personal and universal novel about fatherlessness and identity, about the power of violence and about how we are all
prisoners of time.'
Aftonbladet

'*A Storm Blew in from Paradise* touchingly portrays the
drama, absurdity, and insignificance of life as a political
refugee.'
MO Magazine

'Johannes Anyuru's language hurls itself, like the main character of this book, straight into the sun, burning and scorching.'
Helsingborgs Dagblad

'You feel the breeze from the storm out of paradise, you feel the large movements, you feel the hypnotic effect of a prose that can make you visualize the Angel of History zooming in on a building in Växjö. It is fantastic.'
Expressen

'This is a poignant novel on the shattered life of a man who has only secrets, silence, and painful memories to leave to his son. The violence he endured, the forced exile, and the stupor caused by bloodshed have cut his wings. Johannes Anyuru offers us a moving novel: a homage to his father in a neat, refined, and unsentimental style. Such elegance and stoicism in the face of adversity allow a beautiful portrait to be painted thanks to the son's sublime and celebrated style.'
Le Monde de Tran

'Whoever wants to understand the continuous stream of African refugees, will be provided with a crystal-clear picture by this Ugandan-Swedish writer: run, or die.'
G. BOOMSMA

JOHANNES ANYURU (Sweden, 1979), the son of a Ugandan father and a Swedish mother, is a novelist and poet. *A Storm Blew in from Paradise* enjoyed immense success in Sweden and was awarded two major Swedish literature prizes: the Svenska Dagbladet Literature Prize and the Aftonbladet Literature Prize. It was also shortlisted for the HKW International Literature Prize in Germany. Anyuru has won several more prestigious prizes for his other bestselling novels, including the August Prize and the Per Olov Enquist Literary Prize. His work has been translated into thirteen languages.

RACHEL WILLSON-BROYLES is a freelance translator based in Saint Paul, Minnesota. She received her BA in Scandinavian Studies from Gustavus Adolphus College in 2002 and her PhD in Scandinavian Studies from the University of Wisconsin-Madison in 2013. Other authors whose works she has translated include Jonas Hassen Khemiri, Jonas Jonasson, Malin Persson Giolito, and Linda Boström Knausgård.

A Storm Blew in from Paradise

Johannes Anyuru

A Storm Blew in from Paradise

Translated from the Swedish
by Rachel Willson-Broyles

WORLD EDITIONS
New York, London, Amsterdam

Published in the USA in 2019 by World Editions LLC, New York
Published in the UK in 2015 by World Editions Ltd., London

World Editions
New York/London/Amsterdam

Copyright © Johannes Anyuru, 2012
English translation copyright © Rachel Willson-Broyles, 2015
Cover image © Hubertus Mall / Buchcover / Hollandse Hoogte
Author portrait © Khim Efraimsson

Printed by Lake Book, USA

The Walter Benjamin quote on p. 179 is from *Illuminations*, by Walter
Benjamin, translation by Harry Zohn and copyright 1968 Harcourt Brace
Jovanovich, Inc., New York: Schocken Books, 1969, pp. 257–8.

The quote from the Qur'an on p. 249 is in Surah 14:48 from the translation
by Abdullah Yusuf Ali, published by Tahrike Tarsile Qur'an, Inc.,
Elmhurst, New York, 22nd US Edition, 2007.

Library of Congress Cataloging in Publication Data is available

ISBN 978-1-64286-044-3

First published as *En storm kom från paradiset* in Sweden in 2012 by
Norstedts, by agreement with Norstedts Agency, Stockholm

The cost of this translation was defrayed by a subsidy from the Swedish
Arts Council, gratefully acknowledged.

Twitter: @WorldEdBooks
Facebook: WorldEditionsInternationalPublishing
www.worldeditions.org

Book Club Discussion Guides are available on our website.

He opens his eyes. The floor is shaking. He has the feeling that the area has very recently been full of voices and laughter. Maybe he was just dreaming. He's lying between two rows of seats. The stars move slowly in a window above him. He is lying in a train compartment. He gets up and sits in one of the seats. His body is sore; his joints are stiff. He looks down at his hands, at his knuckles, his thin fingers; he turns his head, tries to get a glimpse of his reflection in the glass. He doesn't remember what has happened to him, what he's doing on this train. The full moon hangs low above the horizon, a grey disc. He can see the craters, the sandy seas. He doesn't remember who he is. The moon, it reminds him of something. Of clouds. Of the wind. He doesn't remember. He doesn't remember his story.

I

'**WHY DID YOU** come back?'

P has been sitting with his chin on his chest; he raises his eyes and looks across the table again. 'I've already told you,' he says. The room is windowless, and despite the fact that both men have unbuttoned several of their shirt buttons, they are sweating profusely; there are large wet spots on their backs and under their arms. The interrogator spreads out his fingers and drums his fingertips against each other. P looks down at the floor again. The concrete looks rough and desolate, like a photograph of the moon's surface.

'I was promised a job at a company outside Lusaka.' P doesn't understand why they're holding him here, why they have brought him here at all. 'I was going to fly a crop duster.'

'You were going to fly a crop duster.' The men are speaking Swahili with one another. The interrogator looks through the papers on the table. His body is wiry, his face is fleshy and his features crude, his moustache is sprinkled with grey, he is nearly bald. His facial expressions are amused, cruel, sometimes artificially friendly. 'A Ugandan fighter pilot travels from Rome to Zambia to fly a crop duster over fruit plantations?'

P wipes the sweat from his brow. They brought him here straight from the airport, and he hasn't had anything to eat or drink all day. He is tired; he has the sense of being caught in a dream that is far too long, of swimming underwater, of being outside himself. The walls of the room are blue. Tendrils of bare cement appear where the paint is flaking. They look like continents on a map from another time, another world.

'Send me back to Rome if you don't believe me.'

A guard is standing in the corner of the room to the left, behind P's back; his presence makes itself known only by the scraping of shoes against the floor. The interrogator changes position, rests his chin in his hand, places an index finger over his lips in reflection. He refuses to believe that anyone would return to this devastated continent without aims beyond the one P has given time and again: that he wanted to fly, that his only chance to fly was at a small company outside Lusaka in Zambia that sprays fruit plantations using propeller planes from colonial times.

P screws up his eyes and feels the exhaustion rising in his head like a white roar. He feels ill.

'It's time you realize you won't be allowed to return to your contact in Rome.'

'My contact?'

The interrogator pounds the table with his hand. 'Who sent you to Zambia? Who do you work for?' The guard behind P moves; his shoes scrape against the floor. 'Well. How could we send you back to Rome? Officially, you already went back there, from Lusaka, didn't you? You signed the deportation order yourself.' The bald Tanzanian points at a document, then takes out yet another piece of paper and places it on the table. 'Right here, you signed a statement to attest that you have been sent back to Lusaka, from here.'

P stares straight ahead, trying to think of something to say. He hasn't been beaten, but violence is hanging in the air.

'You ought to be more careful about where you put your signature. You no longer exist. It's time you start answering our questions.'

Many of the papers that have already been placed on the table belong to P: his passport, his plane tickets. The interrogator takes yet another document out of a folder and looks at it, pretending to be considering something. He places it on the table and pushes it over to P, who picks it up.

P looks at the Greek letters. His name and rank. The insignia of the Hellenic Air Force: a man with wings, white against a sky-blue background. His diploma.

'You were trained at the Hellenic Air Force Academy in Dhekelia outside of Athens; then you went to Rome, and from there to Zambia. Why?'

'I wanted to fly.' The statement sounds like a lie even to him. He wants to shout, to stand up and overturn the table, shout that he just wanted to fly. He feels the letters with his fingertips. He just wanted to fly. Inside him, a scrap of an image flutters by, a memory that feels like it took place in another life: he's standing beside a chain-link fence, watching jet airplanes come sinking out of the sky; it's his first autumn in Greece, and the leaves haven't yet fallen but the crowns of the trees in the playground have turned a colour like cardboard; he and the rest of the future flight cadets from the Third World study Greek on narrow wooden benches, repeating verbs and nouns all day long, but one afternoon they are picked up by a bus and driven through the barriers around the air-force academy and dropped off at that chain-link fence that faces the airfield, and they stand there and look at the airplanes that they're going to learn how to fly, later, after their language course is finished— the sleek murder machines move across the runway, far away, slow and wobbly like gulls.

'Do you want a cigarette?'

P shrugs without looking up from the document in his hands. The interrogator must have given a signal to the guard, because he takes a step forward and holds out a pack of unfiltered cigarettes. P takes one, sticks it in the corner of his mouth; the guard lights it and then backs into the shadows again. P puts down his diploma, waits for a question, or for violence, or for his release, for something; he smokes.

'What is your opinion of Obote?'

'Of Obote?' He lets the smoke curl through his nostrils. 'I wish he were president of Uganda. He is one of my people.'

'Tell me what happened when Obote visited your village in the spring of '69.'

'I was in Greece in '69.' P knows what the interrogator is talking about. John wrote about it in a letter.

'The spring of 1969.' The man pronounces the year slowly, syllable by syllable, as though there were a chance that P might have misunderstood it. 'In the spring of 1969, Milton Obote, your president, travelled around and gave speeches in the countryside. It was a campaign to unite the people after the Buganda kingdom uprising. You are familiar with this?'

'I was in Greece.'

'When he came to your village, he was attacked by a mob that tore down the podium, destroyed the microphone, and forced him to flee.'

'I was in Greece.'

'But you heard the news from your family, didn't you? You were all against Obote.' The interrogator points at P as he says this, as though P were the one behind the general disapproval of Obote's tendency to favour his own family, his own ethnic group, from the presidential palace. P snorts, ashes onto the floor, shakes his head.

'My life was destroyed by the military coup.' He waits for a question that doesn't come; he tries to remember what he has said and what he hasn't said, which lies, which omissions, and which confessions measure out the bounds of this conversation. The three men are silent; only their breathing is audible, and the dull hum of a ventilation duct, and far off, outside the room, the occasional sound of footsteps. The interrogator takes a photo album from a box on the floor. P recognizes it; like the documents on the table, they have taken it from his luggage.

In 1969 he was in Greece, flying the training planes. In 1967 he was in Greece, studying Greek and watching the training planes land and take off, and in the evenings came a chill that he had never experienced in Uganda and that made him sleep with his olive-green training jacket pulled tighter around his body, made him shiver, and some days a breeze came from the sea and brought with it enormous amounts of sand that blew in over the narrow streets of Dhekelia, sand white as pearly shards, or white as broken bits of sky, sand that lay in thick dunes along the edges of sidewalks and the sides of houses. He went to the sea sometimes, on the weekends, on a civilian bus line that carried tourists in the summer but was nearly empty in the fall, winter, and spring. He wandered alone in the swell with his shoes in his hand and his pants rolled up and felt how something from his childhood, some vague thing, was swallowed by darkness, and maybe by forgiveness. He sometimes thought, then, by the sea, that the people who existed at that time would one day disappear, become limestone on the bottom of another sea.

The interrogator takes a photograph out of one of the plastic sleeves and pushes it across the table. A young African man in a pilot uniform stands on a T-37, supported by the large, grey tail fin, almost twice as tall as a person.

'This is you.'

'No,' he says quickly, without knowing why he is lying.

'It's not you?'

The photo is grainy and the face in the picture is shadowed by the pilot's helmet, blurry. It could be someone else. The situation between Tanzania and Uganda is very tense. Uganda's military is shooting grenades across the border. Amin claims that Ugandan guerrilla soldiers who want to overthrow his regime have camps in Tanzania.

'It's someone else.' He shouldn't have lied, but he did and now he has to stick to his lie. He bends down and stubs out his cigarette under his shoe. There are already two butts on the floor from cigarettes he smoked earlier. How long has he been sitting here? 'It's one of my classmates.'

'You persist in lying.' The interrogator shakes his head, makes a disappointed face, folds his hands over his stomach, and leans back in his chair. 'It's not important. We'll start over from the beginning. The man in the photograph is you. You belonged to the second generation of Ugandan fighter pilots. You were sent to the Hellenic Air Force Academy in Dhekelia outside of Athens, which has produced fighter pilots for a number of African countries since the early sixties.'

The first time they went through this, P refused to confirm any of what the Tanzanians said, but the irrational loyalty he felt toward the two states that have now completely betrayed him disappeared as his exhaustion grew. He closes his eyes and nods slowly; yes, he was sent to Greece to be trained as a fighter pilot and an officer in the Ugandan air force. He sits with his chin lowered, his eyes closed.

He remembers the increasingly chilly autumn days and the shouts in Arabic and French and the crowds in the corridors when they all rushed out to the yard, all at the same time to shove each other and brag about the military education in their countries and the planes they'd already flown during the trials. He remembers the days. He particularly remembers the day when they took the bus to the airfield and stood staring through the fence, how their eyes widened when the afterburners on a T-37 lit and comet tails of welding-flame blue slowly grew out of the jet exhaust, and how the plane jerked and hurled away and up, and that in that moment it felt like it was possible to start over, to leave your past behind, to escape. As though history didn't exist.

Uganda had recently become independent from British rule, and they had started to build up the nation's air force by buying MIG-21s from Israel. A first generation of Ugandan pilots had been trained to fly these by Israeli security advisors, but while the Israelis continued to train Ugandan pilots, they began to send small groups of young men to the Hellenic Air Force Academy in Greece. The idea was that they would become familiar with American and French fighter planes and, above all, become officers drilled in the military lifestyle, gentlemen, leaders. While the Ugandan pilots who were educated in their native country only trained for a little more than six months, those who went to Greece would study at the air force academy for three years in order to become the corps and spearhead of the new air force.

They slept in bunk beds and kept their few belongings

in grey metal lockers; they were the most promising members of their generation, their country's future gods of the sky. As they walked from the student quarters to the language-school building, cawing birds ate from garbage cans. P was in a class that was mostly made up of Libyans, Egyptians, and Tunisians, but also students from the Ivory Coast and a young man from Chad.

He received letters from John, his eldest brother; he read them sitting on his bed. He longed for the language course to be over so he could begin his military training and then learn to fly. He jogged in the afternoons, felt his heart beating and his lungs expanding, contracting, expanding; he went to the sea, he bent down and washed his face in the water that tasted of salt, not sweet like the water on the shores of Lake Victoria. Not like home.

On the day when they stood at the fence with their eyes open so wide that the whole sky would fit in them, the sky that would soon be theirs, the sound of the airplanes' motors were like thunder and when the planes descended they had rated the landings, given their future colleagues two points out of ten, or three points, or sometimes one point, and of course one of them would yell zero then, to be the worst: in Greek, *zero*. They had boxed with each other and laughed. That was in the beginning. When he was a child he had wanted to be a bird.

'What did you say?'

The interrogator said something that P didn't hear. P is sitting with his head in his hand, his elbow on the table. His eyes are still closed. Inside him, the image and the sound of hundreds of hovering birds.

'I said that I'm quoting one of the air force academy's own documents.' The interrogator has another piece of paper in his hand; he folds it, unfolds it, reads: "'*Ever since airplanes were first used in military operations in 1912, the Air Force has protected the skies of our country against every threat, and it is with deep respect that we turn to the victims and the heroic deeds that have made it possible for Greece and her people to enjoy democracy and freedom as well as the progress of civilization.*'"

P doesn't understand what the man is trying to get at. He reads the words with a hollow tone that makes them seem empty and silly. 'You recognize this? "*Because of their self-sacrifices, the aviators of Greece occupy a prominent position among the country's sung and unsung heroes.*"' The man puts the paper on the table, smoothes it out with his palm, pretends to disappear in thought. He draws his index finger across his moustache, he looks out into the empty air, he drums his index finger against his lip; then he says, as though apropos of nothing: 'Are you a fascist yourself?'

The guard laughs behind P's back.

'I don't want to get involved in politics.'

'You don't want to get involved in politics.'

'I don't want to get involved in the war.'

'What war?'

'Between you and Amin. Between Tanzania and Uganda.'

'Are you saying that Uganda is at war with us? Is that how they see it?'

'Who?'

'The people you're working for.'

'Let me go back to Rome. I just wanted to fly.'

The man doesn't answer. He reads from the paper as though to himself, fascinated; at first he almost mumbles: "'*The Hellenic Air Force Academy instructs its cadets in the science of flight and develops their military virtue and military discipline. It forms the officer into a man with perfect military and aeronautical knowledge and an advanced education, as well as social, cultural, and political understanding and knowledge of proper conduct, and supplies him with comprehensive professional and scientific training.*" Would you say that this is accurate? Did your friends possess what they promise here?'

'No.'

'It's not accurate? You didn't receive pilot training? Then what did you do in Greece?'

'They weren't my friends.'

'And that's not you in the picture?' The interrogator points at the photograph where P is standing by the tail fin of his training plane.

'I don't remember.'

'You persist in lying. That's you in the picture. You completed the air force academy's fighter-pilot training and now you claim that you returned to Africa to use your—let's see what it said—your "perfect military and aeronautical knowledge" and your "comprehensive professional and scientific training" to fly a crop duster?'

P pinches his temples with his thumb and index finger. He has been taught how to handle interrogations, how to escape from prisons, how to withstand torture. One must go to a place beyond the body. One must not be in the room.

'May I have another cigarette?' The bare cement walls of the room make him sound sharp and tinny.

The thin, wiry man who taught the course on imprisonment and torture, and who was presumably from the Greek security police, said that as soon as you've told them everything you know, your life ceases to be of any worth, and this, not loyalty or nationalism, is why you should not talk during an interrogation. P picks up the photo. The interrogator waits for him to say something.

He never thought about the political situation in Greece, even though it was there like background noise: that a military coup had recently been carried out by three army generals and that King Constantine found himself in exile after a failed attempt to seize power from those who had executed the coup. The communists and anarchists blew up cars in Athens, the newspapers were full of articles about the degenerate, atheist youth culture and the democratic-party politics that had almost brought the extreme left to power in the country. P wasn't interested. They were words in headlines. He would soon learn that the air force, like the navy but in contrast to the army, were royalists and had supported the king's attempt to take power in late 1967. He would hear this in nervous whispers from the Greek cadets later on, and he also remembered, from the later years, from the time when he was going through the flight training itself, the deep respect that bordered on fear he and his classmates were met with when they were in uniform. He liked life in the military, liked that for the first time it was possible to analyze his life, that there were rules, a system. He didn't think about politics. His gaze roams. The light bulb on the ceiling starts to buzz. They will never be able to understand. He remembers the white, short-sleeved summer uniform of the Greek air force. He just has to be able to fly again. That was why he travelled to Lusaka.

'You took language classes before you were trained as a pilot?'

'Yes. We learned to speak Greek,' he says. And their language teacher always tried to drag the African students in particular along to bordellos, because apparently that was what the black Americans from the aircraft carriers that sometimes docked in Piraeus wanted to do. He said *eiste pala kaidia*, 'you're good guys'; they called him the Gull, he had tufts of white hair that he was always stroking into place with his left hand.

They had nicknames for one another, too. Hussein was going to be a helicopter pilot, and had only been accepted into the school because several of his relatives had top posts in the Ugandan army, and they said he was going to learn to fly a mosquito, an eggbeater, what else—a dragonfly; they wrestled with each other in the gravel and laughed.

At the time, P had flown only once, during the trials in Uganda. He had sat in the small propeller plane with an Israeli flight instructor who would evaluate how suitable he was for pilot training in terms of his sense of balance, his capacity for spatial orientation, and his coordination, and when he was allowed to fly the plane by himself for a few seconds, he grasped the controls in his hands and glided through layer after layer of light, and it had felt like freedom, a transformative changing of worlds. He thought of it often there in Greece, back in the beginning when he was conjugating verbs and practising dialogues and scratching his nail against the lacquered wood of the school desk and looking out at the clouds. Of flying again.

'The language course lasted a year?'

'Six months.' For six months he sat in the evenings, cutting pictures of airplanes out of Greek and American newspapers that former students had left behind in the barracks. The F-86s that the Greeks flew, with the air intakes like open mouths hanging under their noses, the T-37s in diamond formation low above a scrap of coastline, in bright sunlight—cross-shaped silhouettes against the breaking waves. His longing redefined him, gave him new contours. On the weekends he and the other Africans in his class walked from bar to bar with their arms across each other's shoulders, shouting so loudly their voices echoed between the buildings, and the waiter poured out Greek spirits into a big glass and blended it with water so that it turned completely white, like a winter sky. And the winter came and the light over Dhekelia turned white and he walked with his schoolbooks under his arm and turned his face into the wind and his future was like the white light from the sky.

If he held his hand out in the wind, it lifted, slowly.

'After the language course, you were moved to the air-combat school?'

'Yes. To the air force academy itself.'

'So you started flying sometime in the beginning of 1968?'

'No. The summer of '69.'

'The language course began in the fall of '67 and lasted for six months?'

P goes through the years and the dates in his head so he doesn't get confused; so he doesn't give the impression that he's lying. He swallows. He says: 'The basic military training started in the spring of '68. It lasted for a year. In May of '69 we started to fly.'

A deep, concerned wrinkle appears between the interrogator's eyebrows. During the interrogation he has been taking notes in a small notebook with a black ballpoint pen, and he flips through them; he says in a friendly, concerned voice, 'Hadn't you already undergone basic military training in Uganda?'

None of this is a secret, nothing is information the Tanzanians don't already know, nothing is anything worth keeping from them.

'Yes.'

'Yet you went through basic military training in Greece? Is that what you claim?'

'That was what happened.'

'That was what happened.' And the interrogator quotes again, in English, from one of the papers in the folder. *"The military training develops military competence in the flight cadet by increasing his stamina by way of long training sessions, and it develops his ability to act correctly and think in a consistent manner under pressure. This is achieved through proper training in the handling of weapons, survival, and training in military organization and procedures."*

P wonders how they have gotten hold of these documents. He hadn't brought them along with him. Maybe they're the official descriptions the academy uses to attract students from the Third World. 'Tell me about the Greek cadets. Where did they stand politically?'

'Politically?'

'Were they fascists like the Americans and the Greek government?'

Fascists? They came to the academy in September, thirty young Greeks, selected from among thousands. They stepped off a military bus, they tossed their dark manes of hair and whispered to one another as they passed the foreign-language students who were sitting outside the barracks. The language course was over, long shadows fell across the barracks yard, it was morning, the Greek men disappeared into the gym, P sat there and watched them along with his classmates, he smoked, he remembers that he was struck by the thought that he could have been one of them, that he could have been in some completely different country, could have had a different body, a different name, a different life, so strange; he remembers that now, that while he watched the Greek cadets-to-be, his life opened before him for a few seconds and he saw how arbitrary it all was: that he had been born in Uganda, the son of a woman who sent him away and a man who died when he was very young, that his name was P, that he was in Greece because his friend had skidded past on his bike one day and asked him to come along to the trials for the Ugandan Air Force, that he had followed his friend and had treated the tests as though they were a game at first but later, naturally, with increasing earnestness—his friend had been eliminated but P had been asked to stay the night and was then sent away to undergo more trials at a camp in northern Uganda. He drew in the gravel with his tennis shoe.

He finds himself repeating the motion with his patent-leather shoes on the cement floor. He stops. He closes his eyes.

After half an hour the Greeks came out again, in a row, in ill-fitting field uniforms, their hair buzzed down to their bumpy, pale heads. Some seemed not to care that their long manes of hair had been cut; others were experiencing total breakdowns. P and the others who were sitting and waiting and who had already gone through this, first in their homelands and then a second time here in Greece, laughed at them. That night, after the Greeks had been given lodging in the barracks inside the fence they had once stood outside, they had all been wakened and herded into a gym in only their underwear, and a group of students in their final year had shoved them and spat at them and taunted them, calling them small fry, *psarades*. This was all part of tradition, of the transformation, of the science of flight.

'I was a Greek cadet,' says P.

The interrogator looks up from his folder with an

expression of genuine surprise on his round face. 'Excuse me?'

'You asked me where the Greek cadets stood politically. We were all Greek cadets.'

'You mean to say you're Greek, not African?'

P continually has to fight the sensation that the walls are closing in on him. The ventilation system rumbles.

'May I have a glass of water?'

'You may have another cigarette.' The interrogator nods at the guard, who gives P yet another cigarette. It tastes like thirst and stress, and he smokes it nervously and with a sense of hopelessness rising inside him like dark, murky water. They don't believe him even when he tells the truth.

'You don't even know whether you're African or Greek, but you expect us to believe you when you claim that your only agenda in Lusaka is to work as a crop-duster pilot?'

'Yes.'

'You may have a glass of water when you stop trying to hide the fact that you took courses in intelligence techniques, espionage, and sabotage during the time when you claim to have completed a second basic training.'

They ran through the spring and the growing shadows of afternoon into the evening that came sweeping over the barracks. The only thing the freshly buzzed cadets did during their military basic training was run. They ran around and around the barracks yard in their grey sweatsuits. The gravel crunched under their feet; they ran while night fell and the summer veered away and the leaves once again turned yellow and fell, a second Greek year. They ran and heard their instructor shout: 'The primary purpose of military basic training is the proper cultivation of the flight cadet's personality. He is initiated into a military lifestyle, a military sense of duty, and the habits and traditions of the academy.' They ran and their breath rose like smoke from their mouths and dissipated into the evening sky and he tripped over his own feet and his gaze was thrown upward and he saw snowflakes unfurling above them. That's how he remembers it now. That they ran for a whole year without ever stopping. He remembers one day when a group of second-year cadets were walking across the barracks yard in their khaki winter uniforms, that they stopped and pointed at the small fry who had always been running there, who would always be running there, but he doesn't know whether, in this image, he is one of those running or one of the older ones looking on, if it's later. He doesn't remember. He holds the cigarette in his hand, his hand against his forehead; the interrogator shoves yet another picture across the table, he looks at it, and the interrogator knocks on it, hard.

'Do you deny that this is you?'

In the photograph he is dressed in the summer uniform of the Greek air force. A short sabre hangs from his waist. He is wearing a uniform cap.

'That's me.' He picks up the photo, holds it up in front of him. 'That was me.'

'Tell me what you did during your basic training.'

'We ran.'

In the spring he collapsed on the ground and lay with his back against the throbbing earth, against the rustling gravel. Clouds glided by up there, and now, as he remembers them, he thinks: *Nimbostratus: rain clouds that gather in a single layer and are blurred by continuous precipitation.* They took a basic course in meteorology later; alongside their flights, they learned about the sky, winds, rain. Things were happening for him. The photo in his hand captures the light from the bulb on the ceiling; a ray of grey light slides across the young cadet's face and he knows that these men will never be able to understand, that they see these photos without understanding the power of the sky and the sun that made him return here, to these wars, to this danger. *Cumulonimbus: vertical clouds whose upper parts are striated and flattened and widen into the shape of anvils and giant plumes.* He looks up at the interrogator for a moment, then down at the photo again. He leans back in the hard wooden chair, the photograph still in his hand. *From the base of the cloud comes precipitation in the form of falling streaks that never reach the ground.*

'We ran,' he says a second time, and he laughs suddenly, snuffling through his laughter and shaking his head. He grows silent, stares down at the table.

The sound of a sudden movement behind his back. A buzzing numbness, like carbonation, spreads through his arms and legs, he feels himself sliding off the chair and it seems to happen slowly, like in a dream; somehow it has already happened even as it is happening.

He is lying on the floor, looking up at the light bulb on the ceiling. Sharp, flashing pain in the back of his head; it radiates down along his spine. His shoes scrape feebly against the cement floor as he tries to get up.

Darkness.

The guard hit him in the back of the head with a weapon, probably the butt of his pistol.

He hears the interrogator speaking but the words have no meaning; they're just sounds, noises.

Darkness.

His head throbs. His body is clumsy; it doesn't want to obey him.

'Sit up.' The interrogator speaks in a tone that one

might use when instructing a less-than-gifted student to perform a dance step. P is still lying on the floor; his shoes scrape, scrape against the floor. The chair has tipped over; it's lying beside him. The guard rights the chair and P curls up on himself because this quick movement makes him think he is going to be struck again. Then the guard lifts P's arm, roughly and simply, and sits him up. His tongue is swollen. He feels the back of his head carefully and gets something sticky on his fingers. He looks at them, smears the blood around with his thumb for a moment, in a sort of shocked fascination. He remembers his childhood. He remembers a man who wasn't his father, a man he lived with for many years. He closes his eyes, hard. The taste of iron in his mouth.

'Shall we continue?' The interrogator wipes his forehead with his shirtsleeve and looks down as his folder, somehow bureaucratic and thoughtful. 'Take off your shoes,' he says. 'Take off your shoes and take off your clothes.'

A black-and-white picture. A young African man standing on a beach in swimming trunks. He is so fit as to be almost sculpture-like, and he is looking straight into the camera. The sun is exactly behind his back, which gives the sense that the summer sky is a tunnel of grey, grainy material. He is standing on a beach; his toes are digging into the wet sand.

A black-and-white picture. Three black men are crouching on a gravel field. Their olive-green clothes look dark grey in the photo. Their faces are hard, serious; the whites of their eyes shine in their faces.

More photographs. Greek flight cadets climbing nets, running in pine forests, making their way through obstacle courses: in one picture they're jumping between cement slabs and their reflections in the muddy water are vaguely discernible as flecks of grey light. Like memories.

A faded colour photo. A swimming pool, outdoors, the diving platform made of bare concrete, eight lanes marked with dark lines on the bottom of the pool. Evergreen trees in the background. The water is grey, like the sky.

No cadets in the picture.

A THIN MOSQUITO net floated up, into the room. For a moment the boy could see the evening outside, how it stretched away, violet and endless. The sun was a burning wafer above the horizon. He sat on a mattress, he rested his chin against his knees. His skin smelled like livestock, dry grass, mud. He had loosened the two nails that otherwise kept the bottom edge of the net in place. If the man came home before he had time to replace the nails, he would say that it was the wind. He wanted to see the sky, disappear into it. He had his arms around his knees.

A light bulb hung in the middle of the room; its cord was wound around a beam on the ceiling and then plugged into an outlet that led to a diesel generator out in the yard. He shifted, tried to avoid sitting on the bruises across his thighs and his tailbone. He would say that it was the wind, that it had blown so hard that the nails came loose. The neighbours' dog barked. The door opened. The man came home.

The man hung up his jacket. His shoes were muddy and large and somehow unwieldy; his pants were worn but had sharp creases. The boy stood up and took the clay jar from the oven, it was hot; he protected his hands with a rag. All of this in a sort of memory of the memory, flickering film images, washed out now by sea and sun. The man sat at the table; he stared at the boy with his lower lip thrust out and his hands before him. His presence was like a roar in the boy's ears; the walls seemed to throb inward like the skin of a drum. They didn't speak to each other. The boy's face was swollen; he had seen it in school, in the bathroom mirror. He picked up an aluminium plate by his mattress, received a few spoonfuls of food. They ate with their hands, semolina porridge; the boy had made it when he came home from school, as usual, while the man, who was a teacher at the school, had gone to the village pub to drink his beer and his palm wine.

They sat there, like always. They ate as the sun went down, a man, a boy, two brothers. Their oldest brother, John, was still in a country called Burma, where he had been at war against the Germans, and their father had died of malaria one day when the boy was very young, so the man with the large, muddy shoes was the oldest man in the family. The boy stopped eating when he heard the man stand up. He sat, frozen, with a pinch of porridge in his fingers and his eyes stuck to the metal plate between his feet. He heard the sound of the bottle hitting the table, the mug being filled. He snuck a peek at the window, at the dusk that was falling so quickly, as though someone were lowering a large hand over the sky. His lip was swollen; when he put porridge into his mouth he spilled it. He quickly scraped it up with his fingers, licked them. The sound of his swallowing was sticky, wet.

'Come here.'

The mosquito net bulged in the wind; he just sat there, staring at the sky. 'Leave the plate and come sit.' He wanted to be a bird. The man kicked a chair and it fell over. The boy started at the sound but didn't move his eyes. 'Mama spoiled you.'

When he sat on the chair, it hurt the undersides of his

thighs where he had been whipped earlier. He slid out to the edge of the seat; he wanted to cry, scream, run away, fly away. The man held the metal mug up in front of his face and stared at it as though he were looking for something in the dull, grey tin surface. 'Why don't you look at me? I'm your brother.'

The table between them was of rough, dark wood. The grooves in it were red in the shallow, dusky light. The boy scraped at the top of the table with his fingernail. There's no getting away. This is life, this abandonment in the abyss. The man drank from his mug and slammed it down onto the table; he sucked air in between his teeth, a sound that meant idiotic brat, spoiled brat that the family has forced him to care for. The boy's hand trembled as he lifted the bottle, he sneaked another peek at the window, at the sun that by now lay like a thin streak of fire in the tall grass. He refilled the mug. Carefully; he didn't spill. He screwed the top back on.

'I have bad news,' said the man. The tin mug looked small between his fat fingers. The boy could feel the man's eyes searching his face. 'John is dead.'

Silence. The boy liked John, even though he had never met him; he liked the stories his other brothers had told of John. John was like their father, they would say. John would take him away from here when he came back. John was a soldier.

'John is dead.' The man took a few sips. 'John has died, our father has died.' He laughed suddenly and then, irritated, hit the back of his own neck—all these sudden movements caused the boy to start. The man laughed. 'We are dead, too.' In his memory, that's how it was: they were dead, the boy and the man; it was as though they were made of wood or stone. The man was struck dumb by his own words. He sat there gaping for a moment, eyes on the wall. 'Don't be afraid of me. I'm your brother,' he said. He took off his tie, unbuttoned his shirt, leaned back. He looked at the mosquito net. It was flapping. He scratched the back of his neck, smacked his lips, seemed to lick his teeth. His tongue was swollen and pink like an animal's. 'Stand here,' he said. His white shirt had a brown streak of sweat along the collar; his voice was calm and controlled, almost gentle. 'Come here.' Almost warm, laughing, as though it contained indulgence, mercy, brotherhood. The boy slid down from his chair. 'Why did you loosen the mosquito net?'

He raised his eyes. It wasn't him. It was the wind it was the wind.

The man struck him with his fist, but just before it hit him the boy turned blank like metal, or like the worn tabletop. He didn't feel the blow. It was always like this. When he opened his eyes he was lying on the floor and his head felt like it was just a piece of meat, wet and heavy and meaningless, and the darkness inside his head was like the darkness inside a piece of raw meat. When he inhaled air, it snuffled with blood, and the blood was the blood that comes out when you cut meat and place it on a cutting board, watery and thin, almost not even blood, some other sort of fluid. His nose was numb; it stung a little inside. He crawled under the table; the man overturned it so plate, silverware, and mug clattered against the floor; the man kicked after him and when he was hit by the man's large, muddy shoe, right in the stomach, everything went almost completely still, yet another blank, empty moment, and then there was a flash of light and the room crashed down over him and he flew into the wall.

His fingers scraped over the dirt floor. He crawled. He hopped out of the way of another kick and got up on his feet, but he was dizzy and crashed into the overturned table. He hit his temple; once again the blankness rose within him.

The man was silent; only his breathing could be heard. He took off his belt. It sounded like the wind. His large shoes stomped around the room; the boy rolled around in a rain of bloody arcs, trying to protect himself from the lashes of the belt that made the world shake; it wasn't him. It was the wind. The man chased him but he got to his feet again and stumbled toward the door, out the door—behind him he heard the man knock over a chair.

The grass tickled the soles of his bare feet. He ran, and the whole time he had the sense that the ground was turning, leaning, that he was going to fall. He heard the man's voice behind him, heard it yelling a name, a name that was his, but he didn't stop, he thought what he always thought, that if he ran all night he might get to the village where Mama lived, so he ran, he ran, but the sky, it was like the sky was turning too, and rotating, and rotating, and his feet moved, but when he threw a glance backward the darkness from the blow to his face or the kick to his stomach came back and knocked him over and he rolled around in the grass, hugging himself, curling up into a fetal position and waiting for the blows.

He sits motionless, with his head leaning against iron bars. He wonders where he is. He must have dozed off, dreamed something. He dreamed something. A row of filthy windows near the ceiling shimmers when cars drive past on a road outside. He looks down at his feet. The cement floor is damp, cold. His memories of the last twenty-four hours return slowly, as though they were trickling in at his temples: that he had been interrogated for hours and now he is in a cellar under the room where he was questioned; that he is a prisoner here; that he never should have returned to Africa from Rome; that it was a mistake.

He thumps his temple against the bars of his cage, just once, and lets his head rest there. A fan whisks up the dirty, urine-reeking air. Voices in the darkness around him are praying, shouting curses, singing, and speaking in a dozen different languages.

After the guard had taken his shoes and clothes away from him, the interrogator kept pressing him for almost another hour. He sat there wearing only his underwear while they went through the same questions again. Why had he returned to Africa? He wanted to fly. Was he against Milton Obote? No. If anything, he is against Amin's regime. What had he learned in Greece, what intelligence techniques, what types of espionage, sabotage, assassination? When the interrogation was over, they brought him to this cellar in what must be some sort of police station. It is full of small cages made of welded metal poles. The ceilings of the cages are lower than the ceiling of the room itself, and they are lined up in two rows so that a long corridor runs between them. He sits motionless, with the back of his head against the bars. He thought they would let him go when the interrogation was over, that he would be allowed to return to Rome, or at least to Lusaka in Zambia. He starts to cry without making a sound. He feels something crawling on his skin; he feels everything slipping from his hands. He thought the sky would watch over him. He's having trouble thinking. He can't breathe. He raises his eyes and sits for a long time and sobs and just stares at the windows, at the blurry lights, and tries to hold back the sick feeling. Maybe they are going to kill him. They say

that he's signed papers that make it impossible for anyone to trace him, that he has disappeared, that he doesn't
exist. He prays to God, a whispering, internal prayer. He
doesn't know what they want him to say. He sits still,
with a storm of whispers inside, until he realizes with a
start what the crawling sensation on his skin is and he
lets out a scream against his will. His scream is a shrill,
birdlike sound; he doesn't like it; it's something foreign
escaping his body. He flies to his feet so quickly that he
hits his head on the low ceiling of his cage. The cell is
teeming with lice. Lice, they're already in his armpits, in
his underwear, between his toes. Lice. He brushes off
his thighs, tears at his hair, at his crotch, shouting for
the guard, grabbing the bars, shaking them, roaring.

A fading Polaroid picture. The weight-training room at the academy. Young men sitting among dumbbells and barbells. The ceiling slants because the room is under the bleachers of an arena. Sunbeams fall in columns from the windows, way up high, outside the upper right corner of the picture.

A black-and-white photo. A young African man standing in front of a two-seater propeller plane with a large helmet under his arm. Clouds tower behind the plane, sharp like in an oil painting. Greyscale, a radio tower is visible on the horizon, the cowling of the plane is open, the motor's silver pistons glitter in the light. The large propeller is a white cross behind the pilot's back.

AUTUMN OF '69. The Piper slowly fell upward, the sunshine caught in the scratches on the glass and turned into white strands of hair, a trembling blindness, his instructor was sitting behind him and carefully moving the controls toward himself as he spoke into the radio; the voice crackled in P's ears, distant; he turned his head, trying to orient himself, got a sense of claustrophobia from the helmet and the jumble of analogue instruments in front of him. He felt his arms become heavy from the acceleration. To the east he could see the sea. As though someone had shattered a mirror into fine dust and swept it up over there, on the ground. He had the thought that he was in the heart of it all.

'I'm going to hand over the controls soon, cadet.' The plane shook and seemed to brake. 'Orient yourself.'

'Yes, sir.' He blinked the sweat out of his eyes, he breathed in so hard that the oxygen mask glued itself to his sticky face.

A liquid or incompressible gas that flows at high speed along a streamline exerts less force along the direction of flow than the same liquid or gas flowing at low speed along the same streamline; later on, the equations of the aerodynamics lessons drew arcs and curves in the empty air when he looked up at the birds that whipped their way up above the city in the dusk, or when he saw the clouds rush in above the runways and the barracks. The sky was inside him now, in his heart; it pumped around his body like a gas. After the flight he went and showered. As he was putting on his uniform, one of the other cadets came into the changing room, out of breath, in his flight suit. He sat down on one of the wooden benches next to P and said: 'We talked about air combat today.' The changing room smelled of soap and sweat; the odour reminded P of the gymnasium at boarding school, an acrid scent of boys, sexuality, hierarchies, pent-up violence. He buttoned his cufflinks and stood in front of the mirror. 'We did manoeuvres that are used in combat.' P turned down his collar, didn't answer. He looked at the guy in the mirror. 'What if there's a war.' The guy drew his palm across his sweat-glistening face, pulled down the zipper of his flight suit; the sound was sharp and crisp like ripping fabric. 'What if Uganda ends up in a war? Then we'll have to bomb people. We'll have to kill other pilots. I hadn't thought of that before.'

P smoothed out his shirt. The guy behind him had his hands clamped on the wooden bench he was sitting on, as if he were about to slip from a ledge, about to fall straight up to the ceiling. P didn't like to talk about it. A meaningless discussion. There couldn't be a war in Uganda.

'We're only going to do exhibition flights. Roll, do loops above people's heads.'

On Sundays they had free time. He went to the Orthodox church with his Greek classmates because he hadn't found a Catholic church close enough to the academy. He knelt in the wooden pew and closed his eyes, his hands clasped. He started to fly the T-37E, a training jet. The seasons changed; rain whipped the coast. They flew at dawn, in formation, wing to wing. In early 1970, Hussein's relative was promoted to chief of the army and the air force, and Hussein treated them to liquor one evening in central Athens. They stumbled around the side-walks in one of the cold drizzles of Greek winter; they called out to women in Swahili, they laughed and stared up at the silent, white down that was suddenly falling in the glow of the street lights that night, the rare Greek snow. John sent a photo of his newborn son, and P put it up over his bed. At night he could feel the horizon sway-ing under his feet. The bare branches of the plane trees and fruit trees splayed out in the photographic brown light of afternoon as he walked from the barracks to the bus that drove the cadets to the airfield, and sometimes he thought of the trees he had climbed as a child, and of the games. He had wanted to be a bird.

Dropping bombs, training on targets; the forces of acceleration closed around his head like a black tunnel, the line of the sight raced over the rocky landscape, the small groves of forest. Air-combat training, the radar system swept the sky, he threw himself from side to side in his seat harness and tried to see his classmate's plane behind him, pressed the plane into a sharp turn to fool the heat-seeking missile into seeking another source of heat, into the sun.

During the spring of 1970 he had a visit from one of his cousins who lived in Rome with her Italian husband. He showed them around Athens; they drank coffee at side-walk cafés, the wind blew P's white summer uniform into a fluttering cloud, he spoke English with them because the husband knew neither Lango nor Swahili; it made him feel distant and strange. Maybe there was something else, too. What he was becoming. He thought of his childhood. He wanted to be free of it, forgive it. He waved at them as they stepped onto the ferry in the har-bour.

Flying at high altitudes. He pushed the plane to its

limits and climbed out toward the layers of the sky where the light that fills the cockpit turns a shade of midnight blue; he felt the metal shaking, he felt more than heard the double jet engines hacking, he levelled out the plane and its heavy metal body seemed to hang perfectly still for a moment, way up there, before he turned the plane and fell down to the deep again.

Love for the Greek Air Force is a crucial element which must be present in the soul of every young man who wishes to become a cadet.

Early summer, 1970. He was sitting in an open hotel window, eight stories above the cool April night. He had just won the high jump at a track-and-field meet where the air force had competed against the army. The trophy with its small gold figurine lay where it had been tossed on the bed. An open bottle of champagne stood on the hotel-room table. The breeze from the Mediterranean brought with it salt and sand. The gullible heart of his life. An evening when they had cheered his name. His muscles felt weak after his golden jump; his head was empty from the mental discharge, his thoughts swam calmly, a bit sadly. It was as though this were the evening when he realized that everything would disappear. Although that wasn't true, either. He rested his chin in his hand. A Greek woman was sitting beside him in the window, looking at him with searching eyes; her name is K and she was probably wondering about him, about this Ugandan flight cadet who had recently hung weightless in the air, in the swarming, roaring curve of the Olympic stadium. She drank the champagne and kissed him, drunker and more careless than she usually was when they met like this at hotel rooms or in parks. He thought that the emptiness after his victory was like the wind, too; had it all just been the wind? It was such a tranquil, strange night, like after a disaster. He missed walking under the trees with John. He would be finished with his pilot training in less than a year. He lost himself in the kiss, in her; there was something lost about her tonight, this night that was coming—something new and vulnerable in her way of being. It was as though he were moving along the edge of something. Athens shone blue-green out there, a city on the bottom of the sea. A large sign with lettering hung in the spotlight above a deserted lot across the street. *All of Greece is a construction site*—one of the slogans of the military junta, and one of the oddities of the dictatorship that he thought about sometimes, that the military was building hundreds of tourist hotels in Athens and on the islands in the Aegean Sea. He smiled and took the bottle from K's hand. Her fingers lingered on his. He spoke to her in Greek and felt like he was many people in one body. A boy who runs out into the grass one evening. A young man who fights in a schoolyard. The wonderful weapons of the skies. He laughed suddenly and she asked what he was thinking about, so he said that he missed his country, but he didn't know if this was true. He said that he had wanted to be a priest once, and this is true, but she laughs at it and doesn't believe him, because he's so military, so much a pilot, she couldn't imagine him as anything else, she said. He breathed a column of smoke out into the night. He talked about his childhood, about his homeland; he said that he had lived with his older brother, who beat him, but he couldn't say everything that the man had done; he couldn't put it in words. It was one of those nights when life was too deep, too long, too large, a night that was like a dream or like a memory even as it is there before your eyes. He blinked, rubbed his eyes. They had shouted his name as he stood there concentrating before his final attempt, for the gold—presumably it had been one of his classmates who had started the cry, but it had spread and grown and suddenly the whole Olympic stadium had been screaming his name in unison, over and over again, as he paced off his approach and as he ran, and pushed off, and took flight.

Altostratus. Blue layers of cloud, streaky. The sun visible as through frosted glass.

He walked across the runway with his helmet under his arm; the sweat was already dripping into his face. He was too tall for the modern fighter planes, and if he had been Greek he would have been rejected, but because he had undergone the tests in Uganda, the Greeks hadn't noticed until now, during the last phase of training: someone had gone through his papers and realized with a shock that if he were to deploy the ejector seat he would break his kneecaps on the instrument panel. He felt the rivets under the wing. He tapped the dull aluminium surface and listened. He didn't know what he was listening for, but he did it anyway. He made sure that the jet engines' air intakes were free of leaves and sand. He brushed it with his hand; stroked the smooth surface of the plane. He climbed up into the cockpit; he belted himself in and pulled down the glass hood as he taxied out onto the runway. He throttled up; the airplane trembled with restrained power, he spoke to air-traffic control on the radio. The motionless glass of the sky. He throttled up, he released the brakes; his head was pressed against the headrest; the landscape receded behind him. Everything fell away. See the ground sinking. See the world sinking. The sky carried him.

Cumulus. Clouds with sharp contours that grow vertically, in mounds, domes, shining white towers. Dark, horizontal bases.

Flying in formation. Half-hidden behind the reflection of the sun on the cockpit glass, he saw the other T-37s in a row, on a diagonal slant, over mountains. He pulled the controls toward him, rose out of the storm of sliver flakes that twinkled, twinkled.

He awoke in his bed, in the middle of a big breath. John was proud of him, he wrote in the letters. Just before dawn. He slipped out of the bunk bed, careful not to wake the others, stood at the window, and looked out at the dark winter sky. It was late 1970. He was far gone in the sun-tunnel of flying jets. The Greeks had offered him the opportunity to become a helicopter or cargo-plane pilot instead, but he had clicked his heels, straightened his back, and said in a loud voice—he had almost shouted it to the administrator there behind the desk—that he was a fighter pilot, sir. He wasn't afraid of death in the jet's narrow cockpit; he was afraid of not being allowed to be the deadly weapon of the sky, the son of the sun, his country's proud hero. He stood with his forehead against the window, breathed out mist. It was a bit chilly. He thought of his father, whose face he didn't remember—he had only been three or four years old when he had learned of his death: one of his many brothers, F, had taken him aside one day and said, 'Our father is dead.' He hadn't understood. He remembered that he'd been hungry and that he had eaten a lot at the evening meal that day, because no one else had had any appetite. A few days later he had moved out of his mother's house, along with the brother who would make his childhood hell. He breathed, placed his hand in the spot, white, blurry. When he took it away, the imprint looked like spread feathers, quills.

The Cessna T-37 was a light, two-seater training plane, originally produced by the United States Air Force. It had two Continental-Teledyne J69-T-9 turbojet engines, built on contract with the French Turbomeca Marboré. Its weight when empty was 2.5 tons; its maximum speed 628 kilometres per hour. The seats were placed side by side so that student and instructor could interact more closely than in an airplane with tandem seats. It had an upper ceiling of around 25,000 feet.

Altocumulus. Ripple clouds. Shaded, grey-white floes, blinding sunshine in the space between the clouds.

The motors of the T-37 were extremely loud, even compared with regular fighter planes: when the air was sucked into the plane's sleek turbojet engines, they emitted a powerful, high-frequency, screaming noise, and the ground personnel who worked in the vicinity of taking-off or landing T-37s wore hearing protection so they wouldn't go deaf.

Exhausted sleep. He hurtled forth through skies crossed by flight paths, parabolas, curves. There was a flight exercise where the cockpit was covered with black fabric on the inside, and one flew according to radar and altimeter. One hurtled forth through dense darkness.

'**WHY DID YOU** come back?'

The small interrogation room feels damp and raw now, as though the night had lingered in the bare, flaking walls. P rubs his bare arms. 'Why did you come back to Africa?' P picks a few lice from his hair, presses his hands between his knees to warm them up and get them to stop trembling. His body is a hollow sculpture of dried mud. He bites his nails. He is not this naked, itching, coughing, crying body. His skin smells like rubbing alcohol. A guard gave him a wet cotton ball yesterday and told him to rub himself with it to get rid of the lice. His underwear is wet. The guard drenched it in alcohol too. The interrogator looks at him and laughs. P is struck by the thought that this is all an act on the part of the Tanzanians, that the letter promising him a position outside of Lusaka might not have been real, either. He wonders if the Zambian or Tanzanian intelligence agency got hold of one of his job applications and answered it to get him to come here.

'Who do you work for?'

'I was going to fly a crop-dusting plane. You've seen the letter.'

'You were in Europe. In Rome. You were in Italy, a NATO country. You received a military education in another NATO country. Zambia is a socialist republic. You chose to return to Africa to spray fruit orchards.'

'Yes.'

The guard behind him places his arm around his neck and pulls back so he can't breathe. P's legs kick under the table, he tries to get loose, the interrogator busies himself with his papers.

'We want you to tell us who you work for. Then you may go.'

P's vision goes black, it feels as though his throat were about to be crushed like a thick stalk being broken off in someone's hands, his bare heels scrape the cement floor. The interrogator signals to the guard, who lets go and backs up.

'What did you think when you found out that Obote had fallen?'

P leans over the table. Coughing. He tries to remember those days. Now, afterward, he can't believe he didn't see the coup coming, can't believe he was so blind. He remembers a different day. K walking toward him with her hair swinging in the street lights and her long, black skirt floating around her legs; she sat down next to him, said his name, she was two years younger than he was, she studied literature at the university and when she said his name it was like he was swept up in clouds and sunshine and he sometimes thought, in those moments, that he wanted to stay with her, that he didn't want to go back to Uganda to become a flight instructor. They sat on a park bench in central Athens, on Syntagma Square, in front of Parliament; it was cold, he was wearing his flight jacket, the olive-green one with orange lining. 'Do you have to go away after your exams?' The birds ate the leftover food on the café table.

He tries to remember. The interrogator looks at him. He remembers the way he felt the death-machine's metal skin, across the protruding rivets, how he brushed a little sand out of the air intake, that he always made a second round and checked everything again, knocking here, listening, knocking there. He remembers that he sat in the gravel with his head between his knees and the taste of blood in his mouth one day, from running, and that the tears came, and it was like the lashes of the whip were running out of him, and his childhood, everything, as though a great forgiveness and mercy were streaming into the universe. That was the last winter before he was to return to Uganda. He would be a fully trained fighter pilot and an officer in the Ugandan air force on the seventh of April, 1971.

'Have a cigarette.' The interrogator tosses a pack on the table. P takes out a cigarette and puts it in his mouth. He has no lighter, of course; he looks around and wants to ask the interrogator for a light but doesn't dare, because of some diffuse fear. 'Where are your manners?' the interrogator hisses at the guard, 'give the man a light,' and the guard leans toward him and lights the cigarette for him. P doesn't know if this is the same man who was at the interrogation yesterday, or if it is a new man; he has hardly seen the faces of any of them. He takes a few quick drags.

'What did you think when you heard about the military coup?'

What did he think. He had been half-lying on a bench outside the main entrance of the academy. He was wearing long pants and a shirt; it was a cold January day, three months until exams, he stared out into the grey and let his pulse slow. His hands were clasped behind his head; he had run almost a mile. A Greek first-year student, a small fry, jogged up and stopped in front of him.

'Are you one of the students from Uganda?' P yawned pointedly before he answered. 'Yes,' he said, 'yes, small fry, I am.' Sonic booms from the F-86s flown by the fully trained Greeks swelled across the airbase.

'Sorry to bother you.' The small fry stood with his hands behind his back, a young man with a narrow face, large chin, and half-open mouth; he fidgeted and looked down at the ground. 'I was on guard duty last night,' he said, but he was interrupted by a whole group of small fry coming around a corner. The sound of crunching gravel grew and died away. *Psarades*. P lay still, his eyes fixed on a distant point.

'I heard on the radio that there was a coup d'état in Uganda.' P looked at him from under half-closed eyelids and felt a muteness trickle into his body. What did he think. He thought nothing. 'A soldier named Idi Amin has seized power.' He thought nothing, not then, not at that moment. Another plane roared past, above them.

'Idi Amin?' he said. He tried to act indifferent in front of the small fry, an instinct. 'Hussein's uncle? Amin?' he said to himself, and for the small fry's sake he let out a short, scornful laugh.

'I think that's what they said. Idi Amin.' The small fry couldn't meet his gaze, he just stood there in front of him with his head slightly bent. He suddenly gave an awkward, hesitant salute, turned on his heel, and jogged off across the yard—his tennis shoes crunching on the gravel, the sound of each step separately carved into the winter air. P stood up cautiously. As he thinks about that day now, almost a year later, he wonders if he didn't sense a political change coming in Uganda after all, if he hadn't known without knowing it consciously that a military coup was on the way, because things he hadn't understood suddenly made sense: a strange tone in John's latest letter, an assassination attempt against Obote last year, small shifts in the tone of conversation among the Ugandans, and in their body language as they placed an arm around the other's throat and pulled him close, violently, and something in the laughter and jokes and Hussein's expression when they said that he wasn't a pilot but what, a chauffeur, a helicopter chauffeur.

P clenched and released his hands as he walked down the stairs outside the academy; his fingers were numb, somehow like stones, petrified. He thought, Idi Amin, commander of the army and air force, Hussein's uncle? He walked down the stairs. He stopped and steadied himself against the railing.

'I was afraid.'

The interrogator has lit his own cigarette, which he smokes in short drags; he seems unused to smoking.

'You were in the same class as Hussein, Amin's nephew, isn't that right?'

'Yes.'

'What did Hussein say?'

'I don't remember.'

'What I don't understand is why you persist in lying. Your people are the ones dying in Uganda. Are you still working for the Greeks? Or for the Americans? Who sent you to Lusaka?' The interrogator turns his head from side to side, as if he were listening for something, as if he could hear P's thoughts, which whirl around, muddled and terrified. 'You work for the Americans?'

'You're all crazy,' P says, opening his mouth so that the smoke billows from it.

'You work for the Americans.'

'Why would I work for the Americans? Let me go back to Rome.'

'You shouldn't have come back to Africa.' The man leans back in his chair and points the burning tip of his cigarette at P; threateningly at first, and then his expressions and body language become reasonable and reassessing. 'Let me explain something to you. Here in Tanzania, we are socialists. Like in Zambia. We oppose the imperialists. It is thanks to the imperialists that Amin has come to power. They have placed him there. Great Britain, France, the US, and so on. Your friends. Greece. They have recognized his regime as legitimate; we don't; nor do our friends in China and the Soviet Union. The Brits didn't like the fact that Obote made noise about their arms sales to South Africa, did you know that?'

'No.'

'Of course you don't.'

P ashes on the floor, and he notices that they haven't even cleaned up the butts from the last interrogation.

'I'm hungry.'

'Tell me why you returned to Africa.'

'I wanted to fly.'

'Obote was threatening to withdraw from the British Commonwealth if the Brits resumed their sale of arms to South Africa. Now they have, with Amin's blessing.'

The interrogator is sitting with his mouth open, silently, looking at P. His chin moves side to side, vegetatively; the muscles in his sinewy neck move under his skin. He says, 'During World War II, the British conducted a census in Uganda.' He stops talking. Maybe he is trying to remember the story. 'The people in the colonies were evaluated for their ability to serve as soldiers in the British colonial army and were ascribed certain traits— aptitude for aiming and firing rifles, aptitude for leading or being led, body, intelligence, aggression. Are you aggressive and disobedient?'

P glances behind him. The guard is standing against the wall, a shadow.

'Look at me when I speak to you.' P turns his head slowly. 'You were created by these censuses. The Brits created nations where there had once been only loosely related clans and tribes. On the whole, the Acholi had no conception of themselves as a people before the Brits started administering them as such. The Acholi and Langi in particular were the two peoples the imperialists took for their armies. Ask me why.'

P shrugs.

'You want to know why?'

He has the sense that the guard is going to hit him in the back of the neck with the butt of the pistol. A fly buzzes around the bulb on the ceiling.

'They chose soldiers based on height, as though you were livestock. And you were, and you still are. Livestock they sacrifice in their wars. This is completely in line with the imperialists' strategy and way of thinking. The Western-Nilotic people, whom Amin belongs to, were sifted out because they are on average shorter than the Acholi and Langi. Do you understand what I'm telling you? I'm teaching you history.' P blinks rapidly and doesn't understand the point of this. Inside him he hears the clatter of locks and barred doors from the cells.

'The Kingdom of Buganda, on the other hand, and certain other Bantu peoples, posed a real threat to British sovereignty with their more centralized societies, so the Brits did not want to train their young men in warfare. And so on. The Acholi and Langi were considered to be suitable soldiers, and when Uganda became independent, you inherited a military organization full of tribal rivalries and suspicion and, considering what the rest of the nation looked like, it was monstrous. You are a monster. In your new army, nearly half of the soldiers and officers were Acholi, an ethnic group that makes up hardly twenty percent of the country's total population. You, the Langi, which Obote belongs to as well, made up another quarter.'

P is familiar with what the interrogator is saying, but he pays very little attention to politics, history, anything that isn't part of his own private life.

'Do you believe that you were chosen to be educated as a pilot because you are gifted?' The interrogator laughs. 'You are Langi. As soon as you showed up on the military base, your kinsmen took you under their wings. Just as the Brits have taught them to do.'

P looks down at his hands, at the lines and grooves in them. Many of the top military men he met in those distant days when he was undergoing tests were Langi, of course, and many of the young men who moved on were either Langi or Acholi. But that was because they performed best on the tests, wasn't it? He picks at his palm with his thumb, he lifts his hand, dries sweat from his forehead. The ethnic conflicts which are tearing Uganda apart right now are something he has only understood instinctively, with a hypersensitivity he learned in his childhood, and even if, since the coup, he has thought daily about the explosive lines of blood that run through his homeland, it isn't until now that he has realized that he *did* grow up with just these sort of crude ideas about different groups: he has known that Western-Nilotic people are sly and hot-tempered, that Bugandans are greedy and lazy.

'Obote.' The interrogator studies him. 'Now we're getting to your enemy.'

'He is not my enemy.'

'He tried to unite the various peoples of Uganda into one people. That's what he was doing when he travelled around the country, giving speeches. When the people in your village destroyed his equipment. You are reactionary. Langi. You are like Amin in that way. You are by nature conservative and backward-looking; you were favoured by the Brits, as well as the Indians and Pakistanis who own all the shops and textile mills in East Africa now. You lack political understanding because you belong to a social class for whom blindness is a condition for the privileges you enjoy. You are parasites. You multiply in the darkness. You conspire. You weed out those who don't belong to your own people. If you are against Amin, it's only because he has seen your true nature. You hated Obote because he belonged to your own people, but broke out of this blindness and started working for the entire nation. He was a great leader. He is your country's Julius Nyerere.'

P recognizes this name, Nyerere. The president of Tanzania cooperated with Obote. Since the coup, Obote has been in exile here, in Tanzania; in all likelihood he is even here in Dar es Salaam, maybe at a hotel just a few kilometres from this cramped room.

'I had nothing against Obote.'

The interrogator pages through his folder. 'Have you met him?'

'Obote?'

'Amin.'

'Have I met Amin?'

'It's a simple question.'

'I'm hungry.'

'Do you want something to eat?'

'Yes.'

'Have you met Amin?'

'No.'

'Never? Me neither.' The interrogator stares into thin air for a moment. P coughs; his throat is still sore after the guard choked him. The military had crushed one of the primitive Bantu kingdoms' revolts in 1966, the year before he was sent to Greece; this increased tensions to breaking point between the Bantu on one side and the Acholi and Langi on the other. After this, Obote changed the constitution of Uganda so that the traditional kingdoms were dissolved and lost all actual power. This power was gathered, instead, in his own hands. Now Amin plays on the Langi's and Acholi's over-representation in the military, implying, as the interrogator just did, that Obote had conspired to weed everyone who wasn't Langi or Acholi out of the military.

Amin's voice has, in fragments, been streaming out all over the world all year. The BBC likes to repeat his joke about no one running faster than a bullet, but his speeches also always include threats against the Acholi and Langi people, as well as the Indians and Pakistanis who live in the country. P rakes his nails over his bare, itchy chest. He thinks that politics are a kind of labyrinth, a house where doors and windows change places.

The first time he heard Amin speak on the radio was the same day he received the news of the coup from the Greek cadet. He had gone to the barracks and sat on his bed; one of his classmates was there, an Acholi. P had passed the news on to him, and both of them tried to call their relatives from a payphone in the corridor, but they couldn't get through. They listened to the BBC on Hussein's transistor radio. They waited to hear something about Uganda. They sat across from each other without speaking. The dry voice recited cricket results and cultural news, evening had come, a light rain pattered against the windowsill, other cadets from their year passed them in the hallway, Tunisians, Egyptians, and Libyans, some of them had heard the news of Amin's coup and hung around in the doorway for a while, asking if they knew anything, while P and his classmate shook their heads and sent them away. Hussein and the other Ugandan who shared their room were on guard duty. The other Ugandans at the academy were nowhere to be seen. Maybe they were listening in their own rooms. P got up and stood in the window, birds were hopping around outside, the sharp tips of their beaks picking at the winter-hardened gravel. He wrung his hands together, his fingers still felt dull and dead and he stretched them out and then they felt unused and new or maybe like the fingers of a very old man. He steadied himself against the windowsill. His knees trembled. He didn't want to die. He wondered if maybe the news wasn't true, that it was just a rumour that had gained speed. He heard the blood rushing around in his head like wind. Everything was far away. The barracks yard out there, where he had been running for a whole year, the barrack where his body stood at a window, they were far away. He sat on the bed again.

'We met him once.'

The classmate looked up.

'Who?'

'Idi Amin.'

'You've met him?'

'I sat at the same table with him to eat. I just remembered. He visited the military camp in Uganda when we were doing our service there. Don't you remember? In the summer? He visited there. He pointed at me in the mess hall, in the food line, and said that I would keep him company. Because I was tall.'

His classmate laughed nervously, then caught himself and became silent. They couldn't look each other in the eye; something had changed, their gazes were naked and darting.

'What did he say?'

'We sat across from each other and ate. There were others at the table, too. He wanted to show us that he could eat with the soldiers. That he was like us.'

They waited. P stood at the window again. Earlier that day as he had walked down the stairs outside the main entrance, he had decided not to go back to Uganda; now he didn't know. He thought it might not be that dangerous, that it probably wouldn't affect his life after all. At eight o'clock there was a short item about a curfew in Uganda's capital, Kampala. Violent disputes had been going on all day and there had been a coup the previous evening. The BBC broadcast a short clip from a speech Amin had given on Ugandan radio, in which he said in English that he was a soldier, not a politician, and that he had overthrown Obote to ensure that the corruption in the country would cease. There would be new elections. People had spread green branches in front of the army's tanks. When the broadcast was over, P turned off the radio. His classmate, who had once spoken to him about the war, that they might be forced to kill, that this was the point of their education, clawed at his scalp with his fingers and said, 'I can't go back.'

'It won't last more than six months,' P said. 'We'll stay here. We'll wait.'

He asks the interrogator for his clothes, and he asks again about something to eat or at least something warm to drink. He rubs his arms, shivering.

'What did you do in the days after the coup?' The interrogator's tone has become tired and impatient.

'We flew. Everything was the same as always. I tried to call the hospital where John worked. My oldest brother.'

'He's still in Uganda?'

'Yes,' P says, yes, his whole family is still there, in the dictatorship; he hasn't heard from them since the coup, he doesn't know if Amin's regime has murdered them. 'I couldn't get through,' he says, and the words feel mute and heavy. When he closes his eyes, he sees an image before him. Skulls stomped to pieces, blood sucked up by a dirt floor.

'What did the other Ugandans say?'

'Most of them said that they were afraid to go home after our exams.'

'Hussein was happy about the news.'

'I don't remember.'

Details from the days after the coup, instants and moments as clear as photographs but dreamlike in their lack of context: he was walking across the barracks yard and the sky very quickly became darker, as though smoked glass had slid in front of the sun, maybe because a storm was coming; maybe because it didn't happen in reality but only inside him. He was standing on a side-walk on a weekend afternoon and the wind came up and scraps of paper and leaves lifted from the ground, as though they had suddenly become weightless. On that day, the BBC reported that Amin was preparing the army for battle, that the tension between Uganda and Tanzania was increasing, that Amin was accusing Tanzania of planning an attack, and that Ugandan fighter planes were patrolling the border.

Less than a week after the coup, they were flying in formation over the sea in a rainstorm. When he got above the clouds, the water ran across the glass canopy like tears. He felt the horizon swing and looked out across the white ravines. The swell of the radio crackled in his ears; he read the instruments; the acceleration pressed the blood down into his feet and made them heavy as iron.

'Correct your position, cadet.'

He turned his face up and the oxygen mask with its thick, ribbed rubber hose hissed. The squadron leader's plane climbed into the sun, which flashed like a bouquet of knives. That was the last time he flew. It is a mark inside him. That there had still been time.

HE WAS SITTING in a house outside the academy campus and looking out the window at the bare branches in the garden; they spread out into the evening like running black ink, the bushes with leaves that turned gold with the chill. It was barely a week after the military coup; he had received a letter from John that morning, and it had been opened and taped up again. He ran his hands across his face. A flowing sensation in his chest. In the letter, John complained about the rain. But it was the dry season in Uganda. John didn't mention Amin or the unrest in his letter, even though, according to the postmark, it had been sent just two days after the coup. When he had finished reading the letter, he decided to finally tell the Greeks about the decision he had made when he had first heard about the coup, on the stairs outside the entrance to the academy. He had gone to the office and told the administrator that he couldn't go back home after the exams, that he would have to stay in Athens. The administrator reacted by calling a military police officer and asking P to go and pack his things. At first P thought they planned to send him back immediately. He had stood by his bunk bed, heart pounding, tossing clothes and documents into the old suitcase he had used on the journey here, but it turned out that the Greeks just wanted to move him to an empty house that was at the disposal of the air force. It was cold in the house, which must not have been heated over the winter. He didn't know what it had been used for before he came here. The Greeks were apparently worried that he would infect his classmates with his opinion. A light drizzle was sprinkling the yard; he could see it glisten in the glow from the street lights past the iron fence. He ran a hand across the leg of his winter uniform. He was a shipwrecked god of the sky, a potential diplomatic crisis. He wondered why none of his classmates had said that they wouldn't go back to Uganda either. He turned on the radio that stood on the bookshelf among old books by Plato, Herod, and others he didn't recognize. He turned on the BBC and sat in the window again. A weather report from the other side of the earth was talking about a storm moving in over New Zealand. He thought that Idi Amin's empire wouldn't last more than six months. He would wait.

There was no more news from Uganda until a week or so later, a mid-February evening. Battles had been fought near a preschool in a residential neighbourhood in Kampala; the Ugandan army and soldiers who remained loyal to Obote had come to blows. He sat at the kitchen table and ate while he listened. He chewed a tough bite of meat, tried to get the static out of the voice, turned the knob on the radio. 'The inhabitants cowered in fear as the rebels and the regime's soldiers fired their automatic weapons with no concern for the lives of civilians. While these battles were going on, Amin formally took over all of Obote's legislative privileges, dissolved parliament, and designated himself head of state, commander of all armed forces, and minister of defence.' The voice disappeared in a wave of static; he moved his fork around on his plate, and when the voice returned it was hollow and metallic, robbed of human nuance. 'Amin's governing forces surrounded the house where

Obote's loyalist troops had taken shelter and set fire to it.' He turned off the radio. He stood up again; he had an uncomfortably distinct sense of his body, of its muscles, skin, and nails. He thought about how Obote was Langi like he was, and that that meant something, that it had been magnetized and given weight by the military coup. *I am Langi.* He stood by the bookcase and turned his hand before him, clenching and opening it. He had a people.

At night, sometimes, K came to him. They had only met at various hotels and restaurants before. They lay in silence, listening to each other breathe. She said, 'Have you talked to your family?'

He touched her mouth with his fingertips; she rolled onto her back and looked at the little square of sky in the window. He said, 'I can't get through.' He hadn't met her family yet. He was her secret. Her eyes were cloudy. 'I met Idi Amin once,' he said. 'He came to our camp in Uganda when I was doing my military service. I ate at the same table as him.' He smiled and turned his head to her, looking at her in profile. He realized that she could sense the icy fear spread through him and that she didn't know what to do with it either, what it meant.

'Stay here,' she said.

'Did you fly any planes besides the ones listed in here?' The interrogator has taken out P's flight log. He has been paging through the sea-green book for several minutes while P has been talking about the coup, about what he thought; then the man places the book on the table between them, presses his palms together, puts them to his lips, a priest-like gesture, pondering some mystery, waiting.

P turns the book so he can read it. He flips through it,

looking at the columns that list types of aircraft, times, who led which flight exercise. He filled the small boxes in himself, after each flight, with neat Greek letters.

'You didn't fly any military planes?'

'The training planes are military planes.' He touches the inked notes with his fingertips. 'T-42. T-37.'

The interrogator waves his hand dismissively. 'You claim that the Greeks isolated you?'

'They didn't want me to talk to my classmates.'

'Because you were against Amin?'

P closes the log and pushes it back across the table.

'Because I didn't want to go back.' He breathes into his hands to warm them; he looks at the wall behind the interrogator, at the chips in the blue paint. He wonders if they appeared when naked bodies like his own have been thrown against the wall. When bones have snapped, when skin has split.

'It was courageous of you to tell them that you didn't want to go back to Amin's Uganda.'

'Can I have my clothes?'

The interrogator opens the logbook again, pages through it, tries to interpret the Greek letters, as though there were some secret code written there.

'Can't I have my clothes? I'm freezing.'

'Your clothes were full of lice. You are a louse. You are a fascist. You are lying. What did the Greeks say about what happened in Uganda?'

'Nothing.'

'Your last flight was in the beginning of February? Is that right? Am I reading that right?'

'They forbade me to fly after I said I wasn't going back.'

He jogged every morning, in a park around the house. Sometimes he ran for hours. It was the first time in his life that he didn't have something to fill the days with. The wet gravel crunched under his tennis shoes; the sun glittered strange and white between the branches; he ran through dense, even silence, a silence and dullness that wrapped around his running feet and his breath like glycerine. One day as he was sitting on the veranda after a run, he felt the panic, which sometimes disappeared in the absolute exhaustion, rise up again inside like a dull, roaring sound in his head. He couldn't control it; he couldn't handle it; he didn't know what he should do. He wanted to talk to his Ugandan classmates; he wanted to know what people were talking about at the academy and what was going on in Uganda. He tucked his T-shirt into his jogging pants. It had been more than two weeks since the coup. He saw someone approaching on the street beyond the yard; the person opened the gate and walked up the gravel path. It was one of his flight instructors, a Greek pilot; he stood up and saluted, stayed at attention.

'At ease.' The man gave P a disappointed, fatherly look. 'What are you doing?'

P looked at his feet, frowned, didn't say anything for a long moment, and then said, 'What do you mean, sir?'

'You signed a contract to fly fighter planes on behalf of the Ugandan air force. That is why you are in Greece.'

P didn't know what he should say; he was angry, nervous; he felt the sweat chill his skin as it ran down his spine. 'You would be lucky to get a job as a janitor at an airport on the other side of the world after what you've done.' P was surprised by the plainness with which the man who had once taught him to fly dismissed his decision. The exams were still two months away. Didn't they understand that he couldn't return, that none of the Ugandans could return?

'Have you thought even once about Greece's diplomatic status in relation to Uganda?'

'Yes, sir.' He said it quietly. He lifted his eyes, squinted above the man's head at the gravelly sky, the clouds, the light. In some ways, what his instructor said was true. P was a soldier, not a politician. He was trained to obey, not make his own decisions. The instructor was still standing with his hands clasped behind his back. He said, very formally and with the new, hard distance in his voice and posture, that P would have to remain isolated until the Greeks had figured out what to do with him, and that the Ugandan authorities were not yet aware of his decision.

'You talk about it like it happened to someone else.' The interrogator chews his upper lip, sucks it into his mouth; his eyes are fixed on P. 'You talk like you're not the one who experienced it.'

'We were trained to ignore our feelings. We were fighter pilots.'

P doesn't dare look at the interrogator, out of fear that the man will read guilt in his exhausted eyes or in his nervous, twitching face.

'Maybe one of your classmates was isolated, but you weren't.' The interrogator's voice is searching and certain at the same time, as if each sentence were something he examines in the light for a while and then lines up on the table. P has tried to answer the questions as honestly as he can, but it's difficult because he must always think twice about what he's saying because he is worried that something that seems like a trivial detail to him might seem like proof that he is guilty. 'You were never kept in isolation because you told the school that you wouldn't work for Amin, because it's not true. Everything you have said is lies. You supported Amin's coup, and you support him now. You were on your way back to Uganda when we intercepted you in Zambia. Is that right?'

'No.'

The interrogator gestures that he should be quiet, that the accused isn't supposed to interrupt this exposition with lies. P's eyes wander but don't find anything to land on in the bare room. The interrogator closes his eyes; his face is tired and seems closed up on itself and when he speaks again, it's as though he were only laying out facts that everyone in the room agrees upon. 'You were on your way to rejoin the Ugandan Air Force. That much is clear. The only thing we don't understand is why you didn't fly straight to Kampala. What were you doing in Zambia? What did Amin want you to accomplish in Zambia?' P clasps his hands together, and they are cold and feel thin and somehow brittle, like dry stalks. That he would have been on his way back to Uganda of all places is a brand-new angle of approach. As the interrogator leans forward in his chair, his forehead casts deep shadows onto his face, as though his face were bleeding darkness. 'Tell the truth.'

P is struck by the thought that one of his former classmates might have defected to Tanzania and given this man information to save himself. He puts his hand to his mouth, feels his stomach turn. Someone else might have sat in this very room and been interrogated in the same way, said his name, told them about him. This is a crazy place, because it's a place where stories are created—this chair where one is forced to remember.

'You'll get your clothes back when you tell the truth.' The interrogator thrusts his head forward on its sinewy neck, trying to catch P's eye. In a mild, almost apologetic voice, he says, 'You were in contact with Amin's regime even back in Greece. You were in contact with them when you were in Greece, and then you went to Rome to complete a task there, or to confuse those who might start to suspect you. You are Amin's man. What does Amin want with Zambia?'

A hushed, heavy silence fills the room. P is tight with tension and suspense. Do they know that he met representatives from Amin's regime while he was in Greece? Might someone have taken pictures of him that summer? How much do they know? P sneaks a look over his shoulder again; the guard meets his gaze and his eyes are like two holes cut out of tin cans.

A gust of wind blew last year's dry leaves across the gravel path outside the barracks. Three weeks after the coup, his isolation had been broken just as suddenly as it had begun: it seemed that the Greeks had decided to pretend nothing had happened and wait for Amin's next move. He still couldn't fly. He sat and smoked with his classmates; they talked about a rumour that had apparently started circulating at the school while he had been isolated: it said that Amin had sent out a passenger plane that was going around Europe and gathering up Ugandan students, military ones in particular.

'The plane has already been to England,' said one Ugandan in the first-year class, a Western-Nilotic like Amin and Hussein, but unlike them he disapproved of the coup, possibly because he was from an upper-class family that had had business connections to Obote. He was playing with a lighter, fanning out sparks into the cloudy afternoon. 'My brother was studying civil engineering in London, and they called him from Uganda and threatened our parents. They said they would kill our mother if he didn't come back with them.' Someone made his lips into a circle and said, 'Ooh,' and they laughed at him. 'The plane is totally black, unmarked, no name.'

P tried time and again to call the hospital in the city of Gulu where John worked. He sat with the receiver in hand, listening to the steady beeping sound. No connection. Exam day was approaching. The foreign students had started to receive uniforms from their home countries. The official word from Uganda: silence.

He saw the other Ugandans come walking back from the airfield after they'd been flying. Sometimes he walked over to the runway and stood looking at the planes taking off and landing, like he had in the beginning. *Stratocumulus. Clouds with wispy bits along the edges.* The bbc was reporting conflicts along the border between Uganda and Sudan, too. Obote-loyalist troops apparently had camps in Sudan.

He was awakened by one of his classmates one night. He swam up out of a nightmare, hunted by something diffuse he couldn't put a face on. Threw off the blanket. The door to their room was open, and people were moving around in the corridor, slow and subdued. Hussein told him that all the Ugandan flight cadets were to pack their bags and gather in the auditorium, and then he disappeared out under the fluorescent lights with a suitcase in hand. P pulled on his pants, his uniform shirt; he tossed his clothes and documents into his suitcase— the second time he'd packed his bags since the coup.

The intense cold of the spring night needled his face and his bare forearms and hands. The cadets from each class walked across the yard, half-asleep and disoriented, more than a dozen shadows in the green glow of the sparse lamps. Everyone was carrying suitcases and bundles of fabric; a few took the opportunity to smoke, while others breathed steam into their hands. One guy was still wearing his undershirt and was wriggling into his short-sleeved khaki shirt as he walked—flapping, grey wing-strokes in the night.

They walked into the auditorium and sat down. A Greek officer stood at the podium; his eyes were red and his face was bloated and sleepy. He cleared his throat and waited for the young men to sit down and be quiet, and then he informed them, in the explanatory and bureaucratic tone that the Greeks had been using more and more with the Ugandans since the coup, that Amin's regime had called all its flight cadets home from Greece and that a plane was on its way through the night to fetch them. The plane would land in forty-five minutes and no matter what their personal opinions were on the matter they would all be aboard it. P closed his eyes and turned his face up to the glow of the fluorescent lights, which coloured the blood in his eyelids pink. He had dreamed something; he didn't remember what. His eyelids darkened to reddish-black as the blood was pumped out into his skin; a night sky appeared and disappeared. A mosquito net flapped. He yawned. The officer up at the podium was still talking.

'Unfortunately this is a matter of an official request from the Ugandan State and we cannot refuse to obey it without doing harm to our diplomatic ties.' The cadets often whispered that this man was an ace from the war in Cyprus, that he had never lost even a simulated dogfight in his entire career. 'You can wait here until the plane lands.' The officer stood there for a moment, silently sweeping his eyes across the young men's faces, and then he nodded with a hint of apology and left the auditorium. A Greek military police officer positioned himself at the door.

There was a raw, animalistic fear in the room; it was an element in the air, a hormone with a flavour and a scent, just as tangible as if it had been a gas that were pumped in through the ventilation ducts. P wiped his sweaty palms on his pants. He wondered if Amin's regime knew that he had been planning to refuse to return after the exams, if any of his former classmates would mention it once they were home. He looked around, searching the others' faces for a reassuring look, a promise of loyalty. One young man, a first-year cadet, was quietly sobbing and being comforted by his friend.

After almost half an hour had passed, the Greek officer returned. He stood in the door and said in a high voice that they were to go back to bed, that the Greek state had decided to refuse to hand them over to Amin, that a minor diplomatic crisis had broken out, but that they were safe.

Then weeks went by without any change in their status. The fruit trees bloomed, pink phantoms that seemed to hang weightlessly above the lawns. *Cirrostratus. Clouds without shadows.* He went out with K on the weekends; they wandered through the warm orange light of the Greek spring evenings, talking to each other about nothing; the future was empty, he still wasn't allowed to fly; on weekdays he jogged and exercised in the gym or sat and listened to the radio in the barracks. He bought a small tape player, and sometimes he listened to Harry Belafonte on it. It was still impossible to reach his family, but from the other cadets he heard rumours of an atmosphere in their country that was even more aggressive toward Acholi and Langi than what the sporadic news reports from the BBC might indicate. In addition, Ugandan troops were now fighting almost daily with rebels who had established camps in Sudan. Open war was close at hand. The airplanes roared over the academy and disappeared over the Mediterranean. They took their exams on the seventh of April. The Ugandan cadets hadn't received uniforms because of the chaos in their homeland's military, so they went to the ceremony dressed in their white Greek summer uniforms with the gold buttons and small sabres dangling at their waists. They received their diplomas from a high-ranking officer, they saluted, they backed into the line again. P observed his colleagues as they performed the ritual, and he felt a sudden disappointment, or maybe it was just clarity: they all looked like little boys in their white uniform caps. He thought of John, and of the games from his childhood. He had wanted to be a bird. The Greek soldiers were scattered along the walls of the hall, in suits of rank insignia and medals.

After the exams, some of the Ugandans travelled home. Several chose to stay in the country. They couldn't remain at the academy after their exams, so the air force put them up in various hotels in central Athens. They wandered the streets. They sat at outdoor cafés and blinked into the sun, blinded baby birds. All the foreign cadets had received salaries from their home countries, but Uganda hadn't paid them since the coup, presumably as a result of the same bureaucratic chaos that kept them from receiving uniforms. Their savings were about to run out. For a few weeks they spoke only of how they would get money, but then the air force arranged jobs for them in the hospitality sector, possibly out of fear that the unemployed pilots would start selling military secrets if they went broke. Maybe it was just a gesture of lingering loyalty.

Despite his stubbornness and headstrong ways, P was made a manager of the restaurant in the hotel where they all lived, and two of his countrymen started working as waiters. He mostly sat in an office behind the reception desk, handling enormous sums of money, often far into the night. He got drunk with his countrymen and the other employees of the hotel. K visited him now and then, and he lay beside her, tossing and turning with anxious dreams in which he fell through endless layers of clouds or swam through the sky. Mornings, he sat and talked to his two countrymen in the taxi exhaust and heat haze outside the hotel. They played cards for money, laughing laconically and without vigour, and when the restaurant opened for lunch they put on their jackets and white shirts. They were airmen without a country. He flipped through thick bundles of bills, put rubber bands around them, and placed them in a safe. It was in the early summer of that year that he started meeting with Amin's men.

Since the coup, Amin had dismissed more than half of all the ambassadors outside the country, along with many other embassy workers, and now he was sending out his own men, almost all of them top-ranked military men, to take their places. These replacements came to Greece, too, and the Greek military asked P to act as a guide and interpreter for them. They asked him nicely. He saluted when he picked the men up from the airport. They laughed as they walked through the arrivals hall, and their salutes were just approximations, as if military tradition were a joke. Their faces were like rubber masks, expressionless and elastic, and they had sunglasses that reflected the sky. P showed them to the limousine and sat in the back seat with them. He was dressed in his Greek uniform, which he had otherwise not been allowed to wear since the exams; he answered the men's banal questions politely and tried not to show any contempt, anxiety, fury. He thought of himself as an unimportant speck, floating between a pair of massive jaws. Yes, he had learned to fly; yes, he had learned to escape from prison camps. Outside the tinted windows, the city flowed by, darkened as if from thunderheads. High-rises, snapping umbrellas, palms. Yes, he had learned to withstand torture, to fire a rifle. The men exchanged glances and laughed. He couldn't read them, he couldn't tell if their questions meant they were truly fascinated by his foreign-officer training or if they were mocking him.

The men always stayed at the same hotel he lived at, and he made sure that they got the best suites on the top floors. In the evenings he went out and ate with them, helped them speak to waiters, to passing women. Yes, he spoke fluent Greek. An army general, promoted to this position after the coup, leaned across the white linen tablecloth.

'Do you know about the scandal when Amin visited Great Britain?'

'No,' he said, taking a drink of his wine. He wondered if the Ugandans understood why he was still here, if they realized he had refused to return. They spoke a Bantu language with one another and laughed together, and he fell into the laughter, spontaneously. Alongside the unease he felt, there was a sticky seduction in the men's power, in the ceremonies at the airport with sabres drawn and boot heels clicking together.

It was late July, the third time he had been asked to perform this task, which he wasn't sure if he hated more and more or was in the process of accepting as part of his life here.

'Amin had an audience with the queen. He gave a speech for her and her staff. Do you know what he called her?' P shook his head. Apparently this was a story that they'd all heard before, and had repeated several times, because the other Ugandans were already chuckling in anticipation. P leaned across the table and felt something sleepwalker-like in his body, in his face, something ingratiating and resigned and awful. He was a bit drunk. He smiled, nodding his understanding.

'He called her "Herr Majesty."'

P let his smile grow. Herr Majesty, that was kind of funny, considering that Uganda had been a British colony until a decade ago. 'Would you like dessert?' He leaned back in his chair and caught the waiter's eye. He thought of John, whom he still couldn't get hold of, and he wondered if these men had taken part in the murder of anyone in his family. Maybe they had only murdered other people so far. The rank insignia on the general's uniform gleamed in the light from the crystal chandeliers. P thought of the letter about rain. He felt a chill grip his innards and squeeze them.

'May I have a glass of water?' He would like to lie down, he does not want to talk more, he doesn't want to remember. His arms hang down at his sides; when he closes his eyes he feels the dizziness sweep through his forehead like beating wings. It must be around lunchtime now, maybe even later.

'Why did you go to Rome?'

'I was on vacation.' He tries to sit upright, but he keeps slipping down in the chair. He absolutely does not want to talk about his superficial dealings with Amin's men, because he's afraid the Tanzanians will interpret it as a sign that he willingly cooperated with the regime. He rubs his eyelids, which are tender and swollen from lack of sleep.

'I was on vacation,' he repeats. 'I already told you I had a cousin there.'

'And while you were on vacation you received a job offer from Zambia?'

P rests his face in his hands; his mouth tastes like bile and nicotine. 'You received a job offer that was mailed to your cousin in Rome?' the interrogator says. 'That's a bit strange, isn't it?' Somewhere beyond the roaring shield of exhaustion, he realizes he's about to get caught in lies, that he is in danger, that he must think, orient himself.

Athens. He sat in the window of his hotel room, looking down at the leaves swaying five stories below him. It was early August in '71, and on that particular evening his desire to fly was like an ache in his body; he poured a glass of whisky and as he drank it he sensed something growing slowly but inexorably, like the tide. Something vital. He put his glass down on the windowsill and looked at his watch. He was supposed to pick up yet another Ugandan military officer at the airport, and he was already ten minutes late. He hadn't even put on his shirt yet. It lay beside him on the bed. His white, short-sleeved shirt with the rank insignia, it was lying there. His patent-leather shoes stood beside the bed; they reflected the light of the setting sun, which fell through the hotel-room windows. One of his former classmates, who was Langi like him, had told him that several of his relatives had disappeared in Uganda and that all of them, though taken at different times, had been forced to take off their shoes before they climbed into the cars that came to fetch them. The shoes had been found later, at the edge of the road, standing neatly. The shoes of the dead. One of the peculiarities of Uganda in a state of emergency. He looked at his watch again. The stifling summer evening swelled into the room, and it tasted like exhaust and he thought about how he hated the Greeks because they forced him to perform this work, and he hated himself because he didn't dare to refuse. He thought about God; he remembered the prayers he had learned during his years at the boarding school, Holy Mary full of grace, he stood up and pulled on his uniform shirt and buttoned it carefully and very slowly. It was a night, a summer, in limbo.

K slept over at his hotel room more and more often. She lay with her hair flowing across the white hotel linen, talking in her rough, whispering voice about a life there in Greece. He marvelled at her, this Greek woman who studied literature and kept his existence a secret from her parents.

At the end of the month, another of his former classmates, one of the waiters, started talking about a massacre that was said to have occurred in northern Uganda, but it sounded absurd. Yet the man was insistent and mentioned it several times: that a hundred or more young Acholi soldiers had been forced into barracks and killed with kicks and slashes of the machete.

'Photographs.' The interrogator's voice wakes P, who is half-sleeping in the chair. The man has brought out P's photo album yet again, and he takes out pictures and places them on the table one by one.

There is a photo of P sitting in the cockpit of his T-37; the photographer is leaning over his shoulder and P is turning and smiling at the lens. It must be from his second year at the academy.

'Photographs make me think of doomsday,' the interrogator says and pushes a class picture across the table.

P searches for his own face in the picture, but he doesn't find it even though he knows that he is one of the cadets.

'You're Catholic?'

'Yes.'

'Do you believe in doomsday? The day of judgment, when the dead will wake?' The guard in the corner moves nervously. 'Yes,' says P.

The interrogator suddenly closes the photo album. 'We are socialists,' he says, as if this settled it—which perhaps it does; P doesn't know, he is exhausted by the questions, his hands tremble with hunger and lack of sleep, and he can't focus his gaze. 'Tell me who sent you from Greece to Rome. I don't want to see you be mistreated by the Tanzanian authorities. Tell me the truth, now.'

The silence in the room clings to the three bodies like a rubber sheet; P takes a few short, jerky breaths through his nose, hunches down, and waits for the blows. They never come. Instead, the guard helps him stand up and leads him back to the cellar. He collapses in his cage, lying on his back while the lock rattles and the guard's steps disappear down the corridor. He can hear the sound of traffic above the other prisoners' whimpering and muttering. The stinging scent of solvent and urine fills his mouth and nose. P cautiously sits up and crawls over to a small elevated portion of cement that resembles a chair and leans against the bars. He tries to sleep. His temples are pounding. He holds back the urge to vomit, claws his hands into his face; he tries to think. Maybe he ought to tell them that he worked as a guide for Amin's men, that he was forced to? Maybe they already know about that, and they're just holding him here because he's lying about it. He thinks about what the interrogator says about photographs, that they're like doomsday—diffuse, jumbled thoughts; he sits still and stares into the darkness. Fewer and fewer cars go by the small windows up there; night is already coming. *If you have been shot down over enemy territory you should never ask a child for help, because sooner or later children will tattle to adults about what they have seen.* He blinks with heavy eyelids; he's close to falling asleep but looks up when he hears a splashing sound: the man in the cage next door has stood up, stuck his genitals between the bars, and is pissing straight out into the corridor. P looks away as the piss runs into his cage. *The information in your head is the only thing that makes your life valuable.* He runs a hand through his hair, grabs a handful of curls, and tears at them to feel real, to feel something. The blinking lights along the ceiling reflect in the urine that flows out across the floor; he thinks it looks like a night sky opening at his feet. He breathes into his hands to warm them. He is a pilot. He will fly again. He will flee.

My mobile phone blinking. *Dad* on the screen. I close my eyes and the shadows of birds of prey race across the ground. It was November when I saw him last. He had come from the hospital by taxi and was standing in the stairwell in the granular blue light; he had the oxygen tube on his Rollator; he stared at me for a long time and then shook his head, turned around, and left. He has been dying as long as I can remember. I don't answer.

I've been reading the history of the Langi this winter. According to one historiography, they are the last off-shoot of a migration stream that came from the Ethiopian empire in the seventeenth century: the Acholi people in northern Uganda and the Luo in Kenya, both linguistically related to the Langi, would then be part of the same migration, traces of a forgotten exodus. Other reports are incompatible with this. One version of the story claims that the Langi were shepherds from Sudan who settled among the more centralized and hierarchically organized Bantu kingdoms around Lake Victoria as early as the fourteenth century, and who appropriated a place in the rigid social order by claiming that they possessed supernatural powers and could control rain and fertility. Dad really only knows one thing about the origin of his people: that he and his family called themselves Nilotic, which meant that they had once crossed the source of the Nile in eastern Sudan.

I'm standing by a crosswalk in a city that isn't my own and thinking about the people who left, in the past, the nomads from Ethiopia or Sudan, that this is an origin as true as any other: those who came before us travelled. I don't believe in origins. I walk toward my hotel; it's a bright spring night, streets shimmering with rain, no cars out. I'm not made of the material of history; if I come out of history I come out of it at every moment the way you come up from the swell and shake off the cold, the sea, the salt.

When Idi Amin looked at Uganda, he saw a loosely connected federation of peoples and kingdoms. To him, history was the future. To Obote, as well as the president of Tanzania, Julius Nyerere, and other African socialists who were active in the sixties and seventies, the nation was above all a circle that would gather those who lived within its borders into a single people, with a common goal, a common blood running through their veins, a common origin.

A boy runs through tall grass. He is running away from a place. Thus he will always be associated with that place.

I sit on the curb. I take a book from my backpack and page through it: Frantz Fanon's *The Wretched of the Earth*. I was sixteen when I found it at the school library and stole it. Read it sitting on electrical boxes in Araby in Växjö. Fanon was a psychiatrist, a philosopher, who was born in Martinique but ended up a spokesman for the Algerian liberation movement, the FLN. He wrote wonderful books about black skin and white masks, about freeing oneself from history by risking one's own life. Tanzania, like Zambia and many other countries, drew its combination of nationalism and socialism from Fanon's ideology. The book made me feel like I could depend on life, that history would take me somewhere. I hold it in the light from the lamp in the hotel lobby, page through it, remembering how I saw the letters come flying across the small-town sky one winter afternoon, black-headed and shrieking like seabirds. A fragment of my youth.

In the hotel room I page through a document that is many years old, something that Dad wrote one fall. He wanted to write down what he remembered of his life. He sat up at night remembering, and it made him sad, he said, but he also said that it had been necessary for him, that for the first time he had started to understand what he had gone through, how strange and violent it had been. *I looked out into the dark African night and wondered where I was.* I think about his hands writing those words on a computer in an apartment. I sit in the window of the hotel; the curtains are fluttering, I have a smoke.

Julius Nyerere dreamed of returning Africa to the paradise of collectivity and equality that he imagined had existed before the European night. To him, too, history was the future. Nyerere liked poetry; he translated Shakespeare into Swahili. With Amin's coup, the wave of socialist African states fractured and turned. *Ujamaa*, the Swahili word Nyerere used as a name for the African form of socialism, means 'family'; it's the closest translation I can find.

I travel between places I try to form into a nation. In the days after I return home, I ring at Dad's door a few times, but he doesn't answer. Soon I hear from one of my brothers that he's in the hospital again, that he's going to have an operation. The Japanese cherry trees are blooming on Järntorget. I'm restless; I stop trying to

contact him, and when he starts trying to call again I
don't answer. I think about how I am a tree with its
roots pulled up. Once again I read what he wrote that
fall, and for the first time I notice that more than a
third of it, or maybe even as much as half of it, is made
up of his memories from the six months of military
service he did in Uganda before he was sent to Athens:
long-winded descriptions of how they march, lists of
commanders' nicknames, descriptions of the routine in
the military barracks and the tactical drills. There's a
strange weight in all those concrete details, a weight
that has to do with death, with the body that touches
the objects, with the hand that writes. I see with new
eyes the images of outcast-ness, scattered-ness, blowing leaves, petals filling the sky. I am a hare, I run
through whirling snow. He stands outside my door on
one of the first summer days. He has a white face mask
on; the oppressive warmth makes the stairwell smell
like garbage. He says he has received a lung transplant
since the last time we talked. He doesn't want to hug me
because he takes medicine that lowers his immune
defence. I think that a wind came one day and blew
away his life. He pulls down the white mask; I see his
face.

P SITS WITHOUT moving, looking at the light and the shadows. His joints are sore. When sleep finally came last night, just before dawn, he dreamed that he was falling toward iron bars and he hit them and kept falling through the darkness, down toward the same bars, and hit them again. His kicking legs woke him up. He yawns; it's morning out there, narrow columns of sunshine in the darkness; the piss that ran into his cage has evaporated or been sucked up by the cement floor. After a while, a guard comes and unlocks his cage and tells P to follow him to the bathroom. He is allowed to wash himself in cold water from a faucet, but he isn't given his clothes. He is led out into an empty exercise yard, he walks around in circles, the wind brings rust, smoke, carbon monoxide, he thinks that life is too big, too violent, too immense, that he can't touch bottom. He sees a bird pass between the walls; its wing feathers flash in the sun and go dark and the image is burned into him. He closes his eyes. A bird against the sky. It hangs on the wind, beats its wings, drops down. The guard gives him a bowl of boiled brown beans; he wolfs them down while leaning against the wall. The chill of the wall against his bare back. The metal spoon scrapes against his teeth. The exhaustion flows through his body, through his life, like grey electricity. The guard yanks the bowl from his hands.

When he comes back to his cage, another man is sitting in it, curled up far back in the shadows. At first he thinks it's he himself sitting there: that he's sitting in the cage and is also outside himself. The guard shoves him in the back. He's crouching in the cage now, observing the man who, like him, is naked except for a pair of underwear. When he washed himself in the ice-cold water and then when he was out in the exercise yard, a chill crept into his bones and now this chill is radiating into his flesh. He coughs. The guard has already locked the door and disappeared down the hall. The man in the shadows extends his hand, his arms are thin and his face is birdlike, shaved smooth; P shakes his hand and says his name. The man says his own name. 'I'm a journalist. From Zaire. Accused of espionage. I've been here for three days.'

'I'm from Uganda.'

'How did you end up here?' They are speaking Swahili. P sinks down to the ground and rests his elbows on his knees.

'I'm a fighter pilot, trained at the Hellenic Air Force Academy in Athens.'

'I have family in Zaire. Two children, a wife. You?'

'I have family in Uganda. Brothers.'

'A Ugandan fighter pilot at a police station in Dar es Salaam?'

It's such a relief to have a conversation that's not part of an interrogation, to be able to speak without being constantly mistrusted and challenged, and P explains briefly about his time in Athens, about his education, about the coup d'état. In a whisper, he also tells the man about what he kept secret during the interrogations: about his dealings with Amin's men during the summer, about his feelings of guilt, his doubt. 'I decided to stop working for the Greeks,' he says, and then he falls silent. He wonders about his decisions, about life, how it becomes bent.

He remembers one night as he was standing in the shower and had shampooed his hair, he stood with eyes closed and his hands against the tile wall and noticed, at first a bit absent-mindedly and with surprise, and then with absolute clarity and certainty, that his fingers were sticking to each other, that the shower water was viscous and gooey. It was late summer. It was a time when rumours among the exiled Ugandan pilots weren't the only thing that spoke of conflicts between different ethnic groups in the army, about murders and disappearances—so did foreign news bureaus. He fumbled for the faucet, turned it off. He cried out when he opened his eyes. Blood had come out of the shower; he was covered in it, his hands scrabbled across his body, panicked and confused, trying to get the warm, sticky liquid off his skin and palms. He squeezed his eyes shut and leaned his forehead against the tile wall. It wasn't real. It couldn't be real. He was supposed to meet a Ugandan official from the department of defence that evening. He stood still, his eyes closed, as the last drops from the shower head landed on the floor with a gooey sucking sound.

He sat on the edge of the bed, out of breath and full of fear. He looked at his footprints across the wall-to-wall carpet. They were red.

The journalist tugs at the elastic of his underwear, as if he were adjusting the belt on a nice pair of suit pants. P feels empty and desolate. They sit in silence; after a moment the journalist gives a laugh, snorting, nervous, and says, 'It helps to hear someone's voice.' P places a hand on the back of his own neck, massages it, feels a high-frequency sound inside. The interrogations have done something to words, smashed them to bits and displayed them as naked as stones.

'I didn't have any sisters,' he mumbles, once again focusing his eyes on the shadow sitting across from him in the cage. 'Just brothers.' The face in front of him gives a quick smile at his strange answer, a white row of teeth in the dim light. 'Brothers who stood in the grass, screaming.'

'You don't have to tell me.'

But he wants to tell. He needs to tell the story to someone.

The telephone had rung several times. He had been sitting on the bed for several hours, staring at the bloody prints on the carpet until they disappeared mid-blink; they were gone. He finished the whisky in three gulps. He was supposed to meet the Ugandan official a long time ago. The window was open; he could hear sounds from the street, faint and distant like in a dream, like everything this summer, a nightmare. It was too late to go to the airport; he took another mouthful of whisky straight from the bottle, stood up, and looked down at the hotel guests who streamed in and out through the glass doors of the hotel. He wondered if John was alive. Why didn't anyone write to him anymore? Taxis cast the beams of their headlights across the asphalt. He couldn't go back to Uganda. Amin had ordered fighter planes to bomb yet another guerrilla camp in Tanzania during the past week, and if he went back, the best-case scenario would be that they would force him to go on similar missions and the worst-case was that they would kill him. He couldn't go back, but he also couldn't spend more time sitting in a limousine and talking to the Ugandan military officers and cabinet members, because he spent every moment in their company wondering if they had murdered his family, his friends. A knock at the door. He swayed as he stood up, steadied himself against the wall. He was slightly drunk.

His flight instructor was standing in the hotel corridor. They stood facing each other in silence for a moment, measuring each other up, two men who had once belonged to a system, an order.

A military limousine was waiting outside the hotel entrance. P saw his own reflection in the black varnish, a distorted and ghostly being.

They left Athens, went toward the sea. They passed highrises, suburbs, farms, villages; they got out, they went down to the sea, and the chauffeur remained by the car, a silhouette against the summer night.

'We're trying to help you.' The flight instructor stroked his neatly trimmed moustache with his thumb and index finger. They were walking side by side in the surf. 'We let you stay here, we give you a job, and this is how you thank us? You stop showing up?'

There was nothing P could say; he walked with his head down, he would listen and then maybe it would be over and he would get to do some other job. His patent-leather shoes sank into the sand, the sea crashed down; the sound reminded him of jet engines. 'Why are you being so unreasonable?' It had been more than six months since P had flown, and now, at this very moment, he missed it all over again, with the same burning intensity as those very first days when he'd sat in the house thinking that his flight ban would only last for a few days. He missed hurtling away. The transparent waves licked the sand. The instructor's voice was nearly swallowed by the surf. 'A lot of people are getting tired of you.'

P stopped; he bent down and picked up a stone, threw it out into the water.

'Where were you today?'

P brushed wet sand from his palms. Once they had shouted his name. The entire Olympic stadium had shouted his name. 'You have to start living in reality.' They stood side by side, gazing far off into nothingness. P was no one now, nothing. The stars were out, above the sea. 'If you disappeared one day, just disappeared, who would miss you? Amin's regime? I have to tell you something. They're talking about sending you back to Uganda. Forcing you to return.'

The lock at the end of the corridor rattles. The guard is walking, dragging his baton along the bars; P turns his face away from the banging, clattering noise. The journalist crawls into the corner of the cage, puts his head in his arms, and whimpers, a pitiful, animal sound. Afraid of being beaten; P recognizes it from his childhood. The guard fetches someone from another cage, and they disappear. The journalist's eyes flash.

'You went to Rome?' Silence. A voice cries out in the darkness. 'You went to Rome after the Greeks threatened you, didn't you? You said that you came to Zambia from Rome.'

P chews his lower lip and doesn't answer. Night is falling again, the sunshine through the window is diluted; the cement dust that shakes loose from the ceiling as cars pass out on the street glows faintly red, like dry, smouldering dirt.

'Did I say I went to Rome?'

'You said you travelled from Athens to Rome and that you came from Rome to Zambia.'

P is unsure of what he told the journalist and what

belongs to the interrogation; it's a frightening sense of confusion, of worlds blending.

'I went to Rome because I had a cousin there.' The bars of the cage are cold and hard against his shoulder blades. He turns his head and looks at the journalist, who is still curled up in the corner. 'And I'm Catholic; I went to a boarding school run by Italian priests when I was little, and we don't need visas to visit Italy.' He gestures with his hand, he could have gone to Germany, Libya, anywhere. 'I just wanted to get away from Greece.'

He and K were walking in central Athens one afternoon in early September. The cypresses and mulberry trees were tossing in the wind, the limestone walls shone like dull white lamps. They passed an old church; they stopped on the square, among the pigeons.

'There are Ugandan saints,' P said. She wiggled in under his arm, held his fingers in hers, played with them. 'Did you know that?' She shook her head. 'Martyrs. Some of the first Ugandan Catholics were burned to death in the 1800s. They were sainted by the Pope ten years ago.'

She held his hand, she braided her fingers with his. He looked up at the old church, at the sky, the endless and billowing summer sky; he had the thought that this was life, all these moments.

'I'm thinking of visiting my cousin this weekend. Going to Rome for a few days and clearing my head. Can you do me a favour?'

'What?'

'Buy the tickets for me? I'll give you money.' The pigeons climbed through the pale sky. 'If the military finds out that I bought a ticket they might think I'm trying to run away and they'll stop me. It's such a strange time.'

There was a ferry between the port of Piraeus west of Athens and Brindisi on the southern coast of Italy. Rich Greeks liked to take the ferry on the weekends. K stood on the quay and waved as he boarded. He had asked her to buy a round-trip ticket. There was a breeze from the islands, a salty breeze; he was dressed in his white uniform even though he was no longer allowed to wear it except on official business. It was a regular afternoon. It was a Tuesday. The metal hull of the ferry swayed under his feet; a man asked for identification and he showed his ID card from the academy and his Ugandan passport. He didn't need a visa; he knew that. He turned around one last time. Her hair was a dark flame in the breeze; she turned around, disappeared out into the city.

He got a table in the dining room and ate as the ferry left the harbour. Quays slid past outside the window; he poked at his fish with his fork, thinking of his brothers and his mother, who had once sent him away. He pushed his plate away; he stared out at the waves. People were dancing around him, slowly and a bit clumsily, to piano music that came from loudspeakers. In his childhood he had had a friend whom he had gone fishing with. They liked to stand on the shore of Lake Victoria and cast their lines into the water. One day when he asked after his friend, he was gone. He had died overnight, from some sort of fever. P rested his chin in his hand, his elbow against the white, slightly greasy tablecloth, and thought about this, and about why he was thinking about it. He ate a piece of fish; it was as tasteless as paper. Had the Greeks really been planning to send him back to Uganda? He felt naked, up against knives. Against history, against the war. He went to the bathroom and changed his clothes, tossed his uniform and ID card overboard. He stood at the railing and watched the white bundle of cloth spread out like a jellyfish as it sank into the darkness. He was dressed in his green bomber jacket, a pair of jeans, a grey T-shirt. It was late summer, 1971. He thought of this, the year and the season, as a sign. The coast had already disappeared behind the ferry. Saltwater spray flew into his face. He went back to the dining room and stood in the door, looking at people sitting and eating or dancing. There were men in suits and Greek women in long dresses, turning slowly. One Greek had already sat down at the window table where he'd just been sitting in his white uniform. He took a bus from Brindisi to Rome. He slept for most of the ride and didn't wake up until the bus was gliding between bluish street lights in the southern suburbs of Rome. He looked out at the dry grass that burned in the bus's headlights; he thought of God as a storm of ragged grass and fallen wing feathers, he thought that he should go to confession, that it had been a long time. Lone figures in dresses strode forth along the highway, disappeared behind the bus. He thought, this was Europe, these visions were more European than Greece was, in some way he didn't understand. Oncoming traffic, flaking façades, squares where people stood in small groups, open bars. He felt to see if his passport was still in the inner pocket of his flight jacket; he got off at Central Station and went into the large waiting room. His footsteps echoed, steel roll-fronts were pulled down in ticket windows and stores, most of the lights were turned off. Signs hanging from the ceiling informed passengers about arriving and departing buses and trains. The names of places flipped up with a quiet, automatic rustling; they were mirrored upside-down in the dirty marble sea of the floor. He stood there for a moment with his two suitcases in hand.

He thought about how he could go anywhere in the world he wanted, now. Anywhere but home. He sat down on a bench; eventually he fell asleep. When he woke, travellers were rushing by him in a swift stream. He tidied up in a bathroom, exchanged his money, and called his cousin from a payphone. She gave him her address. He took his suitcases and went out to the street; pigeons hopped out of his way, and he ended up standing in a crowd of people. He didn't know if he was happy or sad. The people who shoved past him swore in Italian. He was a millionaire in lire. He thought about turning around, going back into the waiting room, calling K from the payphone and telling her the truth, asking her to come. He was a pilot without wings. When he got into a taxi and gave the driver the address, a lot of other taxis showed up out of nowhere and blocked every street. Hundreds of cars honked in chorus, and people shouted through their open windows. The taxi backed up, drove forward half a metre, stopped. A ravine of noise; the driver turned around and yelled in poor English that a taxi strike had just broken out, gestured apologetically, and turned off the engine. P hung out of the rolled-down window and squeezed his eyes shut; his head was filled with the grey wasp-swarm of traffic. Soon the Greeks would realize that he wasn't at work, and eventually they would contact K and ask where he was. She would say that he was just on vacation at his cousin's. She would be calm, she would say that he was coming back in a week. But she would be surprised that no one else knew about it besides her, and it would slowly dawn on her that he was never coming back. Horns honked, engines roared; when the racket became deafening he opened his eyes, as though to silence it with sight. Glaring light was reflecting off the great glass windows of Central Station.

His cousin set him up in a guest room in the large house where she and her husband lived. P showered, standing for a long time and letting the water stream over his face. He laughed when he thought about how he had escaped, of how easy it had been. He would call K when he felt more secure and knew where he was going. He thought this, but he didn't know if it was true. When he thought of the way she stood on the shore and waved, he wanted to cry, scream, punch the tile wall. They ate at an expensive restaurant. His cousin's husband was an architect with his own firm; he was nearly twice P's age and had round glasses and was starting to go bald. He leaned across the table and said that what had happened in Uganda was unbelievable but that Amin couldn't remain in power very long. That's what everyone said. P drank wine. Part of him already wanted to go back to Athens; he could tell the Greeks that he'd just needed to get away for a weekend, apologize, say that he had gone through something big and difficult but now he could see clearly and was prepared to work for them, doing whatever they wanted. His cousin's husband took off his glasses and polished them with a linen napkin. 'You can become an apprentice at my firm. That would be a good life.'

'We'll see.'

'What are you planning to do?' said his cousin.

He shrugged.

'Look for a job as a pilot.'

He felt suspense within himself, like just before a great leap. The days passed. He walked along the wide sidewalks, sat on benches; sometimes he thought he saw K at a pedestrian crossing, walking toward him, but when she got closer it was always someone else. His cousin bought more than a dozen expensive Italian shirts for him. He visited a church, knelt before Christ, and the anonymous, silent face of the wooden carving stared down at him. He remembered the boarding school; he had been a choirboy. He remembered priests' robes flapping in the wind, the simple altar, and the cross where they had knelt to receive communion. He wondered about God, about the great faceless, breathing being. He looked up at Christ. *Why don't you call out for your father?* A group of tourists came into the church; their heels echoed against the smooth stone floor, and they spoke loudly in some guttural European language he didn't recognize. He remained there for a moment, his knees on the floor and his eyes turned to the ceiling, to the images of clouds and radiant angels that were painted on the vaulted surface. There must have been *something* before everything, before history. He went out into the blazing late-summer heat. He had sent applications to Air France, British Airways, Pakistan Air, Air India, and a number of other companies throughout the world, but he hadn't yet received any replies. He sat with his cousin under an umbrella that snapped in the wind, drinking coffee. In her features he saw his mother smiling. She had received a postcard from her sister in Uganda, but it said nothing about the political situation. Presumably the mail was being censored. They didn't talk very much. He thought of his mother, of how seldom she had smiled. He thought about flying, about how it had felt like falling into the sun; he looked at his watch but realized he was in no hurry to go anywhere; that he had nowhere to go anymore. He ordered cigarettes, and the waiter brought them on a silver plate. He raised his eyes and the clouds were a slow rain of downy pink against the evening sky. He woke up, stood naked in the window, and looked out at the millions of lights in the night. Several days had gone by and he had received a reply to one of his job applications. A horn sliced through the night and subsided. He stood with his arms like a cross, resting his hands on the edges of the window, and the city outside glittered. He could stay here in Rome. He could become an architect. It would be a good life. He felt a great sorrow, fateful and heavy, and he felt as though his heart were a butterfly of black velvet sitting deep inside the blood-red darkness, unfolding its wings, folding them up, unfolding them. He remembered it was different to fly at night. To come gliding above the abysses. Idi Amin would be overthrown soon. It had to happen soon.

On his last day in Rome, they went to the restaurant at the Hilton. The taxi glided past the plumes of the fountains; he cooled himself off by sticking his hand out of the rolled-down side window, felt the wind catch and lift his hand. The job he had been offered in Zambia wasn't what he had dreamed of, but it was a job and he would get to fly again. He thought about how he could write to K now and ask her to come to Zambia, but he changed his mind and thought he would call her from Zambia instead, later, when he had saved up some money or found a better job. His cousin said, 'Don't go.' Her husband, who was sitting in the front seat of the taxi, turned around and the headlights of the oncoming traffic flowed across his face, a pair of rapidly beating wings. 'Come be an apprentice at my firm.'

'I'm a pilot. I have to fly.'

'You mean that you came back to Africa voluntarily?'

P tries to hide his disappointment that this man, too, immediately considers his decision to return to Africa to be a joke, madness. The journalist laughs, cocks his head, and nods to himself. 'Now I understand how you ended up here.' The sun has gone down once again on the planet outside; headlights pass in the window, the shadows cast by the cages stretch out across the filthy floor. 'Zambia is governed by Kenneth Kaunda, who supports the communist freedom movements in southern Africa. He gives money and weapons to UNITA in Angola, ZAPU in Zimbabwe, and the ANC in South Africa. He has close ties to the Soviets and China.' The journalist runs his thumb under the elastic of his underwear, scratching himself. 'And to Tanzania.'

P knew that Zambia was a socialist republic, that Obote and Kaunda had collaborated, but he never felt that it had anything to do with him. He sat in the airplane seat on the way to Lusaka. He was just excited about his next life. Blue thunderheads streamed away outside the window. He dared to hope that his family had survived the coup and its aftermath, and that soon enough, Amin would be overthrown or step down on his own, so that he could go back home and start flying the fighter planes he'd been trained for. He slept for a few hours, light sleep filled with the rumbling of the airplane, voices, and light. When he woke up, he could see the rainforests around the equator, like islands of leafy green where the rain clouds parted. For the first time in three years he was in Africa.

Half an hour before the plane landed, the stewardess handed out forms for the passengers to fill in information about citizenship, how much foreign currency they had with them, their reason for visiting Zambia, and how long they planned to stay in the country. He answered the questions honestly. He was going to fly; he was trained as a pilot. If Amin were still in power after the New Year, he would look for a better job again, preferably at one of the large, international airlines. He wondered which model the company used. A Cessna, like the tryouts in Uganda? Pipers, maybe. The plane they were flying in now was an older Russian model. Rain pattered on the metal as the plane descended through the clouds. The pilot must never have stood by a fence, rating landings—they bounced across the runway and some of the other passengers cried out: loud, small, terrified sounds that made P smile. The rain cooled his face as he walked across the tarmac. It was early morning, and the sun was an oval clump of red haze among the clouds above the palms; buses drove them to the terminal, rain-heavy leaves blew in the wind, looking like the hands of a sleeping person, awkwardly fumbling for something. The bus stopped; a customs official swept his eyes over the passengers, came up to P, and asked his name. The fact that he seemed to have been picked out of the group specifically made P feel a bit nervous, but he answered and started to take out his passport. The customs official asked him to wait; he put his passport back, unfolded a newspaper he'd brought with him from the plane, and held it above his head. The raindrops pattered against the thin paper.

His fellow passengers streamed into the brightly lit terminal. The customs official was dressed in a green uniform and a cap that seemed to be of a Chinese style. The cloudy sky and the large, dirty-white airliner were reflected in the wet tarmac, its mirror broken by the rain. P thought that perhaps the company he was going to work for had a relationship with the government and he would be taken directly to his workplace by the customs official, or perhaps he had put the wrong information on the form he filled in on board. When all the other passengers had disappeared, the customs official showed him into the central hall of the airport and told P to wait on a bench beside a closed door. The man disappeared. P's shoes were wet; the water from them spread into a pool on the floor. He thought of the shoes on the side of the road in Uganda. People came in through the glass doors or went out into the warm drizzle to take taxis or buses into central Lusaka. Several soldiers stood at intervals along the walls; they spoke in low voices and had automatic weapons and rifles nonchalantly slung over their shoulders. Each time P met one of their glances, he felt like he ought to stand up and salute. He was unused to seeing armed soldiers among civilians in such a natural way. He blinked and his head felt fuzzy; he put his legs up on the bench and rolled up his jacket to use as a pillow. All this time, he had to keep reminding himself he was a civilian. Half of the lights in the arrivals hall weren't working; they flickered and sputtered above him, and he closed his eyes, listening to the chattering voices and the sounds of shoes and suitcases in motion. He dozed off and dreamed of running in tall grass, of the night sky above him, of a voice calling his name. He woke up. The door next to him had opened. He sleepily turned around to see who had come or gone through it, but before he had time to see anything a hand grabbed his collar and yanked him firmly off the bench. Someone dragged him backward through the door; one shoe came loose as it was pulled across the threshold, a uniformed man picked it up, slammed the door, and leaned over him.

The man extended the same hand that had just dragged him from the bench, but this time it was to greet him and help him up. 'Good day, sir. I am an immigration officer.' P laughed at the absurdity of the situation, at the quick shift from violence to friendliness. He stood up on his own and backed straight into the closed door.

'Have a seat, you must be tired, sir. Please, sit.' The man, who was tall and thin, with almost completely white hair, pointed at a chair.

They were in a small room that looked like an empty storage closet. Two chairs against the wall, no windows, a single bare light bulb in a socket on the wall. The man took papers and a pen from the inner pocket of his uniform jacket.

'Unfortunately you are not welcome in Zambia.' The man glanced through the paper. P brushed off his pants, still standing with his back against the door. He wondered if it had locked when it closed or if he could open it and run right out.

'I'm going to work here in Zambia. I have my proof of employment in my luggage.' He looked around the room, as if it might contain a dim corner where his bags were hidden. Dirt and filth along the skirting boards. 'Where is my luggage?'

'You will be deported and sent back to Italy.' The man spoke very formally, as though it were a perfectly typical part of procedure to drag a passenger from a bench and into a tiny room. 'You have hereby been informed of your deportation order. Please sign on the dotted line.' He held out the paper and pen, the walls seemed to shift position, come closer; P took the paper and pen, held the paper against the wall, and wrote his name. He stood without moving for a long time, the tip of the pen against the paper. He should have stayed in Rome. He remembered the view from his room in the house, all the street lights. The official tore the paper from him, folded it several times lengthwise, and put it back in his uniform jacket, and as if on command another uniformed man entered the small room. He closed the door firmly behind him. He had P's baggage with him, and both bags had been cut open and taped up again. *Zambia Customs Authority* was printed on the tape in black letters. The guard had a pistol in a holster; he stood at attention by the wall. There was a small red metal star on the olive-green fabric of his cap. The thin, white-haired man said, 'The next flight to Italy leaves at half-past one tonight. You may wait in here until then. I will get you something to eat.' The man who had brought the bags stayed behind as the white-haired man, who must have been his superior, left. After a while the white-haired man came back with rice and brown beans mixed together in a metal bowl, and then he left again. P stood against the wall across from the guard; he held the metal bowl in one hand and ate a few mouthfuls. He was supposed to fly a crop duster. The guard shifted his weight from one foot to the other and the leather of his boots squeaked; P thought that it was a good thing that they were deporting him, that he didn't want to stay in this country or even on this continent. He took out a pack of Italian cigarettes and offered one to the guard, and the two men smoked in silence. The room was poorly ventilated and quickly filled with smoke, and when the first official eventually returned he broke out in a coughing fit. The guard immediately stubbed out his cigarette, stamped on its glowing end, and gave a salute, to which the other man responded only with a quick motion of his hand. The guard coughed, too, a phoney cough. 'Come with me.' The white-haired man opened the door.

The central hall of the airport was bathed in warm afternoon light and the scratched, dusty clock hanging on the wall said it was half-past four. 'Is the plane leaving early?' The man didn't answer P's question; instead he grabbed the arm of his shirt and led him across the room.

A group of travellers was standing nearby with their luggage, and several of them were Europeans and P was about to shout something to them—a reflex told him that Europe would defend his rights, his life; but then he thought about Greece, of how he had been treated there. The customs official pulled him along, out the door. It had stopped raining; the sky seemed to be made of liquid gold behind the slowly parting clouds. The customs official held P by the arm of his shirt, pulling him along, P resisting half-heartedly, and they crossed the tarmac, walking between luggage trucks and containers. Some sort of shortcut. P carried one taped-up suitcase in each hand. 'Wasn't the plane supposed to leave tonight?' He didn't receive an answer.

A military DC-3 was on the runway, ready to take off. The propellers were turning, perfect geometric circles storming around in the otherwise motionless, oppressive air. The sound of the engines was sharp and howling. The customs official shoved P up the metal stairs, and as he grabbed the railing and started to resist harder he felt something heavy burst forth above the trees and roll over the runway like a wave, and he realized how vulnerable his body was, how thin the bones were in his hands as they squeezed the railing, how easy it had been to drag him into a closet and lock the door, and then drag him out to this airplane.

'Go, go.'

He half-stood on the stairs; he turned around and met the customs official's eyes, which were unrelenting and hard under the visor of his uniform cap.

'Get on the plane.'

The wind tore at the wet palm leaves that lay on the asphalt edges of the runway; P thought about the way his temples felt like chalk, or like thin walls of mud, like he was about to break into pieces. He stepped into the plane. It was full of Chinese people in grey uniforms, sitting on benches along the walls. In the middle of the cabin stood a number of wooden boxes with Chinese characters on them. It smelled like jet fuel, oil, dirt. One of the Chinese people lazily pointed a Kalashnikov in his direction and said something in Chinese. The customs official disappeared back down the staircase. P stared after him as he crossed the tarmac. Someone poked the barrel of a rifle into his back, indicating that he should sit in one of the seats. He obeyed, and just as he had when he heard the news of the coup in Uganda six months ago, he had the sense that what was happening was already a memory, that it had happened a long time ago and now he was just reliving it. Nightmarish, involuntary movements, events that just happened. He sat down and buckled the seatbelt; his fingers shook and it felt like he was outside his own body. One of the Chinese people said in heavily accented Swahili that he wasn't to move around the plane without asking permission; a third soldier stood up and closed the door, and P searched their faces for an explanation, an answer, but they were expressionless, uninterested. It was as if he didn't exist. The plane started moving; the jungle went by in the round portholes.

A prisoner out in the darkness sings something that sounds like a children's song in some Bantu language, abrupt, lisping syllables.

'They flew you here?' the journalist says, and P nods, yes, they flew him here, to Dar es Salaam, where a police car brought him to this police station. P gets up and pisses through the bars. Someone swears out there in the shadows and the cold. The journalist speaks behind him: 'History is balancing on a razor's edge right now. With Idi Amin's coup, the development of leftist regimes in Africa has been interrupted. Obote is living in exile in Dar es Salaam and running a guerrilla movement from here, and both Tanzania and Zambia hope that he will be able to regain power. They're helping him with soldiers, weapons, and ... information.' P wipes his hands on the bars and sits down. The journalist gesticulates at him: 'You just happened to get caught up in a ... gravitational field.'

'I would kill for a glass of water.'

'As soon as I get out I'll go to the UN's displaced-persons commission. If you like I can give them your information and tell them that you're being held prisoner here. Maybe they can contact your family and tell them where you are, or at least register you as a legal refugee.'

'A legal refugee?'

The journalist sticks his hand in his underwear and takes out a small pencil stub and a scrap of paper he has hidden there. P laughs in surprise. 'If you're registered as a refugee with the UN, you have certain rights. You have the right to seek asylum, and you can no longer be taken away or killed without someone being informed.'

P gives the journalist his full name and his place of birth, as well as John's name and the name of the hospital where John was working the last time he heard from him. The journalist scribbles down the information nervously while P keeps an eye out for the guard, and then they lean back against the bars and keep talking; the journalist asks P about the details of his story, and P expounds, tells it again. The journalist tells him about the paper he works at in Zaire, and about his wife and his two children. It's still wonderful to talk to someone who doesn't distrust him, and both men laugh, touching each other's knees with their hands, looking each other in the eye. After a few hours the guard comes and fetches the journalist, who seems more panicky than the other times they heard the guard's footsteps. Something in his eyes as he gets up and leaves the cage is piteous, broken. The door slams, P is alone in the cage once again, a solitude like iron. The prisoners are served food, the same brown beans they received for breakfast, and afterward P feels ill and heavy and lies down on the cement. He doesn't care anymore about the filth, the urine, the lice crawling over him again. He wonders if the journalist was let go or just taken to an interrogation; he lies there for a long time, staring up at the ceiling and thinking that the sky exists up there, thinking that the journalist might be walking around out there now, under the leaves of the trees and the stars, on his way to the displaced-persons commission, was that what it was called? The UN's displaced-persons commission. Tanzania's and Zambia's underhand games to make him disappear will fail. His mother and John will find out where he is, that he's alive. Everything will work out. He is sleepy; he yawns, scratches his body, curls into a fetal position, tries to get warm, closes his eyes. He thinks about how he liked the journalist not just because they listened to each other but also because the man had neatly combed hair and smelled good and had clean feet and reminded P that there was a world out there. They must have let him use soap in the washroom. He quickly sits up, his eyes darting, one hand moving toward his forehead, slowly, like an object floating underwater. It slowly dawns on him. How would a journalist suspected of espionage be able to sneak in a pencil and paper in his underwear? He presses his nails into his scalp;

something roars inside him but all that comes out between his lips is a low whimper. If the man had been here for three days, why didn't he have any stubble? He pulls at his hair, rocking back and forth, terrified. That man was no journalist. They tricked him. They tricked him into telling everything.

The interrogation room, an hour or so after dawn. The Tanzanian interrogator is sitting at the table with his arms crossed. Behind him stands a man in civilian clothes whom P thinks he recognizes, but whom he can't place. The interrogation has been going on for fifteen minutes, maybe half an hour. The man in civilian clothing hasn't said anything so far. He's wearing dark pants and a white shirt. P is sweating profusely. The interrogator has asked again about P's time in Greece, his reason for travelling to Zambia, his opinion of Amin. Something is different about his tone of voice. They know what he did during the summer. They know he was forced to go to Rome because he didn't want to be an interpreter and guide to Amin's men. And yet P denies this.

'Why did you leave Europe?' the man in civilian clothing hisses. P realizes with a shock that the man said this in Lango and then he remembers where he's seen him before: the man is one of the Ugandan officers who interviewed him during the trials for the air force. The man is ten or fifteen years older than P, with neat hair and a close shave. 'Are you dumb?' Around his mouth and eyes is a tension that P recognizes from other violent men. This man has presumably defected from Amin's military apparatus. Like P, he is Langi.

'What are you doing here?' P says, but the Ugandan just snorts in answer and repeats his question. P answers in Lango: he wanted to fly.

'You wanted to fly? You wanted to fly a crop duster?'

'I'm a pilot. Like you.'

The Tanzanian looks at his papers. P searches the Ugandan's eyes, looking for an answer to some question he can't even formulate, but the man straightens his shirt collar, his face remains hard, immobile, a stone sculpture. The Tanzanian puts his paper down on the table and says in Swahili, 'Are you seeking asylum here? Do you want to be a refugee in Tanzania?'

'Yes,' P says, 'I want to be a refugee.' He thinks a refugee camp must be better than the cages in the cellar. The Tanzanian writes something down on his paper.

'They're sending you to Tabora,' says the Ugandan. 'A train leaves in three hours.'

Both the interrogator and the Ugandan leave the room; only the guard stays behind, and after a while, another guard comes with P's two suitcases, in which his belongings are tossed willy-nilly. He takes out pants and a shirt and puts them on. He buttons the shirt wrong, starts over; he's nervous and has trouble orienting himself. Maybe the Tanzanians suspected all along that he was hiding something and weren't appeased until the 'journalist' revealed exactly what it was. Maybe something totally different had happened instead, something he didn't understand, something that had to do with the sudden appearance of the Ugandan man. P leaves his shoes in the bag and instead he puts on a pair of leather sandals that his cousin bought for him in Rome. An unmarked police car drives him to the train station. Morning, streaks of lingering haze on the streets, white light through the trees. A guard escorts him onto a train and sits beside him as they roll out of the station. P is sitting in the window seat, looking out at Dar es Salaam, a city he has been in for more than three days now.

Houses and factories, shanty towns and avenues of fruit trees, metal shacks. He thinks of a long trip he took as a child, when he, his brother, and his brother's wife travelled in an old, crammed, rattling car to the village they were going to live in. He was crowded in the back seat among bundles of clothes and curtains, and he didn't understand why he had to go with his brother. He wanted to stay with his mother and his other brothers. Maybe he was being sent away because of poverty, or because some illness was running riot. No one told him anything. His brother had already been beating both him and the rest of the family for several years, and everyone knew that P would be beaten every day. Yet they had sent him away. He sits still, his eyes rove about the landscape, looking for focal points in the dry grass, in the dreary sky. The train thumps and thumps. He has never understood. Sometimes he thought he was a gift or a payment to get the man who terrorized the whole family to leave.

The guard sitting beside him is dressed in a uniform, armed with an old rifle that looks almost like an antique, and he's reading a small red book. When the train has been moving for over an hour, P asks to go to the bathroom and the guard waves absent-mindedly that he may go. P stands and walks through the train. There are many other people in the same car, and most of them are in civilian clothes but some are soldiers. He opens the bathroom door but instead of going in, he uses it to shield himself as he sneaks around the corner of the walkway. He reaches back and closes the door. He cautiously opens the sliding door that leads to the platform between the cars. Dry earth blows into his face. The roar of the old steam locomotive is deafening. He throws a glance over his shoulder. Waits. Nothing. He steps out onto a rough, sooty metal grate and closes the sliding door behind him.

Lone trees stand out against the bare afternoon sky, narrow as blood vessels. He looks down at the ground; it rushes by. He is seized by the sudden feeling of being out of his depth in his own life. He grabs a swinging chain so he won't lose his balance. Yellow palm leaves tumble by as the train passes though a grove of trees. When he looks at the horizon, the world seems to stand still, as though the train were a building tossed out into the savannah. Back in the open countryside again. Dirt dusts up over the sky. The train is heading north. The ground slides away. He doesn't have much time before the guard realizes he isn't in the bathroom. The train is near the end of a long downhill stretch, and when the ground flattens out it will slow down. Then he will jump and run straight out into the grass. He will run away. He squeezes the chain.

'What are you doing?' A soldier has popped up in the door to the next car without P noticing, and he's lazily waving a sub-machine gun. P has no idea how much the other Tanzanian soldiers on the train know about him, if they're even aware that he's a prisoner.

'I am on my way to the bathroom.'

'The bathroom is in there.' The soldier nods at the car P came from and drives him back into it with his weapon aimed at his stomach. As P goes into the bathroom, he says, 'I'll wait outside.' He is very young, he can hardly be out of his teens.

Through the bathroom window, the countryside is broken up in blurry spots, approximations of sky and earth; P stands with his arm leaning against the window frame and his face close to the glass, staring into the changing light. He tries to understand what they want with him, why he's being sent to a city called Tabora instead of being allowed to return to Europe. He washes his hands in a small copper sink because he is afraid the guard is listening to what he's doing in the bathroom. Was it the Zambian military that answered his job application? Someone in Tanzania? He stares into his own eyes in the mirror. He couldn't jump off the train; it was going too fast. He didn't dare.

The soldier follows him to his seat and exchanges a few sentences in a local language with his colleague, who had been absorbed in his little red book and who becomes visibly embarrassed. He puts down the book and signals to P to sit down. The train clatters up the gently sloping land. The two men sit across from each other in silence. Trees rush past again; the branches and the large, dry leaves scrape along the sides of the train. P looks out at the countryside, a taste of animal and blood in his mouth. He leans his head against the window, closes his eyes. He is the silhouette of a man clipped from a photograph of the sky. He opens his eyes, sneaks a look at the guard, who is reading his little red book again. P is sleepy, as he often has been since he left Rome and ended up in this existence of interrogations in the middle of the night and cold cement floors. A strong sense that he is travelling toward an abyss, toward thickening shadows. He sleeps poorly, folded up in the seat like a praying mantis.

SUITCASES ARE LOADED on and off; the steam engine puffs. It is a very warm evening, and when P breathes his mouth and nose fill with moisture and a sweet, almost rotting, smell. He is still half-asleep; he stumbles. The guard climbs down behind him. A handful of people are waiting on the platform in front of a station building of cracked brick. At the end of the platform is a man in white pants, a blue short-sleeved shirt, and a white hat; he's leaning against a truck. He and the guard exchange a few pleasantries in Swahili and shake hands; then the man turns to P.

'I'm the director of the camp outside town.' While P tosses his suitcases on the flatbed of the truck, the man professes the city's historical significance to him, as if P were a tourist who must be convinced that the long journey wasn't in vain. P listens without enthusiasm. 'Tabora is an important hub for the railway that cuts through Tanzania, and it is the administrative centre for the region. Hundred-year-old mango trees flank the streets.' The guard points with his rifle to show that P should hop up on the flatbed. P obeys; the director chatters on. 'You can see them over there. They were planted by Arab merchants and slave traders who founded the city in the mid-nineteenth century. In its early days, the city was a local centre for the slave trade, and for nearly half a century after the rest of East Africa was divided up into European colonies and protectorates, the city and its surroundings were described as a lawless region.' The director holds onto his hat as a breeze sweeps in across the train tracks and the deserted streets. '*Terra incognita*. No-man's land.' The guard doesn't come along as they drive out of Tabora. P sits on the flatbed with his suitcases; he considers running away, but he suddenly feels powerless and afraid. He doesn't even know where he is, much less whom he would contact or how he would get back to Europe, to Rome. He sits with his arms around his knees.

The surrounding countryside is dominated by fruit farms: pineapple and melon plantations, citrus and peach trees, apparently endless rows of white and pink. Farmers working in fields look up as the vehicle passes; their faces are like splinters of wood, narrow and sharp. After half an hour's journey, the plantations disappear and are replaced by thickening jungle. Birds rustle up out of leaves. It's evening when they arrive at the camp. The director shows P into his office and pours tea that a servant has kept warm. The servant, an older fat man dressed in shabby clothes, puts out a clay bowl of margarine and a few slices of bread. P spreads thick layers on the bread and starts to eat. Starved. Stuffing his mouth, stopping himself, calming himself down. Outside the window he can see long rows of huts. Fluttering leaves stand out against the glowing red light of sundown. There is an otherworldly silence. P stands at the window. He drinks some tea; it's weak, almost tasteless. Just a few days ago he was sitting at the Hilton in Rome, in clean clothes. Now he's here. Nowhere. The director is talking, but P isn't listening; after all, it's only about the articles he'll receive when he enters the camp. The servant is rattling things around; the director says, 'You will receive a weekly ration of dried brown beans, salt, cooking oil, and flour.' P feels out of place in this situation; he stares out the window, drinks some tea, glances at the two men who are putting his new belongings in order, looks out the window again. The huts out there cast shadows as long as rivers. 'You get a bucket, a washbasin, two plates, a mug, and a cooking pot, all of aluminium. You get a machete, a kerosene lamp, a bottle of kerosene, a box of matches, two blankets, and two empty sisal sacks.' During all of this he thinks about running away. He should run back to Tabora and get on a train there. Ride it someplace. But there is no place anymore. The director and the servant help him carry his new things down the small hill upon which the office, which apparently also functions as the director's home, sits.

'Choose an empty hut,' says the director, gesturing at the rows of hovels with his white hat before he and the servant go back up toward the hill.

P stands with his suitcases in hand and all his other things piled around him. *Civil dusk occurs when the sun has set behind the horizon and the land is in shadow but the atmosphere is still illuminated.* He looks up at the sky, thinking that it is like a glowing bubble around the earth at this time of day. A halo. Swarms of insects rise and fall in the last light of day; their wings hiss against each other. When he lowers his eyes he sees refugees everywhere; they appear out of the landscape, sitting in groups, speaking in low voices. Many are eating something grey and gooey from their aluminium pots. He wanders farther into the camp. He smiles at the refugees sometimes, nodding at them in greeting. Few of them react. Often he thinks that he can see straight into them when they meet his gaze, as if he were looking into empty, broken shells. It is uncanny, violent. All the empty huts have either large, gaping holes in the ceiling or floors that are overgrown with weeds because the earth has lain untrodden for a long time. He stands in one of these unusable huts and looks up through the ruined roof, up at the oncoming night. The first stars. Two weeks ago he was in Athens. Less than six months ago he was a fighter pilot. He remembers the story, can feel how it burns and stings. Everything he achieved, everything that was his life. He imagines God as a sparrow-shaped void deep inside a marble cliff, and as a judge and a saviour, and a father and a son. Other thoughts come to him then, without meaning, without comfort, flowing past. He hasn't been to confession in a long time. He grips the handle of the suitcase hard, and the nails of his empty hand dig into his palm. They would salute when they saw him. Was it even real? He would like to return to Uganda and kill the man he lived with, the brother who beat him. Can't think. He leaves the hut and keeps looking for an empty hut in passable condition. After he's been walking around for more than half an hour, he passes a group of refugees who are speaking Lango. He stops and introduces himself, and two of them offer to share their huts with him, but he declines. He wants to be by himself. He has to escape. He will escape tomorrow, or at the latest the day after that.

Finally, he finds a hut far from all the other occupied huts; he sits down on the dirt floor, leaning against the wall of woven wood and dried mud. He has a kind of timeless feeling in his head, a sense of eternity that has something to do with this place. He could get up now and run along the country road, back to Tabora. Nowhere. He thinks about K and wishes he had called from Rome and to tell her where he was going. Maybe then she would be looking for him now, contacting someone. A long, narrow insect is crawling up his forearm; its shell shimmers, its long antennae tremble and search his skin, and he looks at it for a long time, wondering at it, and then he waves it away. Rests his head in his hands. He scratches his head, he wonders if John is alive, he thinks one of the hysteric, clawing thoughts that keep coming back since the coup: that John might have been killed by the very men he ate with and laughed with in Athens last summer. For a few moments, God feels closer to him than the pulse in his very own neck, and then it's gone. He stands up and walks back to his countrymen. They invite him to eat dinner with them. They sit around the fire and talk about Idi Amin. Sparks from the fire blow up in the thick smoke, dance for a moment against the starry sky, straws and specks of red, and go out. P gets to hear stories from the state of emergency, about the rural areas of Uganda being inundated with soldiers. One man says in a hoarse, whispering voice that he was forced to drink sulphuric acid from a car battery and was then left to die on a country road. He survived because an Englishman picked him up, hid him in the trunk of his car, and drove him all the way from Tororo, a city in Uganda, to a hospital in Nairobi. In Kenya he was tracked down by a Kenyan soldier, who brought him here in a truck along with a group of other Ugandans. P inhales his food from his metal spoon; it's some sort of porridge made of semolina and powdered milk. The stories have a touch of ritual, of magic. One young man, whose eye is a festering boil crossed by a long scar, says that Amin's troops forced him to take part in bizarre gladiator matches in which each prisoner was given a machete and shoved into a dark room, where they had to choose between hacking each other to death or being shot. Those who survived had to load their victims onto a truck and then they were let go. The young man applied for asylum in Tanzania and was then brought here. P realizes that there are no women in the camp and wonders why all these Ugandan men have been gathered up here. When it feels like it's his turn, he tells them about his escape from Greece and what happened in Lusaka. He feels a diffuse sense of shame because he is the only one who willingly returned to Africa after having been in Europe. He glances up at the whirl of astonished eyes in the glow of the fire, puts his plate down in front of him. The last few days, or maybe even the last few weeks or months, feel like a dream he is waking up from, at this place. When the refugees start to get up and go to bed, he realizes why so many of the huts have large holes in their roofs—the refugees have taken the straw and stuffed it in sacks to make a sort of mattress. P stands in the door to his hut. He is exhausted enough to sleep anywhere, but he still goes and gathers a little straw from the roof of an empty hut and puts his sleeping place in order. He tosses and turns in the straw for more than an hour. When he closes his eyes he can still see Greece before him: the cypresses outside the academy, K walking toward him, the jet planes descending out of the Mediterranean sky. A dream. His story is just a dream. At last, though, he falls asleep and when he wakes up at some point long past midnight, thirsty and in a cold sweat, he hears a distant rumbling and wonders what it is, but he falls back to sleep.

In this dream he is running in beams of moonlight, his hands fumbling at the air before him, shoving leaves and branches aside. He is a hare running in tall grass. *Fighter planes from the Ugandan air force destroyed a Tanzanian training camp along the border between the two countries overnight, a military spokesman reported yesterday*—it was a news report he heard in Greece, he hears it crackle in his ear, and then a stabbing pain shoots through his head. He thinks the camp must have been bombed, that an explosion has burst his eardrum. He stumbles through the tall grass; he hears the airplanes above the trees, he trips over roots and fallen branches. The whole time he can feel the splitting pain in his ear. The planes pass above him in waves, so low that the roar of the jet engines shake the leaves loose from branches and they float down through the moonlight and he thinks it looks like the snow he saw falling sometimes in the winter, under the street lights in Greece. The enormous shadows of the planes sweep across the ground.

He lights the kerosene lamp. He pokes a finger into his ear. The straw jabs his skin. He looks around, disoriented. His suitcases and the things he received from the director stand in one corner of the hut, looking ghastly, as if they were staring at him. The pain is still throbbing in his head and he hears a sound like the static on a radio but louder, much louder now, deafening—he throws off the empty sack he was using as a blanket and sits up. He is fully awake now, but the pain in his ear doesn't disappear; instead it towers up over him, rumbling like distant explosions or engines, and when he stands up there's something wrong with his sense of balance and his legs give way beneath him. He crashes into one wall of the hut. What is going on? He crawls over the cool, damp dirt floor; he rolls around and his fingers claw in the darkness, tearing at his ear. He doesn't understand how, but a shell fragment from a bomb must have hit his ear in the dream and then followed him into consciousness. He is hyperventilating; he awkwardly gets to his feet and wanders into the night.

In the moonlight, the huts look like rows of huge

animals with shaggy grey pelts. He runs, he thinks he screams, banging his palm against his temple, opening and closing his mouth. He finds a hut that belongs to the refugees he ate dinner with, and he steps right in. One of the sleeping men flies straight up and peers at the door, up at the empty night sky. The man speaks and the face he turns toward P is like a terrified mask, but P can hear only incoherent, low sounds over the rumbling inside his own head, and it takes him several seconds to put these sounds together into a sentence, a question, 'Are the bombers coming?'

Someone lights a kerosene lamp and one refugee puts a hand on P's shoulder and tries to calm him down. P signals awkwardly at the side of his head and screams that there is something in there, in his ear. He sinks to the ground; he feels something close in on his consciousness like a rotating tunnel. He must still be dreaming. This is a dream that he's dreaming in the barracks in Athens. The pain in his ear is like someone sticking a red-hot poker into his head. He pokes a blade of grass into his ear, scraping it around; it has to be a dream. Finally he gets a few thin, black bristles out of his ear. He looks at them in the moonlight. They're spiny and curved like eyelashes, and while he looks at them there is something like a shadow at the edge of his consciousness, a voice that whispers to him: *Don't be afraid of me. I am your brother.* He sits there with a few strange bristles in his hand, knowing that he could let go of something now and fall and he would never again have to think or run. The realization scares him and he flies up again; he upsets a stack of metal pots, he finds a bucket of water for washing and scoops it up in his hands. He pours it into his ear, shakes his head, tries to dunk his whole head in the bucket. At last he manages to rinse more of the nightmare from his ear: the back end of a termite, grape-shaped and shiny with blood and water. He keeps going; he gets out two scissor-like, sharp mandibles and the large, complex head with a demon face the size of a pin. He sits still, he catches his breath; blood is running over his hands, his pulse pounds in his head, the pain has faded a bit, and a clear and sharp thought comes slicing like a knife through his abating panic: he will never again be able to work as a pilot if his ear is permanently damaged. Worried voices around him, tinny and broken. When things have calmed down a bit and P explains what happened, in a voice that also seems hollow and dull inside his head, the refugees offer to let him sleep in their hut. But he still wants to be alone. He hears them whispering behind his back as he staggers back to his own sleeping place. He wanted to be sheltered by the night, the stars. He wanted to be protected. With shaky hands he constructs a sort of makeshift bed from several thick branches from the roof of the hut, and also a rack to put his suitcases on: he doesn't want termites to destroy his clothes from Rome. He is surprised to be able to think this thought; it's so practical and logical. He sits on his straw mattress and gropes at his ear for a long time, maybe an hour, two hours. He lies down; his ear throbs, his thoughts spiral inward. He remembers the bright blue sky over Dhekelia. The clouds above the brick roofs of the barracks, wisped by the wind like feathers across a floor.

He opens his eyes, stares at the wall of the hut. The dawn has started to glow between the woven branches. He lies with his injured ear carefully pressed against the mattress and hears the delta of blood murmuring deep down, under the earth.

I remember him standing before a window of falling
snow in my childhood. He still has nightmares at that
point, dreams that he's still in the camp. He wakes up,
out of breath in the bed. He doesn't know where he is.
He leaves the woman sleeping beside him and tiptoes
across the scratched parquet floor: he moves to the living room window, stands there for a long time, looking
out at the night, at the snow. He is not there anymore.
It doesn't snow in Africa. He never becomes a calm,
secure person.

It is late February. Cars fly off into the night; expressionless faces behind windshields. I saw him yesterday.
I was struck once again by the fact that he is fatherless.
It just came, in the middle of a gesture he was making.
It was in his eyes, too. My dad. He had a little fabric
badge he glued onto a denim jacket one raw, cold spring
day in Borås: his wings from Athens. He had received
the badge the first time he flew solo. He walks down to
the yard with a large, silver tape player over his shoulder, dressed in a denim jacket with cut-off arms and
small wings embroidered in gold thread on his chest.

Rain mixed with snow, broken through with light, a
cloudy sky; I'm standing in my window and looking out
at the traffic. I'm reading Nyerere's speeches and mani-
festos, and I remember reading *The Communist Manifesto*
and Che Guevara's diaries as a teenager, and how the
vision grabbed me and transformed me. How history

touches us with rustling wings of death. In the Arusha Declaration, which Nyerere presented just after he had won the country's first and only free presidential election, he called upon the citizens to work hard and quit dancing, drinking, and gossiping. They would dig wells and irrigation ditches, construct dams. They would create a new world. New sea, new sky.

I came across my neighbour walking with his Rollator in the slush of the parking lot this morning on my way to the mosque. He wondered if I wanted a beer; he had them in the basket of his Rollator. He and Dad worked together at the harbour in the eighties. The sun is going down. The days are disappearing; they blow between my fingers.

At the mosque there was a short sermon about the Prophet's life, may peace be upon him. The Prophet was born on the first day of spring. He was fatherless too, by the way, and motherless. It's like Dad comes from nothing. From a great solitude that is like the sky. Crystals of snow whirled gently in the sunshine outside the window. The men at the mosque ask about Dad; they want to know how his health is. I shrug and say *insha'Allah* he'll get better, *insha'Allah*, pray for him. But maybe he is finally dying now. When I visited him yesterday, he was sitting in his apartment, looking through a flood of letters from authorities and banks. He tore up a collection letter for an old student loan and tossed it in the waste-paper basket. The shores of death are overflowing with bank giro forms. 'I don't think there's much time left,' he says about his life. His wolf's life. He takes a lot of painkillers and other medicine. We don't know if the transplanted lung will be rejected.

At night, in the recurring dream, I hold a bird in my hands, tightly, its hovering wings close to its little body. My whole life, this loneliness and sense of inevitability.

I read about China's relations with Tanzania, searching for clarity, understanding. The Chinese had started coming to East Africa back in the late nineteenth century to work for the British like the Indians and Pakistanis, building railroads, and another wave of Chinese immigrants came to Tanzania in the late sixties when Mao sent workers to build another railway. It is harder to find official explanations for the Chinese military presence. It is first and foremost Amin who accuses Tanzanian forces of crossing the border and fighting under Chinese command, from 1972 onward.

I asked to look at his photographs again. He took the suitcase out of the closet. Most of what's left now is portraits Mom had taken. I laughed at the bell-bottomed pants. He said that Mom had brought the pants from Europe and that anyway, that was how people dressed back then; it was fashionable. There is a very beautiful photo where he's dressed all in white, standing in a garden, legs planted wide apart. He's laughing. This picture is like the happy ending I hope to have. Before me. Before us. There's a flight logbook: a bound, turquoise notebook with its pages divided into columns. A picture of him and John. John's arm is around him and they're sitting under an arch of red climbing roses. The photographer must have used some sort of filter on the camera, because the picture is sort of blurry, like love scenes in old Technicolor movies. I asked if the suitcase was from Africa, but he said he'd bought it when he was a student at Chalmers University of Technology, where he studied for a few years. The suitcase he brought with him from Africa was made of paper, he said.

He asks me sometimes how things are going with the

book. Once when I was visiting him at the hospital a long time ago, I read a part aloud for him. It was about flying, and he corrected some technical detail that had to do with aerodynamics and what is called 'stall' in English: when the plane starts falling like a stone because it is flying too slowly and has to dive rapidly toward the ground in order to regain enough speed to create lift. Something like that; he used his hand to show how you turn the plane on its side and hurtle down to the abyss.

I was born in Borås. When I was six or seven, I moved to Växjö with my mom and my brothers. Dad moved to Gothenburg, and my brothers and I had very little contact with him after that. I was beaten up on playgrounds; I drifted home alone along the side of the road. My upbringing was like everyone else's. Populated with giants. There was no end, because there was no beginning. I have two brothers, one sister.

Mom mentioned once that Dad had several sisters he never talked about, whom he denied having when she asked. I'm putting off asking him about that. Maybe it just has to do with the way the Langi think of family, that women are considered to be part of the family they marry into rather than the family they come from. Everything is so formless when it comes to him; everything darts away when I grasp for it, everything is shadows, stories that change. It's all history.

Night has come. The rain starts to fall again, grey streaks of lead between the buildings, and I lean out the window and close my eyes and feel the rain hit my skin, my eyelids, my lips. It's all just places where Dad did or didn't come during his escape. Dad used to say that I had to be prepared to flee my country, that I had to get an international education, that I had to be prepared to get up at any moment and leave it all behind. Memories. Splinters. Coincidences. Ideas about fate, that certain things are written down in a book before history, before time.

When I'm sixteen I read *The Wretched of the Earth*, sitting on an electrical box. Nyerere reads the same book and uses the same ideas to recreate Tanzania in the most violent way. Nyerere studies political science at the university in Tabora in the fifties. In the seventies, Dad passes through Tabora on the way to the camp.

Far back in time, a boy at a boarding school plays Antony in *Julius Caesar*, and Nyerere is the one who translated the play into Swahili. Fifty years later, the boy can still recite lines from the play. He says, 'Let me be your mirror.'

At night I see books falling apart the way my cigarettes fall apart in the rain that washes the city. Books falling apart like countries, sculptures of heavy, wet sand; books collapsing like crashing waves.

FEET WALK BY the patch of dirt outside the hut. He is lying on his straw-filled sisal sack. He opens and closes his mouth. He has been in the camp for a month, but his ear is still swollen and sore, and when he is quiet he hears a dull, roaring sound inside it. Cracked, bony feet walking by, walking by.

He wonders if his former classmates think about him sometimes as they hurtle high above the world, sweaty and concentrating in the sunlight, in the heart of the sky. In his heart. The sunshine falls in through the door; a bit of dust and dirt blows capriciously around in the light, and another man walks by outside. Sometimes he lies like this all day, sunk in something that isn't even thoughts, something that's just some sort of empty vortex that washes through his body. Other days he sits for several hours, leaning against a hut or a tree, watching the sky as it filters though the leaves, watching how it shifts in colour and intensity. In the evenings they warm their corn porridge above the fire. With each day, the faces around him become more like pieces of the earth and trees. He pokes at the fire with a stick. Why are there only men here, what happens to the female Ugandans who escape to Tanzania, why has he been brought here? Branches sprawl against the night sky. 'Good night, pilot,' says a voice from the darkness. He wanders out into the tall grass to piss. As he leans his head back, it feels like he is falling up into the darkness, away. He becomes dizzy and closes his eyes. He hears the rushing sound in his head. He hears the sounds of the birds, the refugees' cries in their dreams in their huts, scattered on the endless earth. When he returns to the fire, the only other one who's still awake is a former policeman, a white-haired man who smokes his hand-rolled cigarettes with the lighted end in his mouth.

'Not sleepy?' The man sticks the glowing end of the cigarette between his lips and blows his cheeks out like balloons; smoke pours from the corners of his mouth and his nose. It looks uncomfortable. He's dressed in a ragged piece of burlap, which he has wound around his waist.

P sits on the log and holds his hands out to the crackling flames.

'Would you like a pair of pants?' he says. He has suitcases full of clothes, but he hasn't shown them to anyone because he doesn't want everyone in the camp to start asking him for clothing. The policeman looks at P with sleepy eyes, takes the burning cigarette from his mouth, and blows a few smoke rings with his mouth gasping like a fish. He seems to be pondering something great and unfathomable, and then he looks away again, into the fire. He nods rather absent-mindedly; sure, he would like a pair of pants.

The policeman is Acholi, one of the oldest people in the camp, and his story is one of the strangest P has heard. One day he was sitting at the police station, listening to the radio, and he heard his own name mentioned as one of several authorities who had recently disappeared. One way or another, he must have displeased Amin or another bigwig, and the order had been given for his murder. Someone had made a mistake, however, and the news of his disappearance had been given to the radio before the murder was committed. The policeman heard the news report, stood up from his desk chair, went to the train station, and took a train to Tanzania, where the authorities placed him in the camp.

He had become history, risen out of history, and run back into life.

'If I were still young, I would leave this camp,' the man says, putting the cigarette in his mouth again, and as always P has the spontaneous urge to yell and warn him that he's about to burn himself with the tip. P likes the old policeman; he likes his snake-like gaze that always seems to be focused on some far-off point. He leans forward and stirs up the fire, blowing on the flickering coals.

The camp has no guards; it would be easy to get up and run straight into the wilderness. But a Ugandan passport isn't just useless, it's outright dangerous to use in Tanzania.

'Where would a person go?'

'Go to Nairobi,' says the policeman.

'Nairobi?'

'You can be a registered refugee there.'

P thinks of the journalist he shared a cage with in Dar es Salaam. He, too, spoke of registration. He holds up the stick he's been using to poke at the fire toward the night sky. The stick has started to burn. He realizes he's still thinking of the man in Dar es Salaam as a journalist even though he must have belonged to the police or the military, maybe the security police. Nairobi. He waves the stick after a buzzing insect in the dark.

'Registered refugee?' He blinks; the smoke is making his eyes water. Sometimes, here in the camp, God is so close to him, close like a fine powder of light that crackles and flashes behind the streaming darkness of his eyes. He tries to wipe the soot and the smoke from his face with an equally sooty and dirty shirtsleeve. Embers jump out of the fire, into the darkness above them. Flying at night. Gliding over the abyss.

'Haven't you noticed that people disappear from here?'

'Disappear?'

'There's a guerrilla camp deeper in Tanzania, and people from this camp are moved there. They are taken in the night when the others don't see.' The policeman laughs and throws up his hands. 'They're forced to become soldiers. We're going to overthrow Amin.'

'We're going to overthrow Amin?' P looks into the night. 'You and I?' Amin has fighter planes, tanks, soldiers; P was one of them himself. It's not possible to overthrow Amin with a handful of refugees. He feels the breath of death in his face; he closes his eyes and shakes his head. There are only brothers, brothers who stand in the grass, screaming.

They fetch water from the pump. He holds his bucket up to the morning sun. He sees the sediment, particles of dirt floating around. Sometimes when the others are gathered around the pots of food, he goes to his hut and opens the suitcase of Italian shirts and touches the thin, smooth fabric. Since his conversation with the old policeman, he constantly thinks of running away. He wakes up every day and he is so heavy; it's like moving underwater. He sits up in his sheets made of sacks; he twists his skeletal hands together. He is getting thinner and thinner. It's as though his body belonged to someone else. He is flooded with sorrow, with exhaustion. He has to run away. The days go by. If what the policeman said is right, that they're going to be taken away at night, it will be even more difficult to run away from the new place, because he won't recognize his surroundings. He has to run away. He has to.

The man in the dream takes a step out onto the savannah. The belt in his hand coils like a snake. The boy screams. The man stops. The boy breathes through his mouth. His nose is stopped up with blood. The tall grass looks grey in the starlight. The boy looks at his brother, at the belt in his hand, at his shaking shoulders. Is the man crying?

'I am going to leave and never come back!' he shouts, and in the dream the crying man shouts back at his little brother, 'One day you will be so far from this place that you will miss it with every bone in your body.' He takes a step toward the boy and stops. 'You will miss the trees, and the earth, and this grass!' The man lurches with a prolonged, dreary motion—he moves his open palm, level with the tall blades of grass, a gesture of burial or mowing down, and something about this movement makes the boy realize for the first time that the man over there, his brother, must miss their father.

When he opens his eyes, they are always stuck shut and he feels like they have nearly grown together during the night. He eats breakfast with the dream still inside him, sharp and clear like a long, hard knife. He repeats his brother's movement with his own hand, trying to decipher its meaning by performing it. Maybe it didn't happen in real life, just in the dream. He thinks he remembers it, like the words the man said to him that night. Each time he dreams about his brother, it's as though he were about to break through something, find some sort of forgiveness. He remembers that night. Once he came home after sitting and shivering in the darkness and the grass for several hours, his brother beat him with the belt so hard that he couldn't walk for several days. It continued. That was his childhood, his upbringing. He wanders around the camp with a suffocating weight inside. He remembers his shame over the mattresses he wet, that it was its own thing, an inconceivably real object made of darkness. He can still feel the pressure of it on his chest. He was beaten with fists, with shoes, with books; he was thrown onto the hard wooden floor with a burst lip, with black eyes, with a broken finger, a bloody nose. He limped away from home with his thighs striped with whiplashes in the great, naked dawn. He came home from school and prepared food. The days went by. The fear never lessened. This was his life. His brother, who had been working as a teacher at the school, eventually became the principal, and he was often summoned to his office and beaten with belts, rulers, pointers. The leaves move in the breeze, move against each other; he's sitting outside his hut, squinting at the tree line. No one did anything. The man just hit him and hit him until he was so tired that he staggered around, breathless and sweaty, too tired to continue. Since the night P screamed at his brother that he was leaving, thereby giving voice to a scream that he had perhaps always heard inside himself, something was different: the words he had shouted became a very small, sharp splinter of stone deep inside him; it was wet and shiny with blood and piss and it was hard and slippery; it gleamed. He would leave and never come back. He thought about it as he sat for half the night, reading his lessons with his swollen eyes, and when he went to school. When he stood with his friend, fishing at the beach, he thought about it and felt like a stranger to himself, mean, because he had a secret. Then one day, when his friend died, he stood in his Sunday best and watched the little wooden coffin lowered into the ground and thought about it. Running away. He had to run away.

He must have been nine or ten years old when John

came home from the war. John, whom he had heard so much about. John called him 'wing commander,' a word from the far-off war. He and John. On that day, he believed that he would get to live with John, that it was over.

'John? What was Dad like?'

John had a thin moustache and an unbuttoned white shirt; he was visiting them for a long weekend, and they were walking along the dusty road under the acacias.

'When Dad was young, he lived far up the river,' John said, laughing softly to himself. He pointed north-east, toward the darkening sky. 'When the Englishmen came to his village, they wanted to find a chief to deal with. Because they thought black people were dumb, they thought the whole village would follow Dad just because he was tall, so they didn't bother with the actual leader of the village and pointed at Dad and said that he would be the spokesman for the whole village.' John moved his hand as if he were unscrewing a giant lid at his temple: the Englishmen, what idiots. P looked at John, a giant. The sun twinkled in the leaves above them. 'But Dad was a young man, and he had no family, so he ran off and jumped in the river.' He liked these glimpses of a father he had never met himself.

'Dad swam as far as he could, and when he couldn't swim any farther, he let the current carry him for one whole night and one whole day, and when he woke up the next morning he crawled onto land and started a new life in the village where we grew up.'

P picks up a stone from the grass and the earth. He rolls it between his fingers, feels an inexplicable impulse to stick it in his mouth and swallow it. He tosses it away. He's still sitting with his back against the wall of the hut. He blinks at the red light of the oncoming evening. He was a boy who walked in the grass with his older brother. He holds his thin hand in front of him, clenches the bird-claw fingers into a fist, opens it.

'Do you want a job?' The young man with the ruined eye is standing in front of him. P turns his face toward him as though he were sleepwalking.

'A bakery in Tabora needs wood, and we're going to chop it and the director's going to take it into town on the truck. We're going to split the money.'

He is wet through with sweat after just a few minutes of working with the machete. He and a handful of other refugees are moving around at the edge of camp; they're felling trees and paring twigs and branches from the trunks, which they then chop into smaller chunks and throw up onto the flatbed of the truck. Muscles ache; sweat runs down into their eyes. He chops off a branch, the evening sun flashes out behind the dense leaves, blood-red. There's a rumour that some of them will be allowed to come along to Tabora to help unload the wood. His ear roars, he squeezes the wooden handle of the machete, there's something enduring about this instant that makes him want to cry.

They work until night falls. They work all the next day. When the back of the truck is finally full that night, the director chooses P and another refugee to come along to Tabora the next day. They leave in the morning, the same road P arrived on a month ago, through rainforest that gives way to countryside and cultivated fields. P is squeezed into the front seat with the two other men; he is nervous about a visit to civilization and it makes him sad when he reflects upon this: that he once flew into the sun but now is upset about riding a few kilometres in a truck to a half-forgotten city. The tires of the truck hop over fallen branches. It's harvest time; there are a great many workers out in the fields. P leans his head against the headrest, smokes a hand-rolled cigarette, puts his hand out the rolled-down window, feels the wind in his face, looks to the side and sees a wave of knives raised, flashing in the morning sun, like a rain of mirror shards.

The director parks behind the bakery and goes to attend to a few errands while P and the other refugee unload the wood. The baker is an older, dark-haired European who speaks Swahili almost fluently, and he stands in the back door of the bakery, shouting instructions. The brick walls of the bakery shine reddish-brown. P stands with a log in each hand, frozen in time. He could throw down the logs and run off through the alleys of Tabora, maybe jump on a train. But he has nowhere to go. No money. Nothing. He squeezes the logs, squints out of the narrow, dusty alley. Pedestrians and the occasional car go by. They might as well be on the other side of the sea, on another planet.

When they're done with their work, the baker tells the two men to meet him in front of the bakery so they can be paid. The baker asks if they want something to drink, and when they hesitate he assures them it's his treat. When they then accept, he turns to the open door and calls to a young man, presumably a relative, who is at the cash register, 'Come out with two sodas!' P brushes his hands off on his pants. He tries to remain calm. He sneaks a look at the other refugee, who's leaning against the fender of the truck. The baker spoke Greek. P chews on his lower lip. Greek. The man is Greek. The mango trees that line the avenue bend in the wind; yellow leaves snow down to the street. When the young man comes out with the soda and hands it over, P is almost scared— he's so far off in his thoughts. He tries to conceal the fact that his hands are trembling with nerves; he takes a quick sip of the soda: he spills a little on his chin, dries it with the back of his hand. In as calm a voice as possible he asks in Swahili if he may borrow a pen and paper. The baker almost looks a bit offended, but he takes a small pad out of his shirt pocket and tears off a page, which he hands over along with a pencil that's been sharpened down to a nub. P writes quickly. He writes in Greek that he studied at the Hellenic Air Force Academy in Athens and was taken away by the Tanzanian authorities against his will, that the baker has to notify his girlfriend in Athens that he needs help. The pencil stump scrapes across the little piece of paper; the other refugee looks at him disinterestedly, he writes down K's full name and her address, gives the paper back to the baker, who reads it, distractedly at first, then irritated as if he didn't understand what this writing has to do with him, and finally with the blood vessels in his face swelling. He sounds frightened when he speaks. 'Would you like muffins with your soda?' Before either of the two men can answer he puts the pencil and paper in his pocket and walks through the door.

The other refugee burps up carbon dioxide and laughs. 'I haven't eaten muffins for a year.'

The baker returns with an aluminium platter full of warm muffins, and they each take one and eat them in silence; P watches the baker the whole time, waiting for a reaction that never comes. The other refugee takes a second muffin and wolfs it down. P waits, declines the offer when the baker holds out the plate of muffins. The director shows up with some shopping bags in his arms; they say goodbye, and the refugees hop up on the bed of the truck because the director puts the bags, in which he has a few dozen eggs, among other things, in the front seat. P sits facing backward as they drive out of Tabora;

he tries to catch the baker's eye, to read a sign in the man's disappearing face. Nothing. As if the piece of paper never existed. The dark, staring eyes meet P's, stubborn, until the truck goes around a bend and the man is gone. Nothing. Nowhere. P stares at the blowing dust, at the swaying palm leaves; the wind tears at his shirt, he thinks about K, how she would lie with her head in his lap and her long hair loose. He wipes dust and sweat from his forehead. He sits at the fire, eating corn porridge; it's gooey, his teeth stick together. He remembers the sound of jet engines, and how he hurtled into the sun.

One relieves oneself in a hole in the ground. Flies buzz in eyes.

One fetches water at the pump. One drinks in large gulps to satisfy the hunger; one stares at the sky with an empty stomach, one becomes dizzy and the water is ice-cold and tastes like dirt and one holds back the vomit with a hand and stands there panting, bent over, clear liquid trickling between fingers.

One sleeps, wakes up.

Days go by, and weeks.

He sits on a log, drawing with his foot in the dry earth, circles, mazes. He is worried that they'll never be asked to cut wood again, that he'll never again get to visit Tabora, that his encounter with the baker will never be repeated.

He takes his yearbook from the air-force academy from his suitcase. He pages carefully through its thick, shiny pages. He touches their faces. From another world.

Now and then, new refugees come to the camp. The director picks them up at the train station in his truck, and in the evenings they sit by the fire and share the news from their homelands. P watches their faces as they speak. They don't have that dull gaze of a person who has been in the camp for a long time; instead there's something animalistic and terrified in their body language and facial expressions. They look around and their eyes are almost like the eyes of cats. The glow of the flames flares across their faces, making them appear out of darkness, disappear, appear again.

He dreams about K. They're walking across Syntagma Square together, it's a cool fall day, he has his arm across her shoulders, she twines her fingers in his. The white morning light filters in through the straw roof. He scratches his head and his beard, which has grown long and matted during his months in the camp. A little lizard winds through the dry straw, stops short, moves quickly again, darting across a brittle brown palm leaf. He thinks of the European birds that stopped to eat seeds in the barracks yard, on their way to or from home. He remembers his childhood.

The long hallways of the boarding school were full of running feet and loud, shrill voices. The older children smoked behind the cafeteria. One boy gave him a cigarette and he stuck it in his mouth and inhaled and started coughing. He was thirteen. The boys stood in a circle around him, laughing; he was doubled up with red eyes and the cigarette smoking in his hand. He took another drag, coughed, joined the other children's laughter. When he was first at the school he ended up in the playground fights almost every day. At night he lay awake in bed, digging his nails into his palms and breathing hard and fast through his nose. The moon moved slowly in the dormitory window. He thought that he would never return home. He had received a scholarship, he had fulfilled his promise to his brother or himself. He had run away. He hit the older boys, struck them in the face, kicked them in the stomach when they lay down. They were surprised that the violence he used was so raw, that he remained completely silent, that he hit and hit until he was exhausted. He turned fourteen. He sat behind the cafeteria, smoking with the older boys; he boxed with them in jest, got them to hold up their hands and say they give up, they give up. He was very gifted and got top grades in almost every subject. He was good at gym class, and he was the best in the class at the high jump. He wanted to become an ambulance driver, like John, or a teacher. He was fifteen when they cut open frogs in biology class, and his dreams of working at a hospital died in the slimy, nasty-smelling innards. The Italian priests who ran the boarding school taught him to recite saints' names, and they read from the Bible in Latin. They gave him communion and the oval melted on his tongue. He wanted to become a Catholic priest, devote his life to God, to the unfathomable and vast thing he sometimes felt inside himself like a rain of gentle, pattering wingbeats. He was sixteen and walked into the church with the swinging censer, feeling pure, powerful, new. He was a choirboy. He cried every time the priests told the story of the crucifixion. He thought, *why must they whip God's son, why must they stick him with spears and taunt him? If you are the son of God, why do you not call for your father?*

He sometimes visited his mother on school breaks. There was a strange muteness between them. He sat across from her, eating the semolina porridge she'd made, and he heard her talking about his brothers, about who had gotten married and who had had a baby. He kissed a girl in his hometown and they ran out into the dark and sat under a tree, and he learned to long and to die. He rolled over on his back; they lay naked under the rain-heavy leaves; they lay on the bottom of the starry sky. 'A long time ago I wanted to be a priest,' he said. They laughed. The walls of the labyrinth grew as he did. The world ended in the rainy seasons, every time. In his seventeenth year he could sense the end of his child-hood like a cliff beyond the horizon, on the other side of the fields of shimmering grass.

It was one of the last nights of his childhood, and he ran in the grass, dressed in the shorts and shirt of his boarding school. He climbed up a tree; he was strong and lithe, he heaved himself up and up through the branches. The sun was red; the light was thick as sand filtering through the leaves. He sat with one leg on either side of a branch, dangling his legs. He had played the same game many times, and he was really too old for it. On the other side of time. He took a few scraps of fabric from his pocket and tied them in the twigs around him. The trunk swayed. He looked down at the ground, far below, knowing that he would die if he fell. He was fear-less. Inside him he had a sharp splinter, a promise to leave. He tied another scrap to a twig. He had started playing here many years ago, after John had told him about the planes of war. He let go of the branch and stretched his arms out like the crucifixion in church. The scraps flapped in the wind. Like flying.

HE LIFTS HIS machete, stands still. The sound of a falling tree rumbles through the jungle. Dry yellow leaves whirl up between the trunks. Sometimes it's like the years don't exist, like life is something completely different from what he thought, a world you can wander through. In the tall grass. He stands with his arms raised for a long time, staring ahead at nothing. The baker needs wood again. The refugees are out at the edge of the forest chopping it; it's the second day of work, and it's already afternoon. P has to talk to the baker again. He has to find out if his message to K made it through, if she has answered. He quickly cuts the twigs from a large branch and chops it up into chunks.

He's working hard; he's pushing the others to go faster. He hopes to be chosen to come along to Tabora again, but the next morning when they're finished loading the wood onto the truck, the director chooses two others. P grabs one and offers his share of the money in exchange for the spot. The man wants a pair of pants, too; the policeman must have told them about P's suitcases full of clothes.

They're squeezed into the cab, and P holds his arms firmly crossed over his chest, as if to close in his heart. They arrive in Tabora around lunchtime, drive along deserted streets; the light flows across the scratched windshield like flickering dragonfly wings. They pull up behind the bakery and stop. This time, the baker and the young Greek man help them unload the wood. They stack it along the wall of the bakery; sand blows up into their faces, forcing them to stand with their arms held in front of their eyes and mouths. The baker gives no indication that he has anything to say to P, who keeps trying to make eye contact with him. If anything, the baker seems angry that P is there again. Time passes. P starts trying to win time by working slowly. Once he even pretends to knock over a whole stack of wood by mistake. The other refugee becomes irritated with him. The taste of blood is in his mouth; his hands feel distant and unreal as he picks up logs. They are nearly finished when the baker mumbles, in an everyday sort of tone, in Greek, 'Do both of you know Greek?' The other refugee, who at that moment is standing up on the truck bed and scraping up the last logs, doesn't react. With his eyes aimed at his young nephew but with words clearly meant for P's ears, the baker says, 'I can't get involved in your case. They will accuse me of espionage and deport me.' P rubs his face with his dirty T-shirt, fumbles with an armful of logs, and drops some of them.

'I will lose my bakery. I can't help you.'

P feels nothing. He doesn't think anything, either—just that no one will help him, that no one exists, that there were never brothers, only bodies, alone, wandering across the fields, beating each other, trampling each other. He picks up a log; it is rough, still heavy with moisture. P thinks that the silence between them becomes stifling and thick with disappointment, but maybe no one else interprets it that way. When they're done, the baker's nephew fetches the director from inside the bakery, where he's been sitting and drinking tea. The three men hop into the cab of the truck; the director starts the engine. The bark and dry leaves on the bed rustle as the director starts to back out onto the road. The baker shouts something and the director puts the truck in neutral.

'I just wanted to say thanks for the help,' says the baker, who has hurried up to the passenger side of the truck. He sticks his hand in through the rolled-down window, shakes hands with the three men. He shakes P's hand last of all, and before he does so he makes a movement which P interprets as wiping his hand on his apron, but in the next instant he realizes it was something else: there is a folded piece of paper in the baker's hand. Their eyes meet for a fraction of a second, and then the truck drives off. They leave Tabora again.

Evening comes; they make a fire. P sticks his hand in his pocket time and again, to make sure the paper he received from the baker is still there. He doesn't want to take it out in front of the others, and he's afraid they'll become suspicious if he, the one who is usually up later than anyone else, goes to his hut before darkness has even fallen.

He sat in a hotel room in Athens with her one evening when a whole stadium had shouted his name in unison. He thinks her name, closes his eyes, remembers how she twines her fingers with his. It can't be anything but a letter from her. When only the old policeman and P are left by the fire, he finally dares to saunter off to his hut. He sits in the moonlight outside the door. He takes out the paper; it is wrinkled and dirty. He thinks that she has probably written that she still loves him and that she's contacted his cousin in Rome and is waiting for further instructions. He squeezes his eyes closed. He thinks her name. He holds the paper; he doesn't want to unfold it. She has probably written that the baker has promised to act as a messenger between them. He sits there, not daring to move. He left without telling her. The letter rustles in his hands when he finally unfolds it. He smoothes it out against the leg of his pants, lights a match, reads in the glow of the flame. The letter is from K's mother. She asks P to leave their family alone. She writes that K is engaged to a Greek officer. His hands are shaking; it is almost a mistake when the letter brushes the dying flame of the match. He holds the burning paper; it flakes to pieces and snows away, up into the grey darkness.

One sits awake at night, listening to the noises of the surrounding jungle. One hears the calls of birds, the paws of wild animals rustling in the leaves and the grass. One feels like an animal. A simple, raw vulnerability.

He is getting thinner and thinner. He whisks his spoon over the plate and looks around. The light of the setting sun makes the aluminium glow in the refugees' hands, as if their spoons and pots were glowing and burning. He closes his eyes and tries to swallow, but the porridge just swells in his mouth. The birds shriek and shriek, why do they shriek like that? He remembers the light on the streets of Dhekelia, the small fish restaurants, the white limestone walls and umbrellas snapping in the sea breeze. He remembers the mulberries colouring the ground like dried blood in the fall. In his memory he runs across a gravel field, collecting feathers in the salty wind from the sea. He and hundreds of other boys with shaved heads gather feathers, which they stick to their backs, and then they throw themselves off cliffs. He remembers things he knows aren't true. They fly. He opens his eyes, puts his plate down on the ground, and lights a hand-rolled cigarette.

'Tell me about Nairobi again,' he says to a man of his own age who lived in Kenya for several years.

'What should I tell you?'

'Anything. Where are the embassies?'

The refugees in the camp have all started to fight the madness of melancholy isolation that conquers bodies in this place by talking about their hometowns again and again, with as many details as possible. They describe the colours of the houses they grew up in; they list street names and remember their neighbours' faces and habits—P has described every nuance of the village by the shores of Lake Victoria where he lived with his mother and brothers; he has told about the great round huts, about the school building of crumbling brick and the fishing harbour where tarred wooden boats bobbed on the waves. He has not mentioned the second village.

Every time someone describes Nairobi, he listens extra carefully. He has begun to draw a mental map of the city. *Nairobi. You can become a registered refugee there.* This is all he has left now—the memory of a lie that a liar told him in a cage, and which a half-crazy old policeman reminded him of one night when he couldn't sleep. Nairobi. He has to get to Nairobi.

The man who lived in Nairobi for a number of years has worked as a chauffeur for an English family and starts to give an exact description of the embassy district. He speaks animatedly, describing the large European villas behind walls and iron gates. P listens with his eyes closed, picturing himself arriving at the bus station and walking east from there. The gardens, the multistorey buildings.

'You go along King's Street. On the right is the British Embassy in a large white stone building, and then if you turn left a hundred metres on you are on Victoria Street;

there are cars parked under a row of acacia trees. The French and Italian embassies are there.'

P is walking there now, under the red acacia flowers, on his way to safety. 'What are you thinking about, pilot?'

He pokes at his boiled beans with his spoon.

'I was thinking about flying.' He yawns, takes his plate, and goes to bed. If he can get to the Italian Embassy, maybe they can help him contact his relative in Rome. He can ask her to send money for a ticket. This is the plan, this is the thought that flickers inside him as he falls asleep, falling into unconsciousness through layer after layer of increasingly hazy anxiety. Nairobi.

He ashed his cigarette against the window frame, blew smoke out at the night sky. The wind was cool against his bare upper body. He could hear the BBC from a window across the street. It was during the slow months after his exams at boarding school. He was living with one of his brothers, F, who was the third-eldest in the family. He was eighteen, himself. A young man. He wanted to devote himself to something. He wanted to become a great rock like the priests who glided through the hallways of the boarding school in their black robes, untouchable and silent. A fortress. He slapped at a mosquito, but the movement was sleepy and not very serious, like everything in his life right now. Yes, sometimes he wanted to be a priest, but he had just climbed out of a young woman's window and he was less and less willing to give that up, that thing people did. This unreal stillness afterward. He prayed to God every night before he went to bed, of course. He closed his eyes, inhaled smoke. He liked nighttime, he liked the lack of people. He was eighteen and he would probably be drafted into the military soon. Become a soldier, like John.

He spent days sitting on the verandah outside the local general store, gasping for breath in the stifling heat and the light straight down out of the sky. He drank Coca-Cola, which he got for free because F worked for the mayor and the man who ran the store wanted to ingratiate himself with the family. A guy he had fought with the week before came clattering up on his bike, braking in a cloud of dust, smiling scornfully at him.

'Where are you going?'

His friend—if they were still friends, after that fight—was chewing gum, hanging over the handlebars; he didn't answer. P turned his soda bottle and it glimmered in the sunlight. 'Do you want a soda?'

The guy laughed, looked up at him, something triumphant in his eyes. As if he knew a secret. Did he have a knife on him? Why wouldn't he answer?

'Where are you going?'

The guy smacked his gum. P took a sip of soda, as if to demonstrate superiority or indifference or he didn't really know what.

'There's an entrance exam for the air force at one o'clock.'

'We're black. We're not allowed to be pilots. You just want a soda. I wanted to be pilot when I was little, too.'

'We're independent now. We can be what we want.' The guy on the bike blew a bubble, popped it between his teeth, chewed.

HE IS AWOKEN by loud voices. He is irritated, he lays an arm over his healthy ear and tries to fall asleep again, but he realizes at the same moment that there's someone in his hut, that a figure is leaning over him. He raises his arms to shield his face from the blows. Nothing, just someone laughing softly. Two men in green are standing in his hut; one of them had poked him with his rifle, and the other says, 'Pack and come out of the hut.'

P sits up, dazed. 'Why?'

'Hurry up.' The man leaves his hut with those words, and the second man, who has his rifle at the ready, stops at the door and watches as P gets dressed, scrambles to collect the contents of his suitcases, and picks them up.

'Where are we going?'

The man places his index finger in front of his lips, backs up, waves the rifle: come. P walks out of the hut, still half-asleep and dreaming. He remembers how he was woken one night in Athens, when Amin's plane was on its way to bring the cadets home to Uganda. It's as though every big thing that happened in his life happened in some sort of trance, in the unreal, shimmering landscape of just waking. He catches a glimpse of the white-haired, bent man who is the director's servant; he's rushing around and pointing out which huts the soldiers should visit. Next to the extinguished fire pit is a truck with a covered bed. Its headlights and engine are off. Several soldiers are moving quietly around the camp, walking from hut to hut and gathering people. P is surprised that he didn't hear the truck arrive. All in all, a dozen refugees are brought to the truck; the motor coughs as someone turns the key, and the headlights come on and the jungle blazes up sharp and monochromatic: leaves clipped from a grey surface. P stretches his back, rubs his eyes. He sees the old policeman come limping up with his hand lifted against the headlights of the truck, as though the light had mass and weight and were hurting him. The group of refugees is shoved up onto the truck bed, under the tarp. Yet another armed man is sitting there.

'Do you know where you're going?' They shake their heads. 'Good.' The man leans back sleepily. The truck starts rolling.

They travel through the jungle. The sound of branches scraping against the tarp is whispering, lulling—after a while, P falls asleep and doesn't wake up until they have stopped and are ordered to climb down from the truck bed. They carry their suitcases and bundles in their hands while they walk, frozen and stiff-legged, across the dirt; a hairline stripe of blue light peeks above the line of trees, and mist hangs in the air. They find themselves in a clearing in which stand a handful of wooden buildings and a number of dark military tents. They are brought to a dormitory, where they are assigned beds among fifty other men; some of the men are woken up by the movements of the new arrivals and swear at them to be quiet in thick voices. P lies on his assigned bed. It doesn't have a mattress, and he has only a thin blanket over him; he tugs at it as he stares at the ceiling; he feels totally vulnerable, like a dead body in a grave. Sleep comes slowly, a grey buzz that fills his head in wave after wave. He wakes up after a few hours. Sunlight falls through gaps in the wall, which is apparently made of thin boards. The ceiling is made of wooden slats and large, dry palm leaves. He props himself up on his elbows. Several Ugandan languages are being spoken around him: Acholi, Lango, Buganda, and various Swahili and Bantu dialects. Ten or so worn-out men in very simple clothes are sitting in their beds around him; like him, they're thin and half-asleep. He recognizes four of them from the last camp; the rest are strangers. Those who are new arrivals like himself are picking at their clothes and belongings, as if they were inspecting a series of strange objects that had followed them up out of a dream. He sees a man trying to put on a pair of pants as though it were a shirt. Some men are still sleeping. P thinks that he has found himself on a journey deeper and deeper down into something, some world that always existed under this world. He pulls on his jeans and his undershirt and goes outside. He passes a guard leaning against a tree, a young man who looks like a Ugandan, but it's hard to know without hearing him talk. He has a Soviet automatic rifle in his lap and is chewing on a long blade of grass. A large group of men is sitting around a fire pit that's died out into a smoking pile of ash. Most of them are wearing homemade clothing sewn from the same sort of green fabric the large military tents are made of. Their clothes are rough and angular and the men are very gaunt, with the unfocused movements of starving people—trembling hands, faces grey with blowing ash. P recognizes another handful of men from the last camp; he nods at them in confusion as he sits down. One man hands him a metal plate and shovels corn porridge onto it from a large pot. P thanks him with a silent nod; he eats the porridge and scratches his stubble, aware that he is being observed. He should have run away when he was in the first camp. He searches for the old policeman in the faces around him, but he doesn't see him. He notices that there are a number of half-burned red book covers lying around the fire pit, and now he can see them all over in the dry grass around him, and he realizes that there were lots of the very same red books and the same ripped-out yellowed pages under the beds in the dormitory. He picks up a torn-out, half-burned page, shakes the ash from it, and reads. *Whoever wants to know a thing has no way of doing so except by coming into contact with it, by living (practising) in its environment.* He glances up at the other refugees. A man meets his eyes, searching. The awkwardly constructed garments of tent fabric make his face look small and fragile. P looks away. The page of the book is written in English. *If you want to know the taste of a pear, you must change the pear by eating it yourself.* He raises his eyebrows and laughs. He throws the paper down. He remembers the red book that the guard on the train to Tabora was absorbed in and wonders if it's the same one. Several piles of the book are burning on a smoking pile of trash not far away, and pages from them blow across the yard like angular leaves. He is just about to reach for a cover to find out the book's title when a booted foot nudges him in the side. The guard who was sitting against the tree has stood up and come over to him, and he signals with the barrel of the rifle for P to get up.

They walk past the worn wooden buildings and a number of military tents, to a larger tent at one end of the camp. The guard opens the curtain with his hand. A man at a desk looks up and signals to them to come in. The man seems to have trouble breathing; his face is swollen and his eyes are half-closed. A map is spread before him, and he has a pen in hand; he's using it to mark something on the map. He puts down the pen, leans back in his chair. Light bulbs hang from the roof of the tent, and a large diesel generator hums in the corner. He asks P to sit down at the desk. P sits in the wobbly wooden chair. He feels like he's acting in a play. He turns around to look at the guard who brought him here, but the young man has left the tent.

'My name is Okello.' The man with the swollen face takes a folder from a desk drawer. '*Major* Okello.' He opens the folder to a page and reads it for a long time. 'Former,' he says, gesturing vaguely at his shoulders and his chest to indicate the lack of insignia. Former Major Okello. He's just wearing a regular military-green shirt, unbuttoned at the throat; he laughs at something unknown, and his laugh is interrupted by a coughing fit. 'Tito,' he says, quickly extending his hand. P shakes it.

Again come the questions. Tito interrogates P about the purpose of his trip to Zambia, about his activities in Greece, his political views. He wants to know if P sympathizes with Amin or Obote or some third party. This time, P doesn't try to hide anything. And anyway, it is highly likely that this Okello has been sent the information from the interrogations in Dar es Salaam; P actually suspects that what he told the Tanzanians is summarized in the folder Okello took from the drawer.

'You are one of the most highly educated soldiers we have in the camp.' Okello folds his hands. 'We're going to invade Uganda soon. We're going to overthrow Amin. I realize that you consider yourself to be imprisoned here, and that your loyalty doesn't naturally lie with your jailers, but all of you are soldiers. My soldiers. You will be armed before we cross the border. Be prepared; that's all I ask.' Okello gestures at the opening of the tent. 'Some of the men are a bit unmotivated.' He laughs, starts cough-ing again, gasps for breath, waves his hand—a gesture that appears to mean that P shouldn't worry about his illness, that the weakness of his body is irrelevant. P looks around the tent. There are several piles of red books in one corner, and there's even one on the desk between him and Okello. P leans forward and reads it. It is a selec-tion of quotations from Chairman Mao.

'You can go,' Okello says between two coughs, and P stands up, but as he's standing in the opening of the tent, Okello shouts after him: 'I hope you're not *museveni!*' The last word of this sentence sounds like an adjective that describes some sort of undesirable human trait. P turns around in the opening of the tent. He doesn't know the word *museveni*, and since they've been speaking Swahili P guesses it's a loan word from a Bantu language, or an Arabic neologism.

'*Museveni?*'

'*Museveni.*' Okello makes a drawn-out hissing sound by sucking air through his teeth; he coughs and waves at him to go away.

Food is served in the evening, corn porridge again. P finally sees the policeman and sits beside him and chats a little about nothing in particular, about the sleeping places, about the approaching rainy season, about the food. Both are worried that the others in the camp are listening to their conversation and will report them if they talk about anything important. When P goes to bed, he falls asleep almost immediately and dreams that he is paralyzed. He wakes up and it's still nighttime. He lies on his side. *I am going to leave here.* He blinks, stares into the darkness.

One is served breakfast. One sits on a log, poking at the ashes with a foot. There are a number of guards in the camp, and the majority of them are Ugandans, but a few, mostly the youngest men, seem to be Tanzanians. Those ones shuffle around the camp with their machine guns over their shoulders and seem to be relatively undisciplined—maybe guarding this camp is part of some sort of compulsory service. In any case, the biggest problem with an escape wouldn't be the guards, it would be the jungle that spreads out in all directions, thick and impenetrable as a wall. He woke up in the same way he had finally fallen asleep: slowly drifting over the border, through a flicker of sunshine, an imperceptible and therefore disagreeable journey between worlds. He shuffles around, talking to the others. He asks them what *museveni* means but receives only evasive looks in reply, and sometimes insinuations that it's best to keep quiet about it. At one point he's even close to ending up in a fight because a group of refugees seems to think that his question is a way to make fun of them.

He sits on his bed, looking at the dirt floor. He waits for some form of military training to commence, but life in the guerrilla camp hardly seems different from that in the regular refugee camp. The days go by. Apparently there are people from almost all the Ugandan social classes in this camp, from illiterates who were chased off their farms and forced to leave their families without provisions to a skinny minister from Obote's government who says that when he first arrived at the camp he was so fat that he couldn't crouch over the hole in the latrine. Now he's as thin as everyone else, one of the bird people of the camp. One picks up a handful of dirt, crumbling it in the breeze. One is flooded with something wordless that has to do with the years and the war and which throws one's heart to the ground, and one looks up thoughtfully and sits still for a long time.

One uses the pages of Mao's little red book as cigarette papers. One looks down at the ripped-out page. The sunshine over the thin, yellow paper moves as clouds pass in the sky. *If the imperialists insist on launching a third world war, it is certain that several hundred million more will turn to socialism.* One sits on a stump, smoking, one yawns and squints up at a young guard passing by, and there's something strange about time in the camp. The moment is there and then it's not. A man with a dirty bandage around his foot stops on his crutches and stares. A teenager in a baseball cap and school-uniform shorts walks along, beating at the grass with a stick. There is something gluey, fragmented about the material of these seconds. The light falls upon the rough brown earth, photographic and eternal. It's all meaningless; each movement is empty, dead. A guard says something to the young man in the cap and smacks him with the butt of his rifle, and P watches as the young man crawls across the ground with a bleeding gash on his head. In the latrine, they use pages of Mao's little red book as toilet paper. One waves away the flies and feels some sort of insanity inside, how it whirls, how it gathers momentum and mass. *In a suitable temperature, an egg changes into a chicken, but no temperature can change a stone into a chicken, because each has a different basis.* One toys with the idea of stealing a weapon from one of the guards and forcing him to drive a truck out of the camp. One leaves the latrine, stops, looks at the trees, the leaves moving in the wind. *The world is progressing, the future is bright, and no one can change this general trend of history.*

The last night before he went to Greece he came walking through the grass, dressed in the olive-green Ugandan uniform that he had worn during his basic training. He looked at the houses of mud and planks, at the goats that were tethered at poles driven into the ground. This was his home; this was the village where he'd been born and where he'd lived with his mother, who had later sent him away. The village was full of dancing drunken people because it was a local festival. He shook their hands, telling them that he was on his way to Europe to become a fighter pilot. He was only on leave for a few days, and his airline ticket was already booked. John was there. They embraced. John promised to write. Brothers who had become fathers. The sun went down; the village was sunk in a sea of red shadows. The brother whom P had lived with in his childhood was there, too, huddled at a table under a dark halo of intoxication. He called to P, who ignored him at first but then went over reluctantly and shook his hand. The man kept hold of his hand in the manner of drunken people, squeezing it for a long time, refusing to let go. He said that he was proud that P had finally done something with his life, that it hadn't looked good in his childhood, that P had been far too spoiled. P wanted to punch the man in the face. He walked away. He sat by himself under the far-off trees, listening to the music that poured out of a battery-powered tape player. He felt a great freedom sweep across the grass and the world like a breeze.

ONE GETS UP slowly, yawns, dresses. One sits by the fire and eats. Everything is the same material: the trees, the faces, the flames of the fire; it's all of the same, mute matter, something that is like mud or wet sand. A group of refugees plays soccer every day, and sometimes he asks to step in on a team. He doesn't want to have to think, have to be still. They kick a deflating leather ball across the endless, dusty earth.

One evening, a man who claims to be a medicine man demonstrates his skills. He dances in the light of the flames, his chest bare; he picks up scorpions from an aluminium bucket and hangs them from his huge lower arm by sticking their stingers into his flesh. He is tall, very muscular, surprisingly young. Not even the guards can help being fascinated by the show; they stand off to the side with their mouths open and their eyes wide. One young man, the one who was once struck by the guard, drums his hands against an empty box.

'He has a salve that stops bullets,' an excited voice breathes into P's ear. He turns around with narrowed eyes, demonstratively slowly and indifferently. It's the old policeman, standing behind him, the man's features are twisted into a grinning mask in the glow of the fire; he is almost sexually breathless. 'You rub it on your body and the bullets can't hit you.' The scorpions are crawling across the medicine man's arm, and he takes a long, black snake from a braided basket. It writhes, opens its mouth, and hisses. P licks his cigarette together, looks at the trees swaying against the starry sky; in the light of the fire they seem to be dancing, throwing themselves upward—one instant, it exists; then it is gone. *Once the correct ideas characteristic of the advanced class are grasped by the masses, these ideas turn into a material force which changes society and changes the world.*

The hunger keeps his body awake even when his thoughts are so tired that they lie still within him like stones. Why didn't he stay in Rome? He twists and turns in the warm night; his body feels like a tangle of empty hoses and sacks and tightly strung sinews and ever-thinner muscles. How could he be so stupid as to come back to Africa? The thoughts lie there without moving. The same questions over and over again, the same questions that everyone else asks, too, when he talks about his journey. Why. Why.

The rainy season starts again; torrents patter against the leaves, light flashes across the sky, thunder silences the sounds of the jungle.

Rumours circulate in the camp, above the whispers of the rain. They say that the refugees will soon be moved again, to yet another place, even deeper in the wilderness. They say that they will be forced to invade Uganda in just a few weeks, even though they haven't done any military exercises or been given any weapons. *Yes, we are advocates of the omnipotence of revolutionary war. The guns of the Russian Communist Party created socialism. We shall create a democratic republic.* They say that Amin's fighter planes have bombed a similar camp nearby. An atmosphere of stress spreads among both refugees and guards; groups start to form; divisions based on religion, ethnic group, education, class, bonds of friendship. It's all some sort of insanity that has become heavy and real. The corn porridge is sticky, tasteless; it's like eating mud, eating oblivion, eating a war. The army-green tents where the guards live and the beds in the dorm and the little red books that are everywhere are all of the same grainy, unreal matter. *In order to get rid of the gun it is necessary to take up the gun.* The hand-rolled cigarettes. The clothes sewn of tent canvas. The old worn soccer ball. The medicine man writes down the names of those who buy the salve that can deflect bullets. They will pay after they've survived. P tries to sell some of his Italian shirts to the young man in the cap, because he has noticed that the man smokes regular cigarettes while everyone else smokes home-grown tobacco, so he must have contact with the outside world, maybe by way of a guard he's befriended. But the young man thinks that the clothes are too big and doesn't want to buy them, and he gives evasive answers to P's questions about where he gets his cigarettes.

One afternoon, three months after P arrived at the camp, he is surrounded by a group of men who crowd around him and spit on the ground. Their thin faces seem to consist only of bad teeth and large, wide-open eyes.

'No Langi will survive in Uganda.'

'Not for a minute.'

'Maybe you think that Okello has a soft spot for you because you're a pilot?' A cold, blue rainy light from the sky. One of the men draws his index finger across his throat. P shoves them out of the way; they shove back. 'You're dead as soon as we cross the border, pilot.'

'Obote was enough. No Langi will rule over us.'

'Dead.'

'You are dead.' They laugh behind his back as he goes to sit on his bed in the dorm.

The men are counted now, every morning and evening except on Saturdays and Sundays. The place becomes more and more a prison, less and less a refugee camp. The guards perform inspections of their sleeping places unannounced, poking through their belongings with their rifles, throwing the contents of their suitcases out onto the floor. They're looking for Museveni, grabbing the refugees' collars and shaking them and asking if they're Museveni. By now, P has learned that Museveni, despite being used as an adjective, is the name of a man who worked for Obote in the security service: when Amin took power nearly one year ago, this Museveni made his way to Tanzania and eventually ended up in a camp like the one P is in, in Morogoro in northern Tanzania. There, he immediately began agitating against Okello, who was the camp director. Eventually, Museveni and his supporters led an uprising, or escaped—the rumours are fuzzy and their details conflict—but in any case, when Museveni left the camp, he took more than half the men with him; apparently he is a man who can organize, convince, lie. A politician. After the incident with Museveni's mutiny, which was embarrassing for Okello, Okello moved the camp and the remaining men to this place. P and the others who were brought from the camp outside Tabora replaced the men who had gone with Museveni.

P starts playing soccer by himself, at dawn, before the others have awoken. He kicks the dull ball across the muddy field, runs after it, kicks it the other direction. There's a drizzle of rain. He still hasn't come up with a clear plan, just a feeling. The threat from the men who promised to kill him as soon as they entered Uganda reawakened his thoughts of escape. The white-haired policeman starts to avoid him. He starts lying awake at night, listening to the breathing of the others. If someone wakes up, he whispers that person's name. Asks if they can't sleep, either. Tries to get his nighttime activities to seem like ordinary sleeplessness. In reality, he wants to learn the others' sleeping patterns, how each and every one of them sounds when close to waking or when sleeping deeply, what time they get up to visit the latrine, how loud a sound he can make without waking them. Days, hazy with rain and exhaustion. The rain breaks down the book covers that lie all over the yard into a reddish-black mud. He kicks the ball, runs after it. He has to move, he has to fight the apathy and weakness that glues his feet to the earth, the mud, the camp.

He is sitting alone in the dorm one evening as the others prepare the evening meal. He is holding his passport in his hands; he is looking at the photo of himself and thinking about how young he looks. The passport is worthless here in Tanzania. The passport is dangerous. He puts it back in the inner pocket of his flight jacket, folds up the jacket, and places it at the bottom of one of the suitcases. He massages his temples. There is no chance he can steal one of the trucks. The guards would hear the engine starting. He has to flee on foot. He has to run. Voices that drift into the dorm from the yard tell him that the food is ready, but he doesn't go out; he just casts a glance at the door. He is inside the acceleration tunnel of escape. On the road that leads away. He can tell.

From Tabora he could have taken the train almost all the way to the Kenyan border, he knows that, but it's too far to run to Tabora from here. The journey here in the truck from the camp outside Tabora had taken several hours, and they seemed to have gone straight through the jungle, at least at the end. The tracks have nearly grown over by now. He has no idea which direction he should run. He looks at the door, at the red light that breaks in through the wet leaves, making the rivulets shine harshly like liquid metal. He has to run. If he is to run away from this camp, he must run like they ran in Greece; he has to train for several hours every day and run until he is nothing more than a running body. It will not be possible to train his body on the small, pitted soccer field. He goes to Okello's tent, in the mud and the drizzle, tells the guard standing outside that he needs to talk to the major. The guard sticks his head in the tent and mumbles something insulting about P, but apparently Okello has time to talk to him. He is sitting with a half-eaten plate of porridge in front of him when P steps into the tent; he pushes the plate away and signals to P to sit down. 'You probably thought I sit in here eating meat stew at night.' He coughs into his clenched fist. 'I live in the same conditions as my subordinates. I always have. How can I help you?' P straightens his back, tries to call up the soldier inside him, to play Okello's game, where the emaciated refugees are soldiers in an army. 'They say it will soon be time to cross the border.'

'Who says that?'

'There's talk in the camp. If it's true, I need to train. I'm out of shape.'

'Play soccer with the others.'

'I need to train for real.' P looks meaningfully at Okello: *I need military training; I'm a soldier. The men out there are completely unmotivated.*

'What do you suggest?'

'Running. I'm in worse shape than a civilian.'

Okello considers this; he seems almost nervous about the situation, shuffles a few papers, folds up a map. He smiles, cruelly and scornfully at first, but after a moment his smile breaks into a loud, rumbling laugh. His stomach sways under his green shirt; he claps his hands together hard, a single time, as if to indicate that a decision had finally been made after a very long discussion. 'Excellent. I wish more of the men out there had your discipline. I will tell the guards that you have permission to train outside the borders of the camp for one hour a day.'

'I need three hours.'

'Three hours?' Okello turns his head. It's a birdlike, curious movement that looks grotesque on that massive body. He drums his short fingers on the table. 'Three hours,' he says, impressed. 'I'll tell the guards.' P stands up.

'Sit.' Okello's face is like granite, immovable and filled with some weight P doesn't understand. They look at each other in silence; Okello twists his fingers together, contemplating something. P sits down. 'I knew the coup was coming,' Okello says. It's raining harder now; drops heavy as syrup drum against the tent. Once again, Okello sits in silence for a long time. 'I had been promised that my position would be secure if I remained neutral.' Okello sucks his teeth and coughs. 'Amin was lying. I was forced into exile. Now Obote is the one sitting in Dar es Salaam and promising me that my position is secure if I help him overthrow Amin. Do you understand what I'm telling you?' Okello is insinuating that he's planning to circumvent Obote and take power himself if the untrained guerrillas of this camp manage to overthrow Amin. P doesn't know what he's expected to answer. He just wants to leave this tent, this political intrigue that is like a dream that lasts too long, like swimming underwater without being able to reach the surface.

The next morning, before the others have awoken, he runs out of the camp. Two guards who see him go nod a reluctant approval. He runs along one of two hardly visible paths. He is wearing the sandals he brought from Rome because he doesn't want to wear out his only pair of shoes. It's hard to run in the thick, wet forest; he gets stuck in the undergrowth, slips on wet roots, scrapes his hands. He runs north. The morning sun falls between the trunks at an angle, like red spears. When he returns to the camp after a bit more than two hours, he is wet with sweat and out of breath, not so much from the running as from breaking through the jungle. He collapses onto his bed, lying there for a long time and listening to the blood pounding in his neck, in his hands. Only a few of the other refugees are awake.

The next morning, he forces himself to run on stiff, sore legs. He doesn't have to tear away the worst of the obstacles along the path since he is running in his own footsteps. He increases his speed and pushes his body to its limits, which he reaches all too fast. He runs for an hour and then turns back, jogging slowly through the jungle.

One refugee is trying to get the fire going and P stops in front of the young man. 'Where have you been?'

He catches his breath for a moment before he answers. 'Training.' The refugee shakes his head, crouches forward, and blows on a coal.

In the second week of his training, two men from the camp start to follow him when he goes out in the morning. They don't say anything, they just trail him as he runs out of the camp. They pant and cough, cold and half-asleep; they run a few steps behind him. At least one of them belongs to the faction of the camp that doesn't like P because of his ethnic group and his military training and has threatened to kill him. Perhaps they want to see what he does out in the jungle. Perhaps they have realized that they really ought to be training for the war that seems to come closer with every day. P lets them follow him a few hundred metres into the jungle; then he increases his speed. The men shout for him to wait, but he ignores them. After another few hundred metres, he can no longer hear them.

His feet trample down the creaking branches and the wet earth sways as his toes push off, and his chest lifts, and his body shoots forward, upward.

He draws in air, pants. His body remembers that it has run before, and that it was happy when it was running. When it was on its way away. He breathes out, presses off, his body lifts; it is light.

The medicine man argues with a short man one evening. P doesn't know what the argument is about; he just hears them shouting at each other in the dorm. He is sitting, leaning against the wooden wall of the building, staring at the tufts of clouds that fly above the trees. The medicine man threatens to use magic against his opponent, who grows silent at that and leaves the dorm, a stooped shadow that disappears over by the fire and his friends.

He still plays soccer by himself sometimes, before he takes off on his run.

One morning when he returns from his run, he is met by the old policeman, who takes his arm and leads him behind the dorm. The policeman is smoking nervously and looking back over his shoulder. Three refugees who were security officers in Obote's government have picked the lock on P's suitcases and gone through them. P stands with his hands on his knees, catching his breath; he has hardly exchanged a word with the policeman in a month and he has assumed that the old man was disappointed when he didn't share his ridiculous enthusiasm for the medicine man's salve, or perhaps he suspects that P is planning to escape and is afraid of being taken for a conspirator. P takes a few drags from the policeman's cigarette. He goes to Okello's tent.

The constantly out-of-breath camp director looks up from his strategic pencil marks on the large, dirty map: his plans to return to Kampala as president. His labyrinth. He has a metal mug of steaming coffee on the table. 'How is your training going?'

P tells him what happened; Okello waves his hand dismissively. 'The men are just nervous.'

'I'm not here for you to punish them. I want you to gather everyone in the camp together. I want to show everyone what is in my suitcases.'

'Is that necessary?' Okello sighs, and P insists; he has not wanted to show them his clothes from Europe because they are his only currency here in Africa, but now he's afraid that the people in the camp have gotten the idea that he's hiding something much worse than clothes, and he wants to lay all their speculation to rest. With difficulty, Okello stands up. He escorts P out of the tent. He wheezes something to a guard, who walks off in the morning mist and rouses a pair of men who are sitting at the fire and shouts that the other refugees should gather and line up. Finally, a large group is gathered in the dorm. P takes out his two suitcases. Their locks are broken. He says nothing. Many of the faces around him are eager and open, and P realizes that people have talked about him in the camp, about the suitcases he has tried to keep secret, about his training, about the ethnic group he belongs to. He tosses the clothes out onto the floor.

'It's clothes.' He shouts it; he wants his voice to carry so that everyone in the crowd can hear, but his shout just seems silly and theatrical. Someone laughs. He breathes hard through his mouth, holding one suitcase upside down, shaking it, emptying the last articles into a pile. 'Are you happy?'

'What is that?' The young man who smokes bought cigarettes points at a small tape player that's still in the other suitcase. P picks up the device; he packed it when he was leaving Greece on that windy September morning almost a year ago. There's a Harry Belafonte cassette in it; he hands the player to the boy, irritated. The batteries are almost dead, and only a few tones of 'Jamaica Farewell' come out when the young man presses play. P is still drenched with sweat from his run; he dries his face with his forearm. The two men who followed P on his run have been standing off to the side, observing the spectacle along with the rest of the refugees who have threatened his life. One of them steps forward and grabs the tape player out of the boy's hand.

'Comrades!' He holds the tape player up in the air. 'This tape player could easily be converted into a radio transmitter!' P shoves the man in the chest, rips the tape player out of his hand, and tries to pry open the plastic casing. A buzz goes through the crowd, and for a moment it seems like the man is going to shove him back. P's fingers are too weak; he tugs and pulls at the tape player but can't get its plastic casing open. He feels a vortex close in on his consciousness and he wants to strangle the man or just start indiscriminately kicking and hitting around him, Instead, he throws the tape player to the ground so hard that it finally breaks. The man who claimed that the tape player could be turned into a transmitter pokes at the pieces with his shoe and is going to say more, but something in the air has died away. P carefully and silently gathers up the plastic and metal pieces, walks out of the dorm, and throws them into the latrine. When he comes back to his bed, the others are gone. He lies down. He hears his heart pounding, muffled and strong.

His mouth tastes like blood; the ground sinks away from his sandal-clad feet. He is running. He will run until he falls. He stops. Why did he stop? He stands in the light that filters in through the leaves and listens to his breathing, to the sounds of the jungle. He thought he heard something. A whistling noise. He waits. There it is again. A long, drawn-out whistle. He cautiously starts to walk toward the sound, straight into the thicket. Soon he hears the sound again, but it is much fainter this time. He stops, stands still, strains to hear the sound if it comes one last time. He hears the faint creak as the ground under his feet sinks with the weight of his body. Leaves pinwheel out of the trees. He waits. He recognized the mournful whistling sound from somewhere, but he can't place it. The sound comes again. This time it's nearly inaudible. He sets off at a full sprint, clambering over fallen trees, jumping over thick roots, running as fast as he can in the direction of the noise. The whistle of a train. He gives up and sinks down with his arms on his thighs, staring into the impenetrable vegetation before him. He heard the whistle of a train.

The days go by. His running takes up all of his thoughts, and he runs every day, faster and faster, farther and farther into the jungle. He has trampled a new path that turns off from the existing one. It extends several kilometres through the thick vegetation. Maybe he has gone as far as twenty kilometres from the camp; he doesn't know. He knows that there are railroad tracks out there somewhere. He has no watch, but he has been used to measuring time with the aid of the sun's height above the horizon since his childhood. After an hour and a half, he always turns back toward the camp. He must not raise any suspicions. Around him, camp life continues with conflicts, mealtimes that buzz with rumours born out of sadness and fear, and soccer games in the afternoons. Yet another group of Ugandans arrives. At first they appear to be refugees like the rest of the men in camp, but Okello supplies them with weapons and worn green uniforms: reinforcements for the guard crew. The man who claimed that P's tape player could be transformed into a radio transmitter gives a speech one day to a small group of refugees. He has a copy of Mao's little red book in his hand; he brandishes it as he speaks in a chanting voice: 'The atom bomb is a paper tiger which the enemy uses to scare people. We are without fear. We are Maoists. A revolution is not a dinner party, or writing an essay. The people and the people alone are the motive force in the making of world history!'

In the afternoons, just before dusk, when the rays of the sun fall nearly horizontally against the trunks of the trees, there is a golden light in the world that reminds P of when he had come home from school, milked the family's goat, prepared food, and done all the other chores and was free for half an hour before his brother arrived. A light that reminds him of freedom.

The rainy season will soon be over; another year has gone by. He lies awake at night, listening to the other bodies breathing and moving in their sleep.

Almost a dozen more men come to the camp early one morning. This time, they really are more refugees. Three of them are deserters who have come directly from

Uganda. They say that Amin has now begun a campaign of hate against the Indians and Pakistanis who live in the country. He gives long speeches on the radio and threatens to take their property from them and give it to black Africans; he calls them parasites and bloodsuckers. When these speeches are repeated, many of the men in the camp nod slowly and reluctantly: they agree.

The rhythm of stomping feet, the sound of twigs breaking under his sandals. P looks up between the large palm fronds, sees the sun blink, sinking silver lines, as if they were slowly growing down into his eyes. He stops. The tendrils and leaves in the otherwise dense wall of vegetation seem to appear out of themselves, cut out of light. He has reached the edge of the jungle.

A railway leads from south-west to north in a long curve. Savannah, broken by shrubs and trees. P's shadow flows before him in the tall grass as he begins to walk along the track. After nearly twenty minutes he sees a village. He stands at the edge of the forest, staring at the small station building with its platform, tossed out under the high morning sun. He sees a group of children on their way to school, glimpses them between two brick buildings; he hears their bright voices. He sees women carrying buckets of water on their heads. Store signs, doors opening and closing. Flashes of sun in the rear-view mirror of a truck that drives out along the village's main street. He is bewitched. All of this everyday life is taking place just over an hour's run away from the camp. He casts a glance at the sun behind him. He doesn't have time to stand here. He runs as fast as he can, back along the railroad tracks. He turns into the jungle, rushes back in his own footsteps: it would be enough for someone to become suspicious and follow the path he's trampled to realize what he's up to. It feels like he's going to vomit blood every time he draws air into his lungs.

He collapses on the patch of earth outside the dorm, lying on his back and staring up at the cloudless sky. Birds go by, slowly gliding above him.

When he leaves at dawn the next day, he puts one of his Italian shirts on under the knitted blue sweater he wears when it's chilly out. When he has made it a few hundred metres into the jungle, he pulls off his sweater and the shirt, takes the shirt in hand, and squeezes back into the dirty, sweat-stinking sweater again. He stands still. The shirt flutters in a chilly morning breeze. It is made of silk and has a red-and-black flower pattern. He thinks he can hear the blood rushing in the veins at his temples. Maybe it's just his injured ear. He is afraid that the Kenyans, like Zambia, have a policy of deporting young Ugandan men back to these guerrilla camps in Tanzania, because the stories he heard in the last camp suggested that this was the case. But he's going to Nairobi. There he will try to get the Italian embassy to contact his cousin in Rome. Nairobi.

Just over an hour later, he is wandering breathlessly along the track, then between the brick, wood, and metal walls of the village, hopping up on the platform, and trying to look like he belongs here despite his dirty clothes and his emaciated face, which is also shiny with sweat after his run. He looks for a store that might buy a used shirt. A group of schoolchildren crossing a dusty street stops to observe him; they're speaking a local language, and one of the boys points at his head. He brushes at his hair, and several dry leaves fall from it; the children laugh. He goes into a small store that sells fabric and some jewellery. He asks the man, who seems to have just opened for the day, what he can get for the shirt;

they haggle for a while and in the end he receives a couple of Kenyan shillings, a fraction of what the shirt cost when his cousin bought it for him in Rome, but it is money he can use to run away. The coins jingle in his pocket as he runs back. He has more shirts. The wind in his face, hot tears streaking his cheeks, at first he tries to run anyway but he has to stop and bend over his knees and snuffle and rub his arm across his face several times and feel the great and unfathomable thing deep inside rise up to the surface and turn above the depths. Because he will never get to stay somewhere, never, never. Because he left his home one night when he was a boy. Because he misses it with every bone in his body. He straightens his back.

During the next few weeks, he sells his shirts one by one. Most are bought by the man in the store, but sometimes he sells a shirt to a farm labourer on his way to the fields around the village or to women he meets on the small main street of the village and who buy the exclusive garments for their husbands or grown sons. He sells the clothes for next to nothing; the important thing is that the transaction is quick. For a few weeks at the end of the rainy season he is a mysterious, recurring figure in the small village. To the man in the boutique and to others who ask, he says he lives with his family a few kilometres to the north, that he recently moved there from southern Kenya. At times he is drawn into a conversation and tells stories about his made-up life, stories about relatives who don't exist, places he's never visited. He ends up standing there, gazing into the distance, where the swaying grass meets the sky. Wondering where everything comes from. All this existence out of nothing. When he passes the guards, he's afraid that they'll see the colourful shirt collars sticking out under the blue knitted sweater and ask him why he's wearing two shirts, and he's always afraid someone will go through his suitcases again and notice that clothes have started to disappear out of them and that instead he has a handful of coins hidden on the bottom. After a while, his suitcases are so light that he starts replacing the clothes he's sold with stones. He counts the money at night, sitting in his bed with the coins in his hand, turning them carefully between his fingers, one by one so they don't make any noise. He thinks that the small, dirty copper coins are made of fear, that their material is fear. He carefully puts them away at the very bottom of the suitcase. One morning when he's walking through the village, he decides to find out when the train stops, where it goes, how much a ticket costs. He speaks to an older woman and pretends to be generally curious.

'Does the train that goes through here go to Kenya?'

The woman is carrying an empty basket of braided sticks; she rests it against her hip.

'The train goes to Mwanza.'

'Mwanza?' P tries to hide the fact that he's still out of breath from his run through the jungle; he breathes slowly through his mouth.

'The harbour city of Mwanza, by Lake Victoria?'

'I know it. I was just surprised that the train went so far north.'

'If you want to go to Kenya, you have to take a bus from Mwanza to Musoma. From there you can cross the border on foot or take another bus.'

The woman adjusts the basket against her hip. P can see that there is a sickle in the bottom.

'Do you work in the fields?' She nods. P has a black silk shirt in his hand. He holds it out and asks if she wants to buy it for four shillings, but she doesn't have the money.

'What does a ticket to Mwanza cost?'

'Twenty-five shillings. Are you on your way home?'

He lifts his eyes, looks straight into the sun behind her. 'Maybe.'

'The train goes on Wednesdays, Fridays, and Saturdays.' The woman points at the shirt. 'Kisumu is right on the other side of the border. There's a market there.'

He has pulled his knees up to his body, sitting in his bed, in the hot, steamy evening. He remembers how he stood in his cousin's house in Rome, choosing which shirts he would bring on his trip to Lusaka. He has counted his money one last time. He has enough to buy a ticket and will have a little left over besides, and he has a jacket and three shirts he can sell in Kisumu so he can pay for the bus ride to Nairobi. He decides to postpone his escape until the Friday night of the upcoming week, because they aren't counted on the weekend.

During the week, he tries to act normal. He runs only twice, on Tuesday and Thursday, because he is terrified that someone will go through his suitcases and steal his money. In the evenings, on his way into the dorm, he looks up at the moon. It's almost waning. He plans to use the darkness to flee. Friday night. He sits by the fire and looks at the other refugees with a gloomy, lingering gaze. They're shovelling down porridge; their faces stand out in the light of the flames, dirty and emaciated like skulls picked from a fire pit. He eats his porridge. It all feels so eternal, distant, like a dream. The night. He lies in the dark, blood rushing through his head. He hears how the others' breathing becomes slower and heavier, how they sink into their dreams. He has put his most important documents into the inner pocket of his

Greek flight jacket and he has knotted it into a ripped-up sheet along with his shoes, which he's barely used since he left Rome, and a number of other belongings. He lies on his side and stares toward the open door of the dorm with wide-open eyes. Now is the time he has been planning for in one way or another ever since he sat in the cellar in Dar es Salaam. He would like to say goodbye to these people and this place, but there's nothing to say, nothing to do. Just lie there for a while longer, looking into the darkness. When he's sure that everyone is asleep, he arranges the clothes he's planning to leave behind into a pile in the bed so it looks like a person is lying in it. He takes his sandals in his hand and places his bare feet on the cold dirt floor.

The new moon is a brilliant white eyelash, cast up in the rain of stars. He leaves the camp by a different path than the one he's used to avoid encountering anyone. He sneaks behind the latrines; the knotted sheet is slung over his shoulder, leaves rustle under his feet. He looks over his shoulder one last time and then he starts to run.

He sinks straight down into the earth. His hands scratch in the grass; his leg sinks deeper and deeper. A sharp pain flashes through his knee and at first he thinks something under the ground is biting him. He feels a rush of panic inside, flowing through him like thick, black smoke, and he fights to pull himself up but he can't. He tears away tufts of grass; he ignores the pain in his knee and pulls his leg up.

His foot dangles in the empty air underground. His leg has sunk to his groin. He is stuck. He must have stepped in an old latrine that's been overgrown by brush. He tries to pull himself up further but he can't. He is stuck.

Spring comes for yet another year. Brightening skies over Hisingen. Brightening skies. Dad returns to the hospital, then comes home again. His new lung is being rejected. I move. I leave my apartment on Hisingen where I've lived among those who are alone, among the alcoholics who scream at night, the Volvo workers and the neighbours coming in and out of the place, students from China who live three to each one-bedroom apartment. I was asked if I wanted to rent a friend's apartment on the mainland side of the river.

'I escaped the fields of death. That was my life,' Dad says, in a voice that is almost a whisper. He has one hand in his tangled, uncombed hair, and his chest is bare; he is sitting in his bed, leaning against the nicotine-yellowed wall. It's a night when he's asked me to sleep in his apartment because he thinks he's going to die in the next few days. He coughs. I'm sitting on a mattress on the floor. He woke up because I had a lamp on; I was lying there reading and writing. We can hear the traffic outside, trucks going by on their way to or from the harbour, the endless cargo of things, goods, maybe even a person or two. I have listened to that traffic for more than ten years; he has for twenty, thirty. He leans forward, sits up for a long time to catch his breath. He is a distant shore, a razed bridge, collapsing cliffs.

'We are survivors,' he says. The reading lamp that

woke him up is placed on the floor, and when I sit up my shadow moves across his face.

I walk across the courtyard. There are cherry trees in the yard here, in the neighbourhood I'm going to live in now; they toss in the wind, a storm of pink flakes blows before my feet. I will try to live here, I think; I will try to make this place a home. I look up at the windows and think about how Dad's apartment on Hisingen is empty once more. He's at the hospital again. May turns into June; at night I dream that I'm running in sand that gives way under my feet.

I like that my new apartment is still almost empty, that my things aren't here. It's like my past doesn't exist anymore.

I read Fanon again and read what Dad has written about his life again; it's a text that hurts me with its longing to understand life. I see this incomprehensible thing that is life; I read what Dad wrote about the moment when the baker told him he couldn't help him. *I was very sad and tried not to cry but I couldn't. To hide my tears I pretended I had something in my eye and I walked away to get it out.* Or about the secretary of state who was once so overweight that he couldn't use the latrine. *Like I did, he realized that there were drawbacks to modern conveniences and promised himself never to let himself get so fat again. I suspected that he wouldn't keep that promise, because I had already forgotten my own promise to always sleep with plugs in my ears to avoid getting insects in them.*

I read about aerodynamics, about aerodynamic lift in birds and planes.

In late July I am sitting at his hospital bed and touching his hand cautiously. His hair is white as cloud fluff, white as death, white as forgetting. The blinds in the room are drawn; stripes of light fall on the walls.

'We know that death is not the end,' he says, slowly turning his face to me. 'Don't be sad. This is what life is.' I squeeze his hand gently, and then I stand up and leave him.

I sit on a park bench, smoking, watching the evening arrive above the streetcar wires and the chimneys. It's been many years since I saw him very ill for the first time. My doorbell rang one afternoon and he stood there, supporting himself against the wall of the hallway, having trouble breathing. He had already been coughing up blood for a few weeks, and now he had become acutely ill and wanted me to come with him to the hospital. He didn't want to call for an ambulance because it cost several hundred kronor extra and I didn't have any money either back then, so we took the bus. We sat next to each other in silence. We travelled through the delirious summer day. The city was moving outside the windows. When we passed Wieselgrensplatsen, he couldn't breathe and asked me to call an ambulance after all, and we got off and sat on a bench to wait. His breaths rattled, it was all like a nightmare, I sat beside him, I placed a hand on his shoulder. He was leaning forward in a particular way. He was so out of breath; it was as if he had run an entire life. I blow out smoke and look up into the leaves above my head; they look like glowing foil in the red street light. *I discovered that most people would have chosen security in Europe. I was ashamed that I was naïve enough to believe that there was any future for me in Africa. As a result, I avoided giving details of the story of my escape.* He ran here, to this country. Cars go by, go by, go by, their red tail lights spreading out in the distance.

There is an idea that every phenomenon has its own

angel: that there is an angel of war, one for law, one for love. The angel of history, according to historical philosopher Walter Benjamin, is a man who stares at something outside the picture with mouth agape, something he is recoiling from in fear. 'His face is turned toward the past. Where we perceive a chain of events, he sees one single catastrophe which keeps piling wreckage upon wreckage and hurls it in front of his feet,' in a pile that grows and grows toward the sky. 'The angel would like to stay, awaken the dead, and make whole what has been smashed to pieces. But a storm is blowing from Paradise, and has got caught in his wings with such violence that the angel can no longer close them. This storm irresistibly propels him into the future to which his back is turned.' The storm, Benjamin writes, is progress.

I bike alongside the traffic. My chain is rattling. The summer night, already getting brighter. I don't want to escape history but life. I want the wind to have brought us out of nowhere, and I wish that we were on our way to another nowhere. Somewhere. That everything is in between. All that exists. The bodies that itch and ache and long and laugh and die. That we're not responsible for what comes before us. That the homeland is a lie. That we come from this very moment, that our home-land is hours, seconds, instants, that there is no origin, that history can't tell us who we are. I feel the breeze cool my face; drunken people stagger out of nightclubs and fall over on the sidewalks, and I just come from all these stories that try to figure out my origins. There is no history. I just come from here. From this summer, when my father is dying.

A FEW MEN are playing soccer; the ball bounces off the field, off into the dry leaves. The young man with the cap runs to fetch it. He sits with his back against a tree, watching the men fighting and kicking at each other and the ball. The dry earth rises in a dust devil over the soccer field. There's a rumour that the invasion, when the refugees will be outfitted with weapons and forced into Uganda, will happen in just a few days. An apocalyptic mood has spread through the camp. They say that Idi Amin has sent fighter jets to bomb the camp outside Tabora, and that he might bomb this place, too, at any time. Every day, people line up to buy the magic salve from the medicine man. P gets up with the help of two home-made crutches and hops off to the dorm. He sits in his bed, feels his knee; it's still badly swollen. It's been a few weeks since his failed escape. If he hadn't already dislocated his knee when he fell into the latrine, it happened as he finally managed to drag himself out of the hole. He has explained his injury by saying that he hurt himself when he was playing soccer alone early that morning; he didn't want to use his running as an excuse because he was afraid to reveal how hard he pushes himself out there in the jungle. There is no doctor in the camp, and naturally they can't take him to a doctor, so he has splinted the knee himself with pieces of an old, broken bed that was lying in a corner, waiting to be firewood.

He thinks about the flight to Greece. It was almost four years ago; they travelled on a commercial flight. He looked out the window at the rising sun. It was as though the sky were made of hammered bronze. He felt like a god. A bird god. He remembers stepping out of the plane along with the three Ugandans who would be in his class at the academy. He felt light inside; he smiled as he walked across the tarmac with the others. He turns over in the hard wooden bed. He feels his ear with his fingers, pokes his finger in a little. He still hears poorly; he probably always will. He rocks his kneecap back and forth under the skin. *Contrails appear when ice crystals form around particles of dirt in the exhaust of the jet.* He would like to go to confession. He would like to have a different life.

The new year is approaching. His knee is healing slowly, and a bit crookedly; he's becoming slightly knock-kneed. He prays to God sometimes, sitting at the edge of the bed with his hands clasped. He exaggerates his injury and continues to limp badly even when the torn ligaments have healed, and when he starts running again he totters overly slowly past the guards. Not until he's well out of sight does he start to jog. *Suppose that a wing is moving forward through stagnant air: the lift that develops is proportional to the wing's speed multiplied by the angle of attack.* He blinks, he's sleepy. He sits, leaning against the outer wall of the dorm and staring into the sun. The leaves move; the hours disappear. In his childhood, he and friends his age would set fire to the tall grass at this time of year, when everything is dry and almost ash-coloured. He hears a group of refugees shouting inside the dorm, excited voices threatening each other. He thinks about how words are as empty and meaningless as the aluminium plates they fill with porridge twice a day. The days go by, the weeks go by, he trains every morning but otherwise continues to pretend that he is injured. One day, Okello comes trotting between the tents with one of his subordinates beside him; they're in the middle of a lively discussion about one thing or another; Okello meets P's gaze and stares at him coldly. Perhaps he has started to see yet another rival for presidential power in P. At night, a collective fear fills the trampled dirt floor of the dorm with nerves. Cries from nightmares, coughs, groans.

Friday night, between Christmas and New Year's Eve. P is sitting on a home-made wooden stool, which he has placed just outside the door of the dorm. Loud voices and the clinking of pots echo through the camp. Three guards run across the yard toward the cooking tent, their automatic weapons in hand. Their unbuttoned shirts flap. A young refugee disappears into the dorm and returns with a small, rusty knife he's apparently kept hidden in there. The young man catches sight of P and turns around.

'Someone tipped over tonight's dinner. They're fighting. We're going to kill those Acholi pigs.'

People seem to heave each other out of the tent in a tangle of arms and legs; more and more join in the fight and soon P is the only one outside who isn't taking part. The guards wave their rifles and shout; Okello comes out of his tent and yells at the prisoners to line up to be counted, but no one obeys. P wonders if the guards will start to shoot. He catches sight of the old policeman, who has a whole pile of Mao's little red books in his arms; he throws them around, laughing. P lights a hand-rolled cigarette. He blows smoke through his nose and shakes his head slowly. So this is the guerrilla army that's meant to overthrow Idi Amin. Someone in the pile of people throws a pot straight up in the air, and it seems to hang there for a moment, perfectly still against the sky, shiny and weightless, before it turns and falls to the ground again. The fight continues for nearly half an hour, and then it dies out, only to flare up again after the sun goes down, when a large group of refugees gathers in the yard, waving torches, canes, and knives they've taken from the kitchen tent. By this point, Okello must have sent for help, because a Tanzanian officer drives up in a Jeep along with three soldiers. The officer climbs out of the Jeep and tries to mediate between the various groups; P hears him shouting catchphrases about the people and the history; they sound like they're from the little red book. Someone throws a stone; it bangs the hood of the Jeep. One of the newly arrived soldiers shoots his weapon straight into the crowd. The report of the rifle is sharp and surreal; the men in the yard go so completely and totally silent that they can hear the wind hissing through the leaves around them. P slowly backs into the dorm. Again he hears shouts, loud voices, movements. He tosses his suitcase onto his bed. He takes out the knotted sheet he's kept hidden away in the bottom of the suitcase since his last escape attempt. He tosses it over his shoulder and slinks out of the dorm. He sees men waving torches and two men fighting over a rifle in the light of a fire that isn't the campfire but something else burning, maybe a tent. Smoke rises toward the rapidly darkening sky. Someone is holding back a friend who is brandishing a knife at the Tanzanian soldiers. P walks behind the latrine, hops over the hole where he injured his knee, and starts jogging. He hears himself breathing, his feet tramping through the dry grass, drumming against the earth. He casts a glance behind himself, afraid someone has seen him leave the camp.

No one is coming. He sees only the leaves tossing in the wind, the rainforest closing around him. He remembers a story from boarding school and inside his head he sees an image flash by: a sea dividing itself and then crashing back down. He hears his heart beating. He increases his speed. After ten or fifteen minutes he hears the crack of another gunshot, then nothing more.

The moon is out, but even with its light the jungle is just vague outlines, shadows, grey flecks of perception. He tries to remember what the path looks like: a fallen branch there, he has hopped over it hundreds of times— he hops, lands softly, his foot presses off. He runs.

After half an hour, the moon disappears behind thick rain clouds and he can't see the ground beneath his feet anymore. He stops and puts down his bundle. The pitch-darkness suddenly makes every movement creepy and surreal, like moving deep underground or through the interior of a cliff. The waterfall of night and blood splashes against his temples. He tries to calm down, tries to let his pulse slow. He has torn his pants on some brush; he's fallen down twice. His mouth tastes like he's been licking a piece of rusty iron. Hopefully it will be Monday morning before anyone notices he's gone. He can't see his hands in front of him. He's afraid he'll twist an ankle if he keeps going before the moon comes out again, but he's also afraid that someone is following him and they'll catch up if he stays here for too long. He can hear crickets and night birds; fireflies flash on and off, and now and then some larger animal moves through the leaves, heavy and rustling.

'Kodi mwanainchi?' He is startled. Someone out in the darkness is shouting a phrase in Swahili that is used to ask if one may enter a home, but also to check if a person one encounters is friendly. 'Kodi mwanainchi?' He breathes slowly, his mouth wide open, listening; he hears the sound of twigs breaking out there in the darkness, leaves rustling. After a while he thinks he can see a group of shadows moving among the trees. Could someone else have run from the camp as fast as he did? 'Kodi mwanain-chi?' If one doesn't receive an answer to this phrase, it means 'approach at your own risk.' P casts a glance up between the large, oblong leaves; the moon is still hidden behind the clouds but it is on its way out. Soon the men will be able to see one another clearly. He clenches his fists, opens them; the fear comes sweeping between the trees. He has learned how to press a larynx into a windpipe with his thumbs, how to break a person's neck, how to kill. A stab goes through his chest as one of the shadows calls his name. They have stopped twenty or thirty metres away; it seems to be two men. They call his name again, curiously. He can't go back to the camp, not this time. As he holds his breath, he thinks he can hear them breathing. A voice suddenly whispers, hoarse and with an almost-playful tone, 'How do you know it's him?'

'I recognize the sweater. That Italian sweater he always has on? It's him.' The shadows move again, quickly coming closer. It's as though they could see him plain and clear, even though he can only make them out with difficulty. Maybe they saw him earlier tonight, followed him, and have now lost him? He slinks around a tree as carefully and silently as he can, but he ends up walking straight into a briar patch. Panicking, he shoves the thorny branches aside with his hands, which makes a lot of noise.

'Stop!' Both of the other men are running toward him, and he runs into the briars, which have thorns as long as human fingers, and they tear at his face and arms. He fights his way forward, shielding his eyes and pressing his body straight into the thorns. He goes ten or fifteen metres before he stops. One of the men calls his name again. Again he thinks that he has to fight, that maybe he has to die. The night has its own taste, its own weight; he can feel it roar over his neck and shoulders and squeeze the muscles in his hands. The wounds on his face sting when sweat runs into them.

'Are you sure it was him?'

'It could have been an animal.'

'An animal?'

'Feel these thorns. A person wouldn't go in there, would he?' P doesn't recognize the men's voices.

'Idiot. Come on.' The footsteps grow distant, moving neither in the direction of the camp nor in P's direction, but in a third direction. P waits until he can't hear them anymore, and then, despite the chilly night, he pulls off the sweater. He holds it up in front of himself: it is torn to shreds and he wants to toss it away, but he doesn't want to leave any traces behind. His chest heaves. If the two men are from the camp and they tell Okello what they saw, he will lose the two-day head start he is counting on. He rushes into the night, his feet seek the ground blindly, he stumbles, gets up on his feet again, hurtles ahead.

The sun is rising over the savannah, a red orb like an eye half-hidden by the horizon. The ground is steaming. P goes the long way around the central part of the village and makes his way to the train station by way of the tracks themselves. The platform is deserted; the station clock reads just a few minutes before six o'clock, and the train doesn't go until ten. He wanders back the same way he came, enters the jungle again, and sits down against a tree. His body shakes with dissipating tension. He knew that he would flee; he knew that even as they interrogated him in Dar es Salaam, he knew it even on that January day in Athens nearly a year ago when a small fry told him that there had been a coup d'état. He will never stay anywhere. He lifts slowly from the ground, he hangs with his arms extended, drifting upward, he hears the crackle of the radio in his ear. *I'm breaking formation, bearing 354.*

In the distance he hears the jingling of a musical box. He casts a glance at the instrument panel, looks up; the sun in his eyes. He pulls the stick to the left; the plane turns on its side, and he sees the T-37's shadow rush across the clouds.

Someone jostles him.

He realizes that he fell asleep and is being awoken by guards from the camp, poking him with the butts of their rifles. He clumsily gets to his feet, blinks, runs his hands through his hair. There are no guards around him. He's standing in the middle of a herd of goats who are eating the fallen fruit under the tree, and the skinny animals are nudging him with their moist muzzles and short, curled horns. He shoves away a goat that is trying to eat his bundle of belongings. The sun is higher now. He might have missed the train. The pungent animals have bells on, that's what was jingling in his dream, and when he realizes this it strikes him that the animals must have a shepherd with them. He takes his sheet and climbs into the tree. Not until he is sitting on a branch six metres up does he realize that he should have walked to the train station instead. He hugs the tree trunk; his head feels foggy. The wind makes the leaves whisper around him. He sees the shepherd approaching down there, a young boy in shorts and a dirty, ripped shirt. He has a stick to push the animals forward; he gathers his herd and drives it on through the bushy vegetation. When the boy and the animals have disappeared, P climbs out of the tree and runs toward the railway station. About twenty other passengers are standing or sitting on the platform. The large clock on the wall of the station reads nine-thirty. P sits down on the boards of the platform and puts his bundle down. Many of the passengers are dressed as poorly as he is, and like him they have only knotted blankets or sheets for luggage. He looks toward the other side of the tracks, expecting the whole time to see soldiers from the camp coming out from between the trees. A woman with glasses is sitting at a counter window selling tickets, but P doesn't want to buy his ticket here in the village because he doesn't want the ticket seller to remember him if people from the camp ask about him. The train pulls in with a screeching shower of sparks. He picks up his bundle, climbs aboard, and sits by a window. He looks out at the jungle, still expecting that the soldiers will come, that they'll stop the train and start searching the cars. The savannah moves outside; the landscape reminds him of his youth. He remembers seeing *William Tell* at the cinema, a black-and-white film that was shown on a screen they put up in his home village. The next day he tried to use a hand catapult to shoot a pot his brother F was carrying on his head. He ran away, laughing in the tall grass. He gives a laugh, doesn't know why he just remembered that. He's still in great danger. He buys a ticket from the conductor; it costs a few shillings extra. At the next station, a young polio victim boards the train, and P gets up to give the young man his seat, stands in the aisle, swaying in time with the movements of the train.

Inside him it is like a gentle rain of light and shadow. He is on his way now.

Sometime in the afternoon the train stops in Tabora. He peers out at the station building and remembers arriving on this very platform. A large group of boarding-school students pours in: apparently a break is over and they're on their way back to their school. The boys squeeze past him as he stands there in the aisle; they shout to each other and look for open seats even though there are none. P almost falls over when the train gives a jerk and starts moving again. His legs are shaky from the night's run and from standing on the train for several hours, and after a while he simply lies down across the aisle with his head between two seats and his knotted sheet as a pillow. The sun flickers in his eyes. He lies there for a long time, looking at the wisps of clouds that rush by in the window above him.

From the other refugees' stories he knows that Kenya's president, Jomo Kenyatta, has been in power since the country became independent after a violent conflict between nationalist groups and the Brits. One man in the camp, whose father was a Kenyan who fought on the side of the rebels, told P that the Brits had established prison camps there where the prisoners were whipped and burned alive, and that they used electric shocks, mutilation, and murder in interrogations of suspected rebels. The resistance movement countered the Brits' violence by murdering white civilians. The most famous murder was a six-year-old British boy who was killed by rebels. When the man told him this, P remembered that it had also been discussed in Ugandan newspapers and that a voice on the bbc had called the incident 'a disgrace' and then described the bestial violence in detail. It had happened sometime in P's early childhood. He remembers being afraid that what had happened to the British six-year-old could also happen to him.

Kenyatta is neither a socialist nor on Amin's side, according to the men in the camp. Even though some of them claimed to have been extradited to Tanzania from Kenya, Kenya seems to be a neutral area in the field of tension that runs across all of East Africa.

The wheels of the train clank against the rails. P stares at the sky, which has started to grow dark again. A desolation takes over his body, an exhaustion that isn't only sleepiness but a deep oblivion. He is so tired of his life; he is so tired of fleeing across this continent and of all the violence that constantly threatens to tear apart his body. He turns on his side and closes his eyes. The last thing he remembers before he falls asleep is something the man whose father had helped drive out the Brits had told him:

'They caught my father and two of my older cousins. They had them in a cell. They cut the ears off one of my cousins and poked out one of his eyes while my father and my other cousin watched. The Brits wanted them to say where some other rebels were hiding, but none of them knew anything. In the end they cut off my cousin's testicles. He passed out then. The Brit who was interrogating them put his revolver right in my other cousin's mouth then, and said something. My father didn't hear what the Brit said. Then he pulled the trigger and my cousin's brains flew out all over the wall of the police station.'

He opens his eyes slowly. The car is empty and dark. Maybe he had only dreamed that it was full of children. He stands up, sits in a seat. He likes this oblivion, it's like the crashing of waves, like a great mercy. The movements of the train rock him side to side. He looks out at the full moon. It reminds him of something. Of the walls in a room where he spoke to a man. He doesn't want to remember it, he wants to stay here, before history. He just wants to sit aboard this train and be without a past. He tries to figure out what day of the week it is. He remembers that he can fly. That memory makes him happy. He just sits there, dull, alone, looking out at the darkness streaming by.

HE IS STANDING on a road, resting his hands on knees that tremble. One of his sandals is broken. Its straps flap. Feet pass him, many without shoes. He thinks he can't manage another step, that he doesn't want to move, doesn't want to exist. On the other side of the border is Kenya. The grass of the savannah sways, an eternally indecipherable whisper. He adjusts the bundle over his shoulder, stands there, leaning over, not moving. They're going to have his name on a list at the border. They're going to stop him.

It was Sunday evening when the train arrived in Mwanza, and from there, as planned, he took a bus to Musoma. He arrived in the middle of the night yesterday, and since then he has been walking on this road. His exhaustion is a sizzling white flame in his flesh; he blinks and tries once more to stand up and go on, but he can't. He presses the thumb and middle finger of one hand against his temples. He has to orient himself. It's a market day, a Monday, which also means that the prisoners in the camp have been counted today, if not earlier. With all certainty, his escape has been discovered by now. Okello might have issued a message to the country's border patrol. He sneaks a look up at the people passing by. He wants to ask someone what it's like at the border, if there's a customs station, a fence; if guards inspect these hundreds of sellers; if it's possible to cross the border without showing a passport. He straightens up and catches the eye of a passing man, holds it, and is going to ask but the sound swells in his throat. He doesn't dare to speak, out of fear that his dialect in Swahili will expose him as Ugandan, enemy, outsider. The man looks at him curiously. P takes off his sweater and hangs it over his head as if to shield himself from the heat; in reality he's afraid someone will see his face while he's standing on the road.

He doesn't remember who he was. He doesn't remember where he came from, what he did on the train. He wonders if he remembers correctly, if perhaps he wasn't making up a new history for himself. The feet that pass him crunch in the gravel, across the worn, crumbling asphalt. He wants to vomit. He looks to the left, across the open fields. He can walk straight out into the grass, disappear. But he's going to Kisumu, on the other side of the border. From there to Nairobi. Nairobi. He finally starts walking again. He turns his eyes away from those he encounters.

Sometimes the sellers are stopped by people waiting along the edge of the road to buy their goods, and sometimes someone even runs out of what they're selling and turns back with empty baskets or an empty bike carrier without ever having reached the market. After a while, P pulls off the sweater that's hanging over his head and knots it like a turban because many of the others who are walking on the road have pieces of fabric tied that way. While he's doing this, he is passed by four older women who are carrying baskets on their heads; their dresses of threadbare fabric flap in the warm breeze. P decides to try talking to them. When they are stopped by a younger woman who wonders what they're selling, they put their baskets down on the ground so the woman can choose among cassava roots, sweet potatoes, and other root vegetables, and one of the women notices P, who has also stopped and is now looking at them. She nudges one of her colleagues; they stare at him boldly.

One of them asks, 'What are you selling?'

They will hear that he is a stranger.

'Nothing.'

He hears his own voice as if it were coming from outside himself. He has hardly spoken since he awoke on the train, in his strange amnesia, and he is stricken once again by the thought that he has been lying to himself, that the story he told himself in the dark train compartment wasn't true, that he is someone other than who he thinks he is. 'I have nothing.' Far off across the wide-open spaces, thunderheads tower up, pierced with occasional lightning bolts like thin, white strands of hair. The women laugh at him. Did he say something strange? One of the women accepts a few shillings from her customer and hands over a handful of root vegetables; then the whole group, including the customer, stares curiously at P. He looks down at his feet and it's as though they were made of cracking mud, as though the dry soil that blows across the road came from them. He hears the roar of jet engines in his ears and blinks hard. He has to orient himself.

'Where are you going?'

Orient yourself. His motionless foot, sinking in the vortex.

'What?'

'She asked where you're going.'

He ought to keep moving, but he can't just walk straight into the arms of the guards; he has to have some sort of plan. The fear comes, it arches in his stomach like a fat, shiny snake. He remembers the interrogation, the violence, the confinement.

'To Kisumu.' His mouth is dry. It occurs to him that he could join the women and pretend he is part of their group. If there were a customs station, it would be impossible for the border guards to check all of these sellers.

'What are you going to do in Kisumu?'

'I'm from Uganda.' He says it without knowing why. He squeezes his bundle and tries to smile, but he just feels silly, as if he were grimacing. The women mumble something to one another in their local language, nod, and then start walking again.

'I'm going to look for some people I know,' he calls after them. Why did he say he was from Uganda? He stumbles after them; he holds up his bundle before him and finds support in the concrete things as he speaks: 'I worked in Tanzania as a cleaner for a white family, but they went back to Europe and now I have to go back home. Everything I own was stolen, except this. May I keep you company?' The women keep walking as he speaks. Only the one who first asked him where he was going looks at him now and then, sneaking a glance over her shoulder with an elegant motion, letting go of the basket with one hand, letting the basket nearly tip forward, and turning her head. He should have lied and said he was Kenyan. He should have said he was from southern Kenya. The women keep speaking to one another in their language, and he thinks it sounds hard and dismissive, as if they wanted him to understand that he's not welcome in their company. He thinks about how Tanzania is the homeland of Swahili, that the first state university to use what they call the 'language of the brotherhood' is here, and that it must be impolite to do what the women are doing: speaking a language they know he doesn't understand.

'I know people in Kisumu.' He smiles at the woman who looks over her shoulder. 'I'm going there to see them. Relatives. My brother and his family. They live in Kisumu.' The feeling, all along, that something is not right. The dust in his mouth. The bright light from the sky. He shouldn't have told the women where he was from; Uganda is the country where Kenyans and Tanzanians disappear and are murdered, the country ruled by a madman, the country that shoots grenades at the Tanzanian border, the country that bombs refugee camps. He ought to have said he was from Rwanda; they wouldn't have noticed the difference in his Swahili. He stops and pretends to adjust the strap of his sandal. He decides to let the women leave him. He is standing doubled over, pulling on the strap of the sandal, when the woman who seemed most interested in helping him notices he's stopped and calls after him.

'Come here. Weren't you going to walk with us?'

Do they believe his story? He gets up, and the women laugh and shake their heads when he catches up to them. They walk for an hour. Eventually one of them tells him not to wear his sweater over his head the way he has it, like a turban, that it looks strange because it's obvious that he's not a member of the ethnic group that ties their sweaters like that. He takes off the sweater and puts it in the bundle. They wander along the road, toward the border, the road to Kisumu; the shadows grow as the sun slowly begins to set in the west. They move on, shrunken to insects, across the surface of the earth. They crawl along the endless road. He can't get rid of the feeling that something is wrong, that the four women haven't been honest with him, that he made a mistake by saying where he was from. When they stop a second time to sell their goods, he doesn't bother to wait for them and hurries ahead. He walks very quickly, almost jogging. He shouldn't have talked to anyone at all. He should have picked out a child to talk to if he wanted company. He knows that the Greeks said you should never talk to a child if you're running away, but he himself would never have tattled if a pilot who had been shot down had asked him for help. If a refugee had come to the boy he had once been and asked for help, he never would have betrayed him to an adult. He would have asked to come along. He walks quickly for a few hundred metres, but then he has to stop and rest with his elbows on his knees. He has been walking since before sunrise; he has no energy left and his heart is pounding. He looks over his shoulder. The women are still standing on the side of the road and haggling with their customer. He squeezes his knees with his hands. Two men pass him, going the opposite direction. He peers up. Thin faces, high cheekbones; one of them is chewing on a mango and spits a mouthful of the stringy yellow flesh onto the asphalt. The dry brown dust blows over it. His entire body hurts, his chest is being squeezed, the wind makes the grass along the shoulder rustle, his injured knee hurts, his ear roars. He thinks that he should have asked people on the bus between Mwanza and Musoma about the border instead of standing here without knowing what things are like up ahead. Someone in the camp said that the soil is red near Kisumu. At least he knows that much. When he looks back over his shoulder again, he sees that the men who just passed him are standing and talking to the women now, and one of them looks straight at him and nods, and their eyes meet. The man lazily waves him over. P quickly stands up straight. He wants to run right out into the grass. He feels the adrenaline pump into his arms and legs like spears.

'What do you want?'

'We are customs officials.'

'What did you say?' P shouts, and the man shapes his hands into a horn and shouts.

'We are customs officials. Where are you going?'

The men start walking toward him and he wants to run, but the exhaustion washes through his body like a wave. He casts a glance out at the openness of the steppe and looks at the men again. They aren't wearing uniforms, just pants made of thin fabric and patterned shirts that flap in the wind.

'Where are you going?'

'First to the market, and then to see some acquaintances.'

'Some acquaintances.'

'In Kisumu. My brother lives there.'

'Your brother lives in Kisumu. We are customs officials.' The man with the mango does most of the talking. He chews on his fruit so that its juice runs from the corners of his mouth. 'Show us what you have with you.' The other man has already started to open P's knotted sheet, which he rips open so the things inside fall out onto the ground: his flight jacket, the photo album from Greece, his flight log book, the clothes he's planning to sell in Kisumu. The mango-eater picks up the photo album and flips through it. P tries to hide his anxiety and looks down at his feet, which are shimmering with gravity and exhaustion. The gold cufflinks from his Greek uniform are in the inner pocket of his flight jacket, along with his passport and a number of other important documents. All this time, many people pass them on the road.

'I took the album from my employer's trash.'

'Why?'

'I'm going to put the pictures up on the wall at home.'

The mango-eater pages through the album; a bunch of photographs that have lain loose between the pages since the interrogation fall to the ground. The man pokes at them with his foot, studying them.

'Do you have money on you?' says the other man, whose face is round and hard and reminds P of a boxer. P has a few shillings left of what he got for his shirts, but he doesn't answer; instead he takes a few steps back.

The women catch up with the group; they look over the others' shoulders for a moment, at the things on the ground, exchanging a few words in their language with the two men who are going through P's things. Then they move on down the road, pillars of flapping, thread-bare fabric. Their voices die away.

P lowers his gaze. The photographs that fell from the album flutter around his feet, and for a few seconds he thinks that the white photo paper looks like flames as it blows around.

'My colleague asked if you are bringing money into Kenya.'

He slowly takes the last coins out of his pants pocket and hands them over. He might have been able to buy a meal at the market with them. If the men don't take his clothing, he can still sell them in Kisumu and get the money for a ticket to Nairobi. If these men who claim to be customs officials don't stop him.

'I dreamed that I could fly when I was a child,' says the man holding the photo album. He laughs a hoarse and pronounced laugh. 'When I woke up ... I tried to remember how to do it.' He flaps his arms clumsily.

The boxer has picked up the flight jacket; he pulls it on, zips the zipper, poses for his friend. P swallows hard. No matter whether the men are really customs officials or just two vagrants, they must not find the passport and the documents that are in the inner pocket of the jacket. The boxer notices something; he crouches down and rummages through the photographs that fell from the album. He picks up one of the pictures. He looks at the young man in the helmet who is smiling into the camera. He looks up at P and tilts his head as if he were listening for something in the oppressive silence.

Seed pods rise slowly in the light, weightless in the thermals from the sun-warmed asphalt. It is midsummer, oppressively hot; almost no traffic goes by on the road. I arrived by train from my hometown an hour ago, and because my mom has moved out into the country I have three hours to kill in the city before the bus goes, so I came here, to this bench I used to sit on so often. Sat here and read about the wretched of the earth, about freeing oneself. I would drink beer with S, a friend who also had a dad from Africa, a dad who, like ours, was absent for large portions of his upbringing. Above the tree tops I can see the building where my buddy lived, and I can see the garage wall where I wrote *Chessface* in silver spray paint. They say that history is like a dream. That dreams are first created in the very moment of awakening, when the consciousness that has been immersed in sleep rises to the surface and remembers a story where there was only darkness and unconsciousness. Where we see chains of events, the angel of history sees a single catastrophe, wreckage. I look at my watch. I keep expecting to see friends in passing cars: friends who died, bodies set out in the roar. I keep thinking that they'll wave through car windows, call my name from balconies. The high-rises over there, I come from them. There, beyond the tree tops. Over there. That's where I come from.

Dad stands in the window, watching the snow fall, in my childhood. Sometimes I wondered if he had killed anyone in his years in Africa, during his escape. In my teens, as I ran between these apartment buildings, I often thought that my home was there, on the other side of the planet. But he has almost never spoken of Africa with longing.

He was in a transplant unit and the doctors said that he wouldn't be given another new lung. I was sitting in the room when he heard this. A week or so ago. A death sentence. The machines around his body hissed; outside, summer was swelling toward its peak. Dad told the doctor that he wanted to see all the documents and papers concerning the decision. He wondered if he could appeal.

'They're telling me to lie down and die,' he said when the doctor had gone. 'That's what it means, that I won't get another new lung. Lie down and die, your life is over. But it's not that easy. It's not that easy to just give up.'

The bus arrives; I travel through the summer, toward my mom, who has asked me not to write too much about her. I look out at what was once my hometown, the apartments and the sidewalks gliding past. The lilacs have already bloomed; they hang like burned twists of paper among the heavy leaves, between the laundry buildings and garbage rooms.

A figure is walking in front of me, a shadow that disappears in whirls of photographs. He walks away, too quickly for me to catch up even though I'm running. It's a recurring dream; maybe it doesn't mean anything. Sometimes the figure disappears, turns to wind, shreds into pieces. Is recreated. Torn apart. Dad.

'How can you know that you're living your own life, and not someone else's?' I say to the shadow, but it can't answer me. It no longer exists; it's just a memory of something that once was.

Recreated. Torn apart.

I sit in my mother's garden, I ask her the names of the flowers, she points and says hydrangea, amaryllis, delphinium. She wanted to live in Africa. Dad broke her heart with his escape, his worry.

Queen Victoria, a type of rose. Anemone. Lupine.

Museveni, who is the current president of Uganda, comes from south-western Uganda and belongs to a Bantu people. He has written an essay that was formulated as a commentary on Franz Fanon's work *The Wretched of the Earth*, and in it I read the sentence, 'I used the district of Nangande in the province of Cabo Delgado as my experimental area': in the late sixties he fought with FRELIMO, a leftist guerrilla organization that fought the Portuguese in Mozambique and which was modelled on the FLN, the Algerian resistance movement for which Franz Fanon was a spokesman. Dad recently said that he would kill Museveni if he could, that he sends HIV-positive soldiers to the part of northern Uganda we Langi come from to rape women. It's a type of biological warfare, Dad says. It's a tribal thing, he says. I think of the phrase 'experimental area': I think about our father, of where we all come from, of where we're going. I remember him walking along the sea in Denmark during one of the few trips he takes after arriving in Sweden. It was during my childhood. He stands in the surf with his back to me, he looks at the sea, he looks at the sky.

My mom says, 'Bleeding heart.'

'I DIDN'T THINK blacks could be pilots.'

P doesn't answer; the man's colleague says, 'Who do you think flies Tanzania's planes? Idiot.' His face grows very serious. He turns to P and says, 'This is over. Go.' He waves down the road with his half-eaten, dripping mango and looks at P with staring eyes. P wonders at the quick change—it's almost as if a third man had popped up out of nowhere. 'You have been inspected. Walk until you get to Kisumu. Don't stop again. Go.' The man takes a bite of the mango and seems to lose himself in thought for a second. The wind in the grass. The wind over Earth. 'Walk until you get to Kisumu,' he says. 'Don't stop again.'

'I want my jacket back.'

The fruit juice runs in a thin line straight down the man's chin; it makes him look like an imbecile. He nods at his colleague, irritated, and the colleague gets up and takes off the jacket. P takes it from him, gathers his photographs, and knots the sheet around his things. He slings the bundle over his shoulder and walks quickly. It starts pouring rain, a cloudburst that lasts for over an hour. P tries to drink from the puddles that form in the ditch; he cups his hands into a bowl and brings them to his mouth, but the water is too muddy; he spits it out. He licks the raindrops from his face and his arms. His clothes are soaking wet; his sandals squelch. The rain sounds like underground applause. He feels ill at ease when he thinks about the two men. He happens to think of stories he heard as a child, of spirits you could meet on a country road. The rain stops. The sky is already starting to darken; soon he will have been walking for a whole day. He raises his eyes. It is clear after the rain. Good flying weather.

It was just before the new year, just a few weeks before Amin's coup, and an instructor and three cadets were flying at high altitudes when one of the T-37s suddenly slowed down in a puff of smoke and seemed to split into two parts: a smaller part shot upward while the rest of the plane disappeared toward the abyss in a steep curve. P gasped:

'*Mayday, mayday,*' he shouted into the radio, 'He ejected, *mayday, mayday.*' He heard his flight instructor answer in the helmet radio and was told to return to base and land. Afterward, the instructor explained that the Libyan air force feared that their country would be drawn into a war with Egypt and that all Libyan flight cadets had therefore been ordered to eject themselves from their planes when their education was nearing an end. Libya was prepared to pay for each and every one of the lost training planes in exchange for the Libyan pilots getting to experience using an ejection seat, because they risked ending up in aerial combat with Egyptian pilots who were veterans of the Six Day War with Israel. P thought it sounded crazy; the instructor seemed irritated but also impressed. P told this to K a few days later, as they lay half-asleep in a hotel bed. He searched her face for some reaction as he described the way the ejection seat had shot out, how the plane had sailed down toward the mirrored surface of the sea. When he said that the pilots had been instructed to crash, he made it sound like a joke.

'You are ordered—to crash!'

She was silent.

'If the academy knew that I had told you military secrets we would both be shot,' he said, and *then* she laughed, strangely enough, and punched him in the arm. He remembers the light that morning, a Sunday. He was used to the diluted light that fell from the skies during European winters, but on that particular morning the sunlight through the white linen curtains of the hotel room made him feel like he was inside a clip of one of the old, jerky black-and-white movies he had seen in his childhood. He stroked her cheek and saw the truth of his story sink in for her, with its alarming connections to his own life and maybe, in that way, also to hers.

'There will never be a war in Uganda,' he said. But it was as if the incident had become real for him, too, when he told it, and he couldn't help thinking about the Libyan pilot dangling in his parachute, a solitary toy pilot above the shimmering silver sea.

The photo from exam day, where they're standing in their white uniforms, is a bit damp from the rain that has soaked through the sheet. He has stopped to take the picture from the album. His hand shakes. He looks for the Libyan airmen; at first he thinks he can't find them, that they're not in the picture, but then he sees one of them. Touches the man's face with his finger. He searches for his own face, but now he can't find it. The road is full of small, sharp stones that have cut through the soles of his sandals, and he stands there for a long time, just looking at his feet and the fluttering, torn straps. As long as the earth isn't red, it's still a long way to Kisumu. He takes one last look at the photo before he rips it in two and throws it on the ground. He takes another photo from the album and tears it up. He shovels a little dirt over it with his foot, as if to test it out, see how it feels. He stomps on the ground, hard. He rips up all the photos in which he is wearing a uniform or posing in front of planes; he kicks dirt over their remains. The asphalt has started to steam in the broiling afternoon sun; the air is sticky and tastes chemical, like oil. He coughs. He never should have brought along the album. If someone links him to the pilot in the pictures, they'll wonder what he's doing in Tanzania. He saves only two compromising photos: one where he's wearing the white summer uniform which he loved and which always made him feel like a god, and one where he's standing in front of his T-37 in a flight suit. He hides them inside his passport; a seller with a bike basket who is passing him slows down and looks at him curiously. He meets the man's gaze and aggressively keeps his eyes steady until he has passed. He saves a few anonymous pictures: photos of himself and the other Ugandans in gym clothes or on the beach. He tears apart the spine of the album and throws it on the ground. When he's done, he stands there for a moment and looks at the torn-up faces of the young pilots. Then he looks up, across the expansive landscape. In the camp, someone said that great parts of northern Tanzania, as well as parts of Uganda and southern Kenya, once lay underwater, and from where P is standing now he can feel the sky and the world blending together with the distance, like when one is out at sea. A group of people dressed in white is approaching from far down the road behind him, but otherwise the world suddenly feels completely deserted. It feels as if every step were like pulling thick, tangled ropes out of the ground. Oceans of grass spread out on either side of the road. The light from the brilliant sky above the steppe is slowly changing. He comes across two men who are carrying their bikes on their backs because the road is in such poor shape, and he stops them with an outstretched hand. They put down their bikes.

'Will I pass customs soon?' He gets straight to the point. One of the men lights a hand-rolled cigarette and leans against the frame of his bike.

'What customs?'

'The customs station at the border?'

'There's no customs station.'

'When will I cross the border?'

'You've already crossed it.' The men lift their bikes onto their backs again. 'You're in Kenya,' one of them calls over his shoulder. P stands there, looking mutely after them as they move on. He feels no sense of relief. He tries to walk faster. He feels no sense of security. The sun is going down now; the shadows become very long.

During his education in Greece, MIG-21s were treated as enemy planes because they were used by a number of socialist Mediterranean countries. The Greek cadets studied the strengths and weaknesses of the plane to learn how to shoot it down; they watched films of dog-fights between American fighter planes and Vietnamese MIG-21s. They learned that the plane lost speed when it yawed, that it climbed very quickly, that it was fully capable of defeating its American generational siblings, the F-4 Phantom, F-5 Freedom Fighter, and F-104 Star-fighter. The superiority of the MIG-21 in the beginning of the Vietnam War had prompted the Americans to start two schools of aerial combat in the late 1960s—Top Gun and Red Flag—which had quickly attained legendary status on the other side of the Atlantic, too.

Among the photographs P destroyed were a few pic-tures of MIG-21s that he had cut out of American and

Israeli magazines. The MIG-21s that are used in Uganda are unpainted, of polished aluminium. He would have flown a plane like that in the Ugandan Air Force if he had returned. He used to trace the streamlined shape with his finger and wonder how it would feel to move faster than the speed of sound. If it would be like finally leaving everything behind. Now the pictures are lying torn up in the dust behind him. He takes out his passport and from it the photograph where he is dressed in a flight suit and has his helmet under his arm. He remembers the short, back-swept delta wings of the MIG-21, the heavily fortified cockpit, the air intake inside the nose cone. He is thirsty. Needs water. Dust in his mouth. His legs give way, he sinks down, ends up sitting on the side of the road. He doesn't want to go on, there is nothing for him there, in Kisumu, in the world. He brushes off his hands, holds them up in front of him against the darkening sky. His hands are red. The dirt on them is red. Red dirt. He gets up with a final, despairing bit of effort. The dirt is red near Kisumu.

He reaches the market. It extends to the west; there are market stands and sellers who have placed their wares on blankets out on the savannah and even along the road. Far off over the great expanse he can see a Kenyan flag, limp in the gentle evening breeze. He jogs on along the edge of the road with his bundle. He could sell the clothes he's carrying in the sheet to someone here, but he thinks he'll get more money for them in Kisumu. He leaves the market behind, sees a group of buildings to the east, and turns off the road. He staggers in between the tethered goats, the cracked mud walls; his sandals trail in the grass; he loses one of them and hardly has the strength to pick it up and put it on his foot again. This is not Kisumu, this is just a small village. He doesn't see any people. He supports himself against the door frame of a hut. He is saturated with sky, rain, escape.

'*Pii*,' he says into the darkness. It is the word for water in his language. He whispers it again: '*Pii*.' He has heard people speaking Luo, a language that is related to Lango, for the last hour, and he repeats the word again in hope that someone inside the hut will hear him and understand. '*Pii*.' A boy comes to the door. He looks at P, his mouth is half-open, he is missing a front tooth, he backs into the darkness of the hut again. There's something eerie about the way he disappeared completely in the shadows inside. *Never ask a child for help.* P stands there alone, leaning into the hut, and his voice is so hoarse and tired that it sounds like it's not him speaking but the dry grass and the red earth. He must get water. Water.

The boy returns with a woman who is holding a calabash. He takes it and drinks, and when it's empty he hands it back and points: more. The boy tugs at the woman's colourful dress, saying something in Luo that P doesn't understand. When the woman comes back with the calabash, she hits her head on the door frame and smiles at him, as if excusing her own clumsiness. She is young, P thinks, but then he realizes she must be older than him and then he feels filled with dry leaves, dust, red book covers, insanity, years, kilometres, miles, clouds; and he drinks, breathlessly, he wipes his mouth with the arm of his sweater and points that he wants more. *Give me a waterfall. Give me the sea and the sky back. Give me my life.* When he has drunk a third calabash, he asks in Swahili if it's far to Kisumu, but the woman doesn't answer. He says the same thing in Lango and then in improvised sign language, but the woman just stares at him with her intense, almond-shaped eyes. Has he offended her? Without taking her eyes from him, the woman shouts something straight ahead into the empty air. P backs up a step. He thinks of the man who said he shouldn't stop before he got to Kisumu. But that man was a robber. The woman shouts again, one word. Nothing happens. She just stands there in the door, staring at him and seemingly waiting for something. He can't tell if she's frightened or threatening. It is as though she had uttered a word meant to wake him from a dream or cause the earth to open up and swallow him. He hears the wind, he hears the faint sound of voices from an open door far away. He waits. Everything waits. A boy comes running out of a neighbouring hut; he is barefoot but his feet are clean and smooth: he goes to school. She must have been calling the boy's name. The woman and the boy speak in Luo for a moment, and then when P asks about Kisumu again, the boy explains in English that Kisumu is only a few kilometres away.

A few isolated electric street lights are burning in the darkness when P wanders in among the brick buildings and the huts of nailed-together, corrugated sheet metal on the outskirts of the city.

Kisumu is Kenya's third- or fourth-largest city, and it is the second-most important harbour on Lake Victoria, after Kampala. He read about it in school. He walks through the alleys, past bars, dark shop windows; he asks night-walkers for the way to the bus station and eventually finds his way there. An older woman is sitting in the ticket window, and she tells him that the bus to Nairobi leaves in an hour, that a ticket costs two Kenyan pounds, that Nairobi is a ten-hour bus ride away. He sits down on a bench. Takes off his ragged sandals. His feet are swollen and cracked. He unfolds the knotted sheet and takes out his leather shoes from Greece. When he's tied them, he turns his feet in the street light for a moment. He tosses the sandals in a waste-paper basket. He finds a bathroom on the back side of the bus station and washes his face. A piece of polished aluminium is fastened to the wall above the sink for a mirror. His eyes are blank. He is almost there. He blinks. He has escaped. He is almost gone. He finds a bar and sells his coat and his last three shirts to the first person who is willing to pay enough for him to buy a bus ticket. He eats at a cheap restaurant. On his way back to the station he passes the harbour, where a cargo ship is gliding over the inky black surface of Lake Victoria. The surf roars against the massive metal hull. He remembers the sound of the shore. He remembers the beach in Greece where his flight instructor told him that he could disappear without anyone noticing. Now he has disappeared. Now everything has disappeared. Solitary seabirds circle above the quays; the undersides of their wings capture the lights of the city: orange, green.

He steps off the bus in central Nairobi the next morning. Cool highland air, mist. Taxi drivers and vendors stream up to him, offering him their services. It's raining, a light, sprinkling rain that smells like exhaust and mud. He pulls on his flight jacket and tosses the dirty sheet into a rubbish bin. He is freezing. Cars splash by. Acacia trees, vines with purple flowers that climb over gates and walls. He walks along King's Street, between the colonial villas of white stone. The British Embassy is to the right, and after one hundred metres one can turn and walk in under the trees. The sound of the leaves in the rain. The sound of the sky against the leaves. White people climb into cars; they look at him with suspicion. The Italian Embassy is guarded by a Kenyan military-police officer, who is standing in a sentry box. He lies and says that he is going to apply for a visa. The guard picks up the telephone, says something into it, and lets him through the gate. Inside the embassy building is an Italian guard in a uniform with a diagonal white band across the chest, a cap, a moustache, and an automatic pistol in a white leather holster. The man is reading a magazine with glossy pages, some Italian fashion one. He looks up lazily as P comes in. 'Show me your passport.' English. The rain against the glass door of the entrance. An older Italian woman with short, greying hair is sitting behind bulletproof glass; the guard doesn't look at the passport but hands it to her through a hatch. She beckons to P. His wet shoes squelch as he walks across the marble floor.

'You are a Ugandan citizen. You don't need a visa to travel to Italy.' She closes the hatch. P stands perfectly still for a long time, staring at his reflection in the glass. He looks like a shadow in his dirty clothes, a phantom made of rain and mud and shadows. When the woman notices that he's still there, she opens the hatch again.

'I'm not here to apply for a visa.' The words stumble out of him; they sound absurd. 'I need help; I need to contact a friend in Rome to get money for a ticket.' He sticks his head through the hatch, but the woman has turned away to speak in Italian to someone in another room, farther inside. 'Please, I need to call someone in Rome.' The woman stops talking to the person in the other room. She writes something on a piece of paper and hands it to him.

'Go to the American Embassy.' She taps the paper with her finger. 'The address.'

The rain. A rain made of pinpricks of darkness. He walks slowly through Nairobi, reading the street signs, trying to find the American Embassy. Cars go by, splattering him with red mud. He thought the Italian Embassy would help him contact his cousin. Maybe he ought to have said he wanted to contact an Italian citizen. The marine standing at the gate of the American Embassy salutes as he walks by. He returns the salute, a military reflex in his spine. *The habits and traditions of the Academy.* It's gone now. It disappeared. The wind blew it away. He walks through the garden with his head hanging. It was the wind. The lobby of the American Embassy reminds him of the lobby of the hotel in Athens where he worked. A crystal chandelier hanging from the ceiling, marble floors, a woman sitting at a switchboard.

'I am a fighter pilot from Uganda. I was trained in Greece. I flew American planes there,' he says. 'I need help.' The woman asks him to sit down and wait; she pushes a button and speaks into the phone. He takes off his flight jacket and sits on a chair.

'Sir?' He looks up. A man in a dark suit has entered the lobby.

'I am a political secretary. Would you please come with me to my office?' They walk through hallways, they pass guards, and heavy wooden doors are opened. An office. 'Please have a seat, sir.' He sits down. The embassy official sits in an enormous leather chair behind a desk; he rocks it backward and folds his hands in front of him. 'So. What can I do for you, sir?' If P tells his story and the Americans believe him, they might help him because he was educated in a NATO country. If they don't believe him, they might hand him over to the Kenyan authorities, who could deport him to Uganda or send him back to Tanzania. He chews on his lower lip and looks at the man in the big leather chair. Then he starts taking objects from the inner pocket of his pilot's jacket: his passport, his service insignia, the wings sewn with golden thread, his flight certificate—he lines these things up on the mirrored surface of the mahogany desk. The last objects in the universe.

The swings on the playground far behind us are moving in the wind; their chains flash in the oblique sunlight. Peter and I are walking on the shoulder of the road, in the angel dust of the dandelion globes that whirl in the red light. We have finished the sixth grade, we're going to start the seventh, I have a long plastic straw in my hand, I slap at the grass with it. Peter has the hood of his black sweatshirt up; he says we're a secret ninja clan, the last of a large family. His mom is from Croatia; he was there last summer, in his homeland. He is my best friend. I stand there with my straw and look over at the playground, but the guys who were there are gone now. I hit one of them until he started blubbering. My mom says where have you been, I answer nowhere.

August 27, 1972. The leader of Uganda, Idi Amin, has set a date for the expulsion of the majority of Asians in the country.

I run with my arms spread out like an airplane. A few boys always tease me; one of them sends my basketball flying, for example, and their faces are like porcelain masks. The ball sails across the sky. They say things about my kinky hair, about my body, about my skin; they laugh and their laughter belongs to this country, to the terrace houses, to the trees. Tonight I hit one of them, and he blubbered and got a bloody nose. Some of it is on my shirt. Peter saw it. They don't tease him, only me. We balance along the centre line; a car honks and gleams and swerves. Tag me if you can.

August 28, 1972. According to Amin, the Tanzanian forces that threaten the borders of Uganda are fighting under Chinese officers. The body of a man described as a Chinese colonel, dressed in a uniform belonging to the Tanzanian army, was displayed outside Uganda's international conference centre.

Dad is visiting us this summer. He smokes on the balcony. He keeps his clothes in a large sports bag in the hall. He lives in Gothenburg now; he's going back there soon. I lie on my back, looking at the sky, and every time I look at the sky I think about my dad, who comes from up there. Peter shouts that a car is coming and that I have to get up, and I see the shine of the car's headlights and I get up and I see my own shadow fluttering before me. It is running.

I have a friend from Africa, too: S, he's my neighbour. We play basketball together this summer. His dad is also from a war in Africa, and at his house the TV is always on with no channel selected and his laughter belongs to his body and to the metal of the bike frames, to the wire fence.

August 30, 1972. The expulsion order surprises Great Britain. The British authorities considered General Amin to be a man they could work with. Ugandan radio has begun broadcasting a countdown to the expulsion date.

I breathe onto a glass stairwell door and write my name in the fog. I'm white on my hands and under my feet, and the others tease me about that, too; they say I was standing on all fours when God painted me. But God loves me.

September 4, 1972. Sixteen desperate and upset Asians from Uganda land in London and say they have escaped from 'a living hell.'

Passengers who have had stopovers at Entebbe airport say that they were ordered to pull down the window shades, but they peeked through the cracks. 'I have never seen such chaos,' said one Indian businessman who was coming from Kampala. 'People were running around that airport in all directions.'

Peter has made ninja stars in shop class; he cut them out of sheet metal and sharpened them. He throws them, they clink across the road, we gather them up and throw them again, they blink in the street lights like big, unwieldy metal snowflakes.

Peter turns one star in the last rays of sunlight, feeling its sharp edges.

S gathers saliva in his mouth and spits and says we're *svartskallar*, black-heads—that we have to destroy the things that destroy us.

One holds one's keys like brass knuckles.

The leaves move above our heads. I wish Dad would take me with him when he goes away again. I always do. I want him to take me away from this country that hates me.

Peter takes my hand and presses the sharp point against my skin. We're going to mix our blood. I let him hold the point there. Against my life. I think of how I made a fist and struck. It was nice. I could feel my heart, there inside my body. We moved here from our beloved Japan; we're the last of a large clan, me and Peter. I pulled the other boy's hair; we screamed. Peter lets go of my hand, he shows me the bloody star, I close my fist around the cut, a drop of blood hits the asphalt. I become dizzy. The breeze makes the grass billow along the road. The old dynasties are gone now, Peter says. They are dust in the wind. They are the air we breathe.

October 5, 1972. Panic and confusion have ruled in the capital of Uganda during the last few days. Military personnel are everywhere, especially around the parliament buildings. Armoured vehicles inspect passers-by, especially Europeans. At one blockade, Asians are robbed of their valuables. Tanzanian forces at the border are pushed back. In Kampala, all the stores are closed. The expulsion of Asians continues.

S throws his empty gold beer can across the road. We hate this country. No one has ever extended a hand to us. We are seventeen; we are sitting on a park bench. I take another beer from my bag and give it to him. I look at his face, and everything shrinks as if I were speeding away: the high-rises, the trees behind him; it all sinks away, already disappearing, already disappearing. But he is my brother and I will put my arm across his shoulders as we walk away, or maybe homeward if it exists; all that exists is friendship like metal and beer we steal from the gas station and cassettes we record our own voices on and Dad says I have to become a civil engineer like my big brother because the war might come, but I'm going to be something else. I'm too tall to be a pilot like I used to want to be, but I'm going to be something.

Shadows flicker across the walls of my childhood room, across the worn plastic floor of the youth centre, across the underpasses where we write the names of our souls in spray paint. Shadows, dads, distance. The fall drizzle drifts across the city. S and I drink beer on that bench every night, almost, and we bullshit and freestyle into our clasped hands, and I love the buzz that comforts me and my girl who loves me and the night that carries me and I'm good at school and S is bad, that's how it goes. I stand up and shadow-box with him, hit his shoulder; he shoves me hard and we laugh. He beat up some nerd recently, in the city. He fights for something inside himself—I don't know what it is—and for my childhood. I hang my head. I want to risk my life; there's no middle ground inside me, it's all moving so fast the world is blurry: bloody noses, orgasms, friends, slow dances, kickers, niggers, hip hop, life, and I walk home and the scent of wet leaves is metallic and the rain is falling in the spaces between the buildings and there is a desolation there that is mine, and that is me, too. I am a Marxist-Leninist. I shout up to a balcony. I am Kwame Nhrumah. I am the black lumpenproletariat and nerds can't even pronounce my last name and this country has pissed on all of our dads, that's how it is. I draw a chrome line across a building, just let the can of spray paint go the whole walk home, or away, if that exists.

A CYCLIST PASSES him: the mirror image slowly gliding in the puddles. P has a wad of Kenyan bills in his hand. He received them from the American. He takes ten steps outside the gates of the embassy; the evening turned to night as he sat inside, talking. Sun-coloured mango flowers against the darkening sky, petals strewn in drifts on the ground, washed there by the rain. With the money, a simple instruction: stay in the white part of Nairobi and the money will last a day, stay with the other Africans and the money will last a month. He pulls on his pilot's jacket and puts his hands in his pockets. At least they didn't hand him over to the authorities. Wandering aimlessly through Nairobi. Just before sunrise, he lies down and sleeps at a bus station where other homeless people are lying on benches and along the walls. He wakes after only an hour or so and slides up with his back against the wall. Morning commuters are walking by. They don't look at him. He is freezing in his wet clothes. He looks at his nice shoes, which he has saved for so long. Why didn't the Americans help him? He was educated in Greece, by NATO. He ought to go to the UN and register himself. Half the reason he came here to Nairobi. But he doesn't know how to go about it, and he's afraid of being sent to Tanzania or Uganda if he goes to the Kenyan authorities. He buys food from a shed outside the station, meat stew with rice, served piping hot in a paper cone. The city's black neighbourhoods, tin roofs shaking in hard, quickly abating downpours. He thinks of his family, he thinks that he can contact them now, that he will do it soon. When the night comes, he pays for a room at a cheap hostel, but after that he sleeps at the bus station again to save money. He drinks beer sometimes, staggering under the night sky, collapsing under trees, into bushes. He stops dreaming of flying and instead the camp invades his nights. In his dreams he is running and falls, or he's sitting against the wall of the dorm and watching the others play soccer. His tape player turns into a radio transmitter, which receives the news that his family has been murdered by Amin's men. Wakefulness and sleep blend together, and his existence as a homeless person in Nairobi becomes indistinguishable from his life in the camp. They are of the same material.

One afternoon he walks into a run-down high-rise and climbs up the stairs. Finds himself on the roof. The breeze cools his sweaty face; Nairobi swarms at his feet. There are enormous slums in the centre of the city, and large shanty towns are growing beyond the city's borders; they were formed in the first half of the twentieth century when farmers were robbed of their land by the British and travelled here to search for work and housing. Birds circle above the garbage dumps. He stands there for a long time. But he doesn't remember what it felt like anymore. It is gone. He doesn't remember what it felt like to fly.

Just before sunrise, a truck comes and places a bundle of *The Nation* on the sidewalk outside the bus station, and sometimes he grabs a paper before the man who runs the kiosk has arrived. Most of the homeless people in Nairobi come from the countryside and are illiterate, and he doesn't want to raise any suspicions so he holds the newspaper upside down to make it look like he's only pretending to read. The morning commuters point at him and call him an idiot; some are friendly and helpful and say he should turn the paper the right way around. Most of them laugh, even the ones who try to help him, and he can see how small conversations about him spring up, how people talk about the stupid homeless man who reads the paper upside down. One day, when he has been in Nairobi for hardly a month, he is sitting under an overhanging roof and paging through the national news about Kenyatta's agricultural reforms and the tension between ethnic groups that developed as a result of the aftermath of the Mau Mau Uprising. In the world-news section of the paper, he sees an item about Uganda and recognizes a face in one of the photographs. A roar in his ear. He reads, 'Ugandan dissidents invaded Uganda last Thursday, in an attempt to occupy the border town of Mutukula.' In the photograph, the medicine man is lying dead on a street, dressed in a green uniform. 'The invading forces suffered major losses when they were forced to retreat by Ugandan infantry and mechanized battalions.' He quickly folds up the paper and puts it down, because it feels as if he were about to be revealed. As if the photograph in the paper were of himself. He presses the back of his head against the wall behind him, breathing rapidly and heavily through his mouth. His eyes rove from side to side. He picks up the paper again with trembling hands and reads another sentence: 'The poorly equipped soldiers were obliterated to the last man when they were surrounded in the city and bombarded all night long by artillery and bombers.' He puts his face in his hands. When he speaks to the other homeless people, he usually lies and says he is from Sudan or Tanzania. He uses fake names. He leaves the paper on the ground and walks away. White sky; the high-rises sink into the exhaust.

He sits on a bench, staring into traffic. He is always afraid. He is afraid of becoming ill and ending up at the hospital and being asked for proof of identity. He is afraid that someone will stop him on the street and ask where he is from, that the police will seize him. The trampled ground under his feet is covered in shredded paper, boxes, and withered leaves, rummaged by the wind. They were obliterated to the last man.

He walks under rows of apricot and mango trees with a braided basket on his back. He has been in Nairobi for just over six months, and he works as a day labourer—trucks come from the fruit orchards outside the city and gather up the homeless people outside the bus station and let them pick fruit for a few shillings per day. He picks an apricot, bites into it. It is sweet, the taste of the sun. He thinks of the boy with a cap who smoked bought cigarettes, of the old policeman, of others he knew in the camp.

One night, he puts his flight jacket, his passport, his flight logbook, and everything else he wants to save into a plastic bag, which he buries in a park.

When he's not working in the orchards, weeks disappear in half-slumber against a wall, in an exhaustion that belongs to the street and the gravel and the constant buzz of traffic. He feels vortices rotating behind his forehead, something inside him that isn't him, something that is dead and heavy and cold being flung around and around.

Laundry flaps, hung out in alleys where waste water

runs out of the houses, straight into the street.

When he wakes up in the morning, rolled up in his rags, he sometimes thinks he is lying in a grave. His mouth tastes like dirt. His tongue is made of dirt.

The boy. The man in the door. The boy shouts something.

He pokes a long, dried blade of grass into his heart and it grows into a savannah of flickering shadows. *Don't be afraid of me. I am your brother.*

He blinks; the sun flashes on a tin roof and seems to linger in his eyes for a moment. He is on his way out of Nairobi by bus. Soon he will have been in Nairobi for a year, and he doesn't understand how time can have passed like this. When he gets off, his feet are sucked down into the mud and he falls over, powerless; he catches himself with his hands, they sink up to his wrists, he tries to get up, he is very drunk, he has been drinking throughout the bus ride. *The poorly equipped soldiers were obliterated to the last man.* He has travelled to one of the shanty towns to die, to take his own life. The mud consists of dirt that has blended with rain, urine, and excrement and has turned into a sticky river that trickles into the houses and flecks the people's faces. His legs go weak and he sinks down against a tin wall. Everything around him is clear and sharp. The boxes that people use as houses, a boy with a stump instead of a foot sleeping in the shadow of half-rotted plaited palm fronds. A thin, tethered goat tugs at its rope and bawls. *I am your brother.* He wonders what he thought he would find in Nairobi. He picks up a shard of glass, holds the sharp edge against the skin of his wrist. He has no future. No future. *Don't be afraid of me.* Hens cackle. No future. His hand shakes.

His mother picks up a handful of dirt. Her hand is furrowed, steady, thin. She pours the dirt over him; it is dry, it blows in a thin stream against the dark skies of the overcast afternoon. He is lying in a hole in the earth, looking up at her. His brothers and sisters are there, too, he can see them now, their hollow-eyed, stiff faces lean over him. They are crying. He is lying in his grave. One of his brothers picks up some dirt and pours it over him.

The tears in his eyes feel like melting tin; he squeezes the piece of glass until his fingers start bleeding, trying to make his hand do the cutting. A newborn cries somewhere nearby, the blood from his fingers mixes with the dirt, he holds the edge against his wrist as the newborn cries, why is it crying—he looks up and sees a woman crouching and nursing her child, sunk to her waist in the red, nasty-smelling mud, and then he thinks of his own mother, Mama, who held up her children on her finger, and looked at them, and said their names, and
  blew—

The coastline sinks under the plane; in the distance he can see the outermost islands of the Greek archipelago. He increases the fuel injection. Rain showers to the east, the control tower chatters in his helmet radio, Morse code, whales singing in the deep: *Istanbul's airport Athens' international*
  airport Rome—
  He flies west. *I'm breaking*
  formation, sir, bearing 354—

His clothes are red with dried mud when he returns to central Nairobi, to his sleeping spot at the bus station, to his work in the orchards, to his life, his life which goes on even though it is impossible, even though it is only his life, naked like a piece of offal on the street. His heart keeps beating, the tree of blood grows through his chest and arms, impossible, he wanders around, thin and penniless and when he sits outside and it starts to rain he doesn't seek shelter but lets himself be washed in the black water, lets it flow through him. Porridge steams on tin plates. Months pass. He fights, he screams, cries; years pass, they just blow through his fingers, he laughs his genuine, rippling laugh sometimes when one of the other homeless people jokes around, he yells at the stars when he is drunk on home-made palm wine. Sometimes he dreams of a man standing with his back to him, and he wakes up and thinks that God is just a distance to everything, a turned back. He writes letters to his family, to John and to F, to the addresses he has; he writes that he usually sleeps at the bus station in Nairobi and that he needs money, that they can find him there if they are alive. But no one comes. He sleeps in the arms of death. He sleeps in the arms of his brothers.

Feral dogs root through garbage. The plastic bags they claw out into the street fill with wind, take off, and are knocked to the ground. It is as if all the things and beings around him were sliding out into an ever-stronger surge, a growing roar of waves that crashes onto a shore.

1975. The last day of February. Thousands of people have been murdered by Amin's military and security service: the papers he reads upside down are filled with increasingly alarming reports of mass executions, of uncontrollable ethnic conflicts. He walks slowly, aimlessly; it is morning, he looks at the sky above the broken roofs and remembers how he used to fly up there, in what is now truly another life. He laughs to himself, grows quiet, stops walking, becomes confused. How did they do it when they marched? You put your heel to the ground and swung your body around, like this—he smiles to himself. He passes a beggar on the edge of the sidewalk, places a handful of coins in his extended hands. Stops mid-step, checks his pocket. He has no money left. He had been planning to buy bread with those coins; they were his last. It was in another life that he used to toss a few coins at beggars. He stands there with his hand in his pocket and wants to turn around and ask for the money back.

'You sleep at the bus station.' The beggar rattles the coins in his hand. 'I've seen you there. At the bus station?' The man, who is about the same age as P, shows a toothless grin and stands up. 'Don't sleep there tonight,' he says. Then he turns around and starts to walk away, and even though P is calling after him he doesn't stop; instead, he disappears around a corner and is gone. It makes an impression when someone says something like that and then just turns around and walks away, and something about this strange encounter stays with him during the day, and at night it turns to worry inside him, and he sets course for a hostel where they usually let him have a room on credit, even though the approaching evening is warm and comfortable and just the sort of night he usually spends at the bus station. He gets a room and promises to pay for it when he gets work in the orchards again. He sits in the window. There is mosquito netting in front of it, and he works out two of the nails and leans out and tries to catch a glimpse of the sky. He only sees buildings. But he sits there for a long time, listening to the voices of early night. The mosquito net flutters. *Don't sleep there tonight.*

Sometime during the night, he is awakened by thunder. He turns in the thin, worn sheets, lying in bed with his eyes open; the street light falls on the brick wall outside the window, painting it blue.

In the morning he walks down to the bus station to take the truck to the orchards. A pillar of smoke is billowing toward the dawn sky. Fires are not particularly unusual in Nairobi. The street outside the bus station is full of police in dark-blue, short-sleeved shirts. He stops. The police are smoking and talking; a few emergency vehicles parked along the street have their lights on, and they rotate silently and make the officers' faces blink blue and orange. He starts to worry that the police will ask to see his identification, so he backs up a few steps. It looks like the bus station has burned down. A hand on his shoulder—he turns around. A policeman.

'What are you doing here?'

'I was on my way to work.'

The policeman looks him up and down. A younger man, about P's age. 'Day labourer?'

A gust of wind blows thick ash into P's face and when he raises his eyes to the palms above him he sees that their dry leaves have burned; they hang like flakes of soot against the light.

'Yes,' he says. 'What happened here?'

'A bomb exploded aboard a bus. Twenty-seven people died.'

He thinks of the other homeless people, who must be among the dead. People walk by; some are crying or screaming. He is cold, even though the morning is warm.

'A bomb?' He shouldn't talk, but he can't help it. He keeps looking past the young policeman, at the chaos, the smoke.

'The headless body of the ticket seller was found several metres outside the bus.'

What a strange, violent thing to say.

Several hundred metres from the bus stop, P still comes across burned pieces of wreckage strewn on the ground as he staggers away. A few days later, a newspaper article says that a movement called the Poor People's Freedom Army has taken credit for the bombing. The bomb tore a two-metre-wide hole in the bus and broke windows almost a kilometre away. An eyewitness who was in the station when the bomb went off describes 'a rain of bodies hitting the wall.' P stops sleeping outside and at the station. He travels to and from the orchards, looking at the other workers who are crowded together, hollow-eyed, in the bouncing bed of the truck. The speed at which it moves causes the glowing ends of their cigarettes to flicker. The earth is mottled by the shadows of the trees. In the evenings, rows of birds sit on the ridges of the tin roofs. He lies in his bed at the hostel, thinking about the sound of human bodies hitting a wall like rain. He thinks about surviving. When he closes his eyes, clouds well forth under his eyelids. Schiphol. John F. Kennedy International—he learned the names of airports in Greece. Paged through atlases at night. Luton, Newark. His arms crossed behind his head, his eyes dart under their lids, dart and lose themselves as a dying man's would. White mountain ranges. Zenata, Diagoras, Ministro Pistarini.

SHE WAS TWELVE or thirteen; she rented a room from an old widow and sat in her bed, doing homework. When she was done, she looked out onto the street at the fallen leaves blowing across the sky, the snow whirling in the street light, the flowers of fruit trees that fell in the spring. She had moved from the farm where she grew up to an urban area to go to secondary school. She held her life up to the evening light like a glass ball and studied it, and learned that she wanted to leave.

Blueweed.

Hepatica. Snow star.

She studied sociology in a small, central Swedish city; in the hallways of the student housing were notices about socialist youth camps in Denmark, Yugoslavia. She took off. She stood with a shovel over one shoulder and red flags behind her.

Poppy. Delphinium.

She travels by bus from the airport into central Nairobi. She sits in the window of the hostel, in the loud, warm evening, listening to the voices in the corridor, the voices out on the street, the voices in the world.

The sound of passing cars dies out. He blinks. He sits up in bed. He hears footsteps out in the hallway, and it sounds like clogs even though he knows that no Europeans come to this part of Nairobi, that he is deep inside the black core of the city. And yet there *are* clogs clip-clopping against the planks out there, and the only people in shoes like that are European women.

She stands in the hallway in her red clogs, speaking to the personnel of the hostel in poor Swahili. She has a basket of laundry in her arms.

They wander along beaches. They see each other every week, and then every day. Acacia. LaGuardia. Blowing petals, their hands grope in front of them, braiding fingers in each other's fingers. Climbing rose.

Everything is condensed; everything becomes innate. They move into a small apartment together and furnish it; she lies in bed reading and her eyes are green-blue, turquoise, like the colour of an overcast sky. Insects buzz around the street light outside the window. Hyacinth. Indira Gandhi. She says she wants to stay here in Nairobi, that she loves Kenya, that this place is her home. He sits in the window, smoking.

Sky Harbor.

The leaves of the trees are nearly transparent with drought when, one evening late in the year 1975, he gives her the two photographs he saved from the Greek album, in which he is dressed in uniform and posing in front of his airplane. She puts them in her wallet. He tells her about his life, his escape, about flying. He writes to John again; he writes that it's raining in Nairobi and he signs with an initial. He doesn't write his name because he's afraid that the Ugandan security service reads the family's mail. He is afraid of the world. He is afraid of the dim forces that have torn apart his life time and again. He is afraid of his own fate. He is afraid of people from whom he has the sense of having escaped; he thinks that pedestrians linger behind him for too long when he walks home at night, that cars sit outside their home with their engines running far too long.

The wedding picture is a backlighted silhouette; the sky is full of pollen and whirling red petals. They sit under an arch of climbing roses. The camera clicks. John has his arm around him.

John has shown up in Nairobi to come to the wedding, and he and P sit there in their bell-bottomed pants, with the smiles of brothers.

'They come at sunset to get the people who are to be executed.' John hands P a cigarette; they are smoking, even though P had actually quit. 'They've started shooting them on the streets. I'm so used to hearing the shots echo over Kampala that I can't sleep if I haven't heard someone get shot. Until I've heard someone get shot I am afraid they're going to come and get me.' John laughs bitterly, grows quiet. They look out into the light, waiting. John tells him that F has been imprisoned by Amin's security service. P puts his head in his hands.

'They've asked about you.'

'Who has?'

'The security service. They want to know where you went when you disappeared from Athens.' John had put his beer down for the photograph; he picks it up again and takes two sips. 'But we buried you,' he says, and once again he laughs that laugh that isn't a laugh. The sun makes the beer bottle glow like a dim, brown lamp when he balances it against his knee. 'Two years ago. We performed a ritual. It was Mama's idea. There's a kind of mock burial that we do if a family member dies far away, or if there's no body to bury. A special fruit is buried instead of the dead body.'

P blinks hard, looks up. Just across the street, in the body-temperature evening, cars and pedestrians go by, shadows gliding away. Soon he must return to his wife.

'It's a tribal thing,' John says. The family performed the ritual partially because they really believed P was dead and partially because they hoped that he was alive and thought that if the Ugandan authorities were informed of the burial, they would believe that the family had received reliable news of his death and they would stop looking for him.

He lies in bed next to her. It's nearly the new year; John has returned to Kampala where he now lives with his wife and children. There's a TV on in the room, a sports show P is half-watching. American professional boxing, black and white, men hopping around in bathing trunks and face masks. She's going back to Sweden to finish her sociology program now that they're married, and they're both worried that the police will start to harass him in her absence. She has promised to write to him every day, so the Kenyan authorities will see that he is missed.

The evenings, running their hands through each other's hair. She wants to stay. She goes. She sits in her student-housing room and writes every day for almost a year. Forget-me-not. He reads the letters; he saves them in a dresser drawer.

In early 1976, while she's still in Sweden, he is offered a job by one of John's friends. He can find work as a statistician at a government agency in Dar es Salaam that is supervising the large Tanzanian agricultural reform that has been taking place in the last few years. Of course he doesn't want to go back to the country he fled from four years earlier, but neither does he want to stay in Nairobi where it seems he can only find work as a fruit picker. John's friend promises him that he'll be safe in Tanzania, and he also arranges new identification papers for him, with a different last name. He goes by train. He looks at the swaying grass and feels something within him thicken.

Every day he walks to the large, new agency building in Dar es Salaam and studies diagrams, discrepancies, percentages. He becomes part of the great collectivization of agriculture. He calculates how much seed must be purchased to feed a certain number of people, and how much labour will be needed to sow and harvest the large fields. He walks under the acacias in his short-sleeved shirt. He shares an apartment with a young man whose father was European and whose mother was a Tanzanian woman. The man is quiet, studies at the university, and keeps to himself. One night, when both of them are sleepless, the man tells the story of his family. His father was a Jew living in London. At the start of World War II he believed that the Nazis would conquer all of Europe and maybe the whole world, and he thought then that the last place the Nazis would look for a Jewish refugee was a former German colony. The man sold all his belongings and travelled to Tanzania in the early forties, moved to a village in the country, and married a Tanzanian woman. By the time the war was over, he had made himself a home and a family here, on the other side of the earth.

He sits in his office, looking out at the sky, the clouds that flow in an endless white river across the city.

She comes back to him, tumbling into his arms. She says that she wants to stay in Africa now, that she wants to stay and work here. But he talks more and more about her country, Sweden. He says he wants to travel there. He is afraid.

They are seized by the police outside his home in August of 1976, after she's been in Tanzania for hardly two weeks. Two men in civilian clothing ask them to get into a car; they are driven to a police station where they are questioned about their activities in Kenya, what they're doing in Tanzania. They are asked about their history. Why they are together, a white woman and a black man. They lie about P's time in the Ugandan military; they say nothing about Greece or his fighter-pilot education; they say nothing about the camp. The police start looking through their pockets and ask them to empty their wallets.

She asks to be allowed to use the toilet and is taken to a tiled room with a drainage hole in the floor. She fumbles with the two photographs P gave her, which could expose all their lies and erase the world they have created. She is cold in a way that surprises her, sharp and clear with fear. She tears up the pictures so they can be flushed down the drain; her fingers work frantically, tearing, tearing; she flushes water over the white shreds and watches them disappear into the darkness.

They fly from Dar es Salaam to the Copenhagen airport. He looks out at the clouds that tower up in front of the setting sun. His last flight was in the plane with the Chinese soldiers, a journey that took him out of the world. He has his travel documents in his pocket, a sort of temporary passport they made for him at the Swedish Consulate, a pale-blue booklet with his photo and name that is only valid for a single journey. His old passport had expired. They take the train ferry across Øresund; they stand up on deck as the ferry glides out to sea, he squeezes the rail, the wind is ice-cold. It is late 1976. He has a sensation of his life being played backward, that this journey to yet another new country, with a different woman, is a reflection of the journey from Greece to Italy, where he stood on a different ferry and left K behind. He is backing into the future. He closes his eyes. The heavy wingstrokes in the dark. He is tired, he can't think, he doesn't know if he feels secure or terrified. He goes down to the train compartment and half-lies on the seat. He thinks of when he woke up on the train to Mwanza and didn't remember who he was. The waves lap against the hull, metallic and dull; he feels the horizon sway. He thinks of his upbringing, the night he stood in the grass, screaming that he was going to leave. He thinks about God, that God is a storm of feathers and the footsteps of children. After a while, she comes down to him. She sits beside him. She holds his hands, and her hands are cold with the wind, with the sea.

'Tell me when we cross the border,' he says. 'Tell me when we're in your country.' He closes his eyes. He drifts on the tide.

When he wakes, the train is moving and evergreens are rushing by outside the window, shadows.

THE LIVING-ROOM TABLE the men are gathered around is made of glass. The falling snow outside is reflected in it. A man leans forward and ashes into a half-empty glass of beer. People come and go as they wish in this apartment, because his friend B who has the lease is a wonderful person. He gets up from his chair, staggers over to the open balcony door, and lights a cigarette. Wet snow, about to turn into rain. Someone he doesn't know turns on the stereo: hard, electronic rhythms. He likes Harry Belafonte, himself. 'Jamaica Farewell.' Sam Cooke. Things like that. B stands beside him, pours more whisky into a large water glass. B is Langi, too. They ran into each other on the street a few years ago, and here on the other side of continents and seas it is a small miracle. Almost like encountering a brother.

P blows smoke out into the winter night, the doorbell rings, more people come in, they step over the mattress he's going to sleep on later, when his tipsiness turns into unconscious darkness. They don't take off their shoes; the snow they track in ends up in his bedding. He shoves a guy who is standing with his boots in his sheets, and who seems to want to start a fight at first, but then he sees something in his eyes, something that is steel and distance. He looks away, looks down at the courtyard. Suburb, thousands of identical windows.

A few years after the divorce. They come flying from Somalia, Uganda, Gambia, Senegal, resting their talons here, on the floors of small apartments. He suddenly feels so alone among all these people. Like in his childhood. Alone among all these violent men. He presses a hand to the glass, breathes on it, moves it. Studies the night through the handprint. It was so beautiful to fly at night.

'What are you thinking about, pilot?' B nudges him, and when he doesn't react, his friend starts to wrestle with him. They fall to the floor. They sit up against the radiator afterward; B pours yet another glass of whisky for him, pats him on the knee.

'We've called a taxi.'

The snow rages in the car's headlights. He ran across the barracks yard. He ran in the grass. B sits beside him in the back seat, with the street lights' play of light and shadow flowing across his face.

'Museveni will resign soon. Then things will calm down. We'll wait.' P doesn't answer. Fresh conflicts in northern Uganda, having to do with Sudan, Amin's legacy, tribal things.

Idi Amin was overthrown in '79 and replaced by a series of military leaders before Obote returned to power. For a few years, P planned to return to his homeland at last, but three years ago, in 1985, Obote was overthrown by Okello and less than a year later, Okello was overthrown by the mysterious, absent Museveni, whose intrigues and secrets had struck fear into Okello even back in the early seventies. A few years ago, P was at a Ugandan party in Bergsjön. He was sitting between an older Ugandan man and the man's wife, talking about the political situation in their homeland. P told them that he had met both Amin and Okello. The man he was speaking to nodded, interested. 'They were idiots, both of them. I tricked Okello like a child.' People around him were drinking. It was an autumn evening.

'And Museveni? What do you think about his chances?' said the older man.

At that time, strangely enough, Museveni lived in Hjällbo, another suburb of Gothenburg. Since Okello's coup, P had heard the name several times in the Ugandan diaspora, and a group of Ugandans had once asked him if he wanted to meet Museveni to discuss Uganda's future. But he had dismissed the suggestion with a laugh. He didn't want to return to war.

'Museveni?' He held his glass up to the light. It was well known that Museveni had fought Obote militarily for several years, and even though he now found himself in exile, there was yet another conflict going on between his guerrillas and Okello's army in northern Uganda, among other places in the area where P grew up. Many had already started to say that Okello was about to fall and that Museveni would be Uganda's next president.

'I was in a prison camp outside Tabora in Tanzania. Museveni had just run away from it.' P tossed the whisky into his mouth. Closed his eyes. Branches and palm leaves rushed by under his eyelids.

The man he was speaking with had hard, intelligent eyes.

'Wait. Museveni had run away from another camp, outside ... Morogoro. But it was one of Okello's camps. The people in it had just been moved to the camp I was in. Museveni is an idiot. I was invited to meet him. He thought I wanted to be part of his war. Idiot. Idiot.' P gestured with his hand the way John had always done, as if he were screwing a large lid to his temple, idiots. He was irritated; he drank from his glass, stared out at the high-rises shimmering in the drizzle. He kept talking to the old man for nearly an hour and took unfathomable pleasure in blurting out insults about Museveni. Because he could. Because he wasn't there anymore, where his life didn't mean anything.

As he was standing and freezing at the tram stop after the party, one of his friends came up and asked what he had talked about with Museveni. It took him a few disoriented, confused seconds to make the connection. Then he laughed and heard his own laughter bounce against a high-rise and back into the night. Museveni had been the one sitting on the sofa. Museveni had asked about Museveni. Museveni took power in Uganda just over six months later, in a relatively bloodless coup.

The snow in the headlights of the taxi. They enter a pub, a whole gang of African men; they drink, play roulette, he loses his last hundred-krona bill, they tumble around inside a deserted shopping mall, losing each other. He stands with his head bent back, looking at a pigeon that has gotten caught inside the mirrored eternity of the mall ceiling. He sits down on a motionless escalator. Once he was walking down some stairs and decided to give up on life. He watches the bird as it flutters around under the fluorescent lights. Flutters. He falls straight forward, down onto the mattress on the floor. He blinks. Is it morning already? They walk to the bus stop in the ice-cold drizzle. They work in the harbour. His children are farther away than the sun. They sit on the bus; it turns through a roundabout, he looks out at the streaming darkness, the light. He writes letters to his brothers' children sometimes, whispering his own name into the wind.

They walk between the warehouses and barracks at the harbour, past wire fences and containers. Their work is to load boxes and drive forklifts and loading cranes. B is a mechanical engineer, but his diploma is Russian and thus worthless in Sweden, like everything else. They play cards for money, drink cans of beer that they buy from the truck drivers. They take a bus home at night. It's around the start of the AIDS epidemic and the first newspaper articles have singled out Africans as carriers, and sometimes he can feel white people's eyes stabbing him like red-hot wire. He thinks he should have stayed somewhere else. Somewhere other than here. Workers climb in the dry dock, their welding torches blinking like blue fireflies in the gigantic steel-joist structures. And the refinery glitters like a fallen sky. The colonized world is a world divided in two. He sits on his mattress, looking at his Swedish passport. He can sit like this for an hour. He fled the fields of death. That was his life. He borrows books about religion from the library, reads about Gnosticism and Judaism, and the snow rains away in the drizzle that sprinkles on the laundry rooms and underpasses. In a book about Buddhism he reads about the people of the distant future who will live in another universe, where matter is psychic energy, light. He searches for the pure faith, the faith of the first man. The trucks roll off the ships; he wipes his forehead with his rough gloves and looks up at the red sky. Gulls shriek in the ravines of containers. He kneels on his mattress with his hands clasped. The cloaks of distance flutter inside him; the thicket rustles in the dark. The Gnostic priests thought they were God, thought they could become God. He read a strange book where it was Judas, not Jesus, who was the true Messiah. He is running through the jungle, the heavy palm fronds hitting him in the face. He opens his eyes. Once he woke up on a train and didn't remember who he was, where he came from. He has told his friend that if he dies it's important that he receive extreme unction from a Catholic priest, but he doesn't know if he believes in that anymore. In the rituals of his childhood. Which seem so empty and silent now. From here, on the other side of time.

He sits at bars and says that he isn't afraid of death. Bringing everyone else down.

He writes his name on a list and borrows a yellow helmet of hard plastic. The foreman checks him off on a list and he climbs up into the truck, turns the key, and pushes the stick forward. The Ku Klux Klan burns crosses on TV, they burn and flicker in the night and he sits on the sofa with his hands dug into his hair and he doesn't understand why God lets them use the cross, *if he is Your son, why?*

One night at one of the bars he meets a recently divorced man who says that he is going to kill himself at midnight. They agree to jump from Älvsborg Bridge together. They just need to get sufficiently drunk first. They sit there drinking until they fall asleep against the bar counter.

One night he is working on repairing an oil tanker and he is alone, the only one in the whole dry dock. He welds two-metre-long steel joists into letters, which he erects along the dirty wall in the empty space between the outer and inner hull. He writes his last name, his family name. Then he welds the space closed. On the way to the bus stop, where he's going to catch the first bus of the morning, he stops and watches the snowflakes float down into the leaden, oily water. He just stands there staring at the waves for a long time. He had a friend who drowned one time, when he was a child. He has started to think about death so much. He thinks about it all the time. Hussein is dead. Strangely enough, he read about it in *The Times* when he had just arrived in Sweden. He used to go to the library and read English newspapers, and a British journalist who wrote a column about Amin's rule used Hussein's story as an example of the madness in Uganda at that time. Hussein would fly his military helicopter to a village outside the air-force base where he was stationed, land on the patch of ground outside a bar, go in and get drunk, and then fly back to the base. He did it often, and in the end he crashed right into a house.

The snow drifting against the troubled surface. He wonders what they were a part of. Those who were part of history. Those who were part of the state of emergency, the war.

John is dead. John's wife wrote it in a letter a few years ago. John died of some kind of lung disease. His mother is dead, too. It's as if all of them over there died, in the fields of death.

B buys a computer, a used PC, and P digs out the old folders and books he used when he studied at Chalmers, and they teach themselves to write computer programs. The code flows across the black screen.

'There must be a system,' says B, who has a thick folder full of all the lotto results going back five years. They search for the equation that will predict the numbers for next week's lottery draw. It is 1989. He stops drinking when the spring comes. He gets his own apartment and stands there with key in hand, in the hallway, and his whole life is within him, his entire long journey. When he steps inside the door and locks it behind him, he starts to cry.

The Soviet Union falls. He sees the pictures of tanks moving through the winter landscape and thinks of the camp that was full of little red books. He thinks of the war, history, of the bodies that are sucked into vortices and destroyed. *If the imperialists insist on launching a third world war, it is certain that many hundred millions more will turn to socialism.* He walks across the docks; the cranes stand out against the twilight, and two other workers walk on either side of him. They have helmets in their hands, reflective vests flap in the chilly, salty, North Sea wind.

'God is justice.' P tosses this out because he talks like this with everyone now, doubting and searching. Fork-lifts rumble by, giant and slow like ancient animals. They just stopped him on the road and took his money, they sent him to a camp, locked him in a cage, they forced him to work for Idi Amin's men even though he didn't want to. He continues to list what he believes, holding his fingers up in the air; the steam rises from his mouth: God is almighty, God forgives, God punishes, God is merciful—one of his colleagues, a Moroccan man, puts a hand on his shoulder.

'God loves you.' A darkening March sky above them. Warning lights mark out the buildings and the ships against infinity.

He stumbles off a tram and someone shouts after him, a voice that is as raw and violent as a frozen piece of chicken hung from a hook.

'Go back!'

The wind tosses drizzle into his eyes as he turns around, and he closes them, and when he opens them again a stairway leads up and away, and someone is walking down it, a young flight cadet who is walking there one January afternoon in his training suit. 'Go back where you came from!' Sneering skinheads disappear in the rain.

He does laundry one night in his new home; he carries the white towels across the courtyard and stops. Row after row of pants, shirts, and underclothes are flapping in the wind in all of his memories of the military barracks in Uganda, because the eighteen-year-old soldiers had to have clean uniforms and clean underwear every day. Someone took his own washing and walked off, someone who was tall and calm as a tree, like John? What was his name? P doesn't remember, but they were best friends for a few months. A face that blows away among the sheets.

The Qur'an is a sea with no shore. A cliff, he can rest against it. He sits in his window and reads it. He looked it up at the library. *One day the Earth will be changed to a different Earth and so will be the Heavens.*

He goes to a Turkish prayer centre; he received the address from his Moroccan colleague. He sits on the rug with his legs crossed. Streaming light in his head. Birds call through the open windows. It is one of the first days of spring. People are sitting in a circle around him; one man says words and he repeats them.

'I bear witness that there is no other god than God.' He looks out the window at the clouds and the grey light as he speaks. Feels like he is dying, breaking into pieces. Being born, maybe. The light stings his eyes.

In his last year in Kenya he ran across a young homeless man who recognized him. It took him several minutes to realize that it was the guy who had smoked bought cigarettes in Okello's camp. The man said that he and one other man had survived after they crossed the border. He had put on his old school uniform under his military clothing on the night before they crossed the border, and in that way he managed to trick Amin's troops into thinking he was just a schoolboy who had wandered into the combat zone. The former secretary of state had taped bundles of money to his body, money he had somehow saved, and he bribed his way out when the rebel troops were surrounded and bombarded by the mechanized battalions. P sits there with his mouth open. Crying. The clouds fly swiftly past the window. He escaped the fields of death. He prays with his head against the rug, against the earth. Wanting to stay there.

I walk across the courtyard with the black plastic bags, emptying my old apartment on Hisingen. I have been putting it off for several months. I carry books and clothes to the rubbish room and toss them among the bags of garbage. I don't want all of these things; they are my history and I want to start over even though I know now that you can't. I sit on the bare apartment floor, running a hand through the dust. Dad called this afternoon. His brother's children found him earlier this fall via the Internet. Now one of our cousins in Uganda has died, in another war. All the relatives write him and call him to seek solace, because he is the head of the family now. It's a tribal thing, that he's the last one of his generation, the one who survived. He is very sick now; I visit him almost every day at the hospital. He laughed when he told me about all the letters about rain that are suddenly arriving. But he sounded sad, too. He says that those who write and call are all looking for someone who doesn't exist, someone he can't be. They are looking for a patriarch. The African way of thinking. We sit and talk for a long time, often, and he tells me about his life yet again. He tells me about his childhood, about his brothers. He tells me about the airforce academy. One night at the hospital he uses his insulin syringe to show me how he learned to fence with an épée. He says that history is a waterfall of chains. It sweeps the bodies along with it. When I walk across the courtyard with the plastic bags, I look up at his apartment window, which is a black square high up in the night.

He dies with his eyes open one January day. My brother and I are standing on either side of the bed. It is morning. There is his body. It has an oxygen mask on. His chest stopped heaving; his eyes stopped seeing. Here is the body. It is made of oblivion.

I walk over to the window and pull up the blinds. I lean against the wall. I say a few words. I go over to the body; touch its forehead. It is surreal that this body is lying here under the blue-and-white county hospital sheets, in the grey light that falls in across the machines and the tubes and across what was once a face but is now an object of survival and some material that resembles stone or marble. He was eighteen; he hopped onto his bike and pedalled off behind his friend, off to the airfield and the air-force trials. It has its own history. This thing that was a face.

Here is the body, sculpted from death; here it lies in a bed. This body that comes from his life.

Later, during the funeral, we will stand in a rainstorm and our feet will slip in the mud while the body is lowered into the earth and I will freeze in my black suit and the wind will drown out the voices. When we pray one last prayer over the man who was our father, our brother who told us where he came from and whose words filled us with impressions and questions without answers and pride. We will pray for his sins to be washed away with rain and snow, and we will be embraced by others who knew him, later. When the body is lying in the muddy earth. Which was its home. His friends from the years after the divorce will be there, white-haired and silent and broken men, and colleagues from the harbour and from schools he worked at, and many people from the mosques of Gothenburg, and a young man will come up to me with eyes cried out and say these words: 'He was my teacher, you know.' Then he won't be able to say more because of his tears.

Here is the body; it had its history, it came out of a life that could have been a different life. But a storm blew in. I stand beside my brother. Soon we will have to push the alarm button and tell them. But for a moment we stand on either side of the body. I take off the oxygen mask and hang it beside the bed. A storm blew in from paradise. The storm was life.

On the Design

As book design is an integral part of the reading experience, we would like to acknowledge the work of those who shaped the form in which the story is housed.

Tessa van der Waals (Netherlands) is responsible for the cover design, cover typography, and art direction of all World Editions books. She works in the internationally renowned tradition of Dutch Design. Her bright and powerful visual aesthetic maintains a harmony between image and typography and captures the unique atmosphere of each book. She works closely with internationally celebrated photographers, artists, and letter designers. Her work has frequently been awarded prizes for Best Dutch Book Design.

The photograph on the cover is taken from the archive at Hollandse Hoogte. It is an image of storm-blown palm trees in Tunisia. The angular font, Refrigerator, was inspired by the industrial letters used on refrigerators, dashboards, and machine panels.

The cover has been edited by lithographer Bert van der Horst of BFC Graphics (Netherlands).

Suzan Beijer (Netherlands) is responsible for the typography and careful interior book design of all World Editions titles.

The text on the inside covers and the press quotes are set in Circular, designed by Laurenz Brunner (Switzerland) and published by Swiss type foundry Lineto.

All World Editions books are set in the typeface Dolly, specifically designed for book typography. Dolly creates a warm page image perfect for an enjoyable reading experience. This typeface is designed by Underware, a European collective formed by Bas Jacobs (Netherlands), Akiem Helmling (Germany), and Sami Kortemäki (Finland). Underware are also the creators of the World Editions logo, which meets the design requirement that 'a strong shape can always be drawn with a toe in the sand.'